Heritage Publishing House

We are pleased to send you this review copy and if reviewed would appreciate a tearsheet.

A VESSEL OF HONOR
by Margaret Miller

Publication date: October 1997

ISBN: 0-9657389-5-7

LC: 97-93383

Page count: 254

Adult fiction

$23.00 hardcover

Distributors: AllBooks, Baker & Taylor, Ingram

Contact: Sylvia Bambola, Publisher
Heritage Publishing House
PO Box 277, Westhampton, NY 11977
Tel: (516) 874-2210   Fax: (516) 878-3809

A Vessel of Honor

Margaret Miller

A Vessel of Honor

Heritage Publishing House
Westhampton, New York

This is a work of fiction. The events described are imaginary: the setting and characters are fictitious and are not intended to represent specific places or living persons.

Published by Heritage Publishing House 1997

Printed in the United States of America

Cover design and illustration by Melissa Sleasman Neely

Library of Congress Catalog Card Number: 97-93383

ISBN 0-9657389-5-7

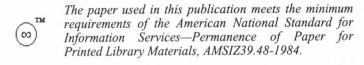

The paper used in this publication meets the minimum requirements of the American National Standard for Information Services—Permanence of Paper for Printed Library Materials, AMSIZ39.48-1984.

97 98 99 10 9 8 7 6 5 4 3 2 1

Special Thanks

To my daughter, Gina,
for never getting tired of covering the same ground, for her honest criticism, for her infectious enthusiasm, and for her wonderful ability to always make me laugh. Thanks, I needed that!

To my son, Cord,
for his help in keeping my computer running smoothly and for his endless patience in removing all those "flies in the ointment" that constantly presented themselves.

To my son-in-law, Michael,
who redefined the phrase, "True Grit." Rooster Cogburn had to face outlaws, but Michael had to face a mother-in-law after editing her book. Thanks for all those helpful suggestions!

And finally: *To my darling husband, Vincent,*
for his encouragement and love these past thirty years, and for helping to keep a dream alive.

Dedication

To Vincent, Gina and Cord

"But in a great house there are not only vessels of gold and of silver, but also of wood and of earth; and some to honor, and some to dishonor."

2 Timothy 2:20-21

One

A sudden explosion ripped off several metal locker doors. Spears of green shrapnel, hurled twenty feet away, injured a dozen people. A small boy fell to the floor as his splattering blood painted a macabre fresco of red on the wall.

"Security, code-four! Security, code-four!" shouted a voice over the Everman Airport loudspeaker.

A squad of guards appeared from nowhere. "Everyone stay calm!" bellowed the security force in unison.

The directive had little effect. People continued running in all directions, not knowing why or where they were going. A news commentator had recently described the year as "the best of times-the worst of times." Could Charles Darnay's "worst of times" be worse than this? No. This was the worst of the worst of times.

"Everything is under control. You are safe now," the guards repeated over and over, as they moved among the crowd.

One by one, people stopped running. Some fell exhausted into nearby chairs, others slumped against the walls, and one man simply dropped to the ground as though finishing a marathon.

Two nurses came forward and began assessing the condition of the injured, and mentally separated them into three groups:

slightly, seriously, or fatally wounded. First aid kits were retrieved from every corner of the terminal, and immediately the nurses began cleaning and bandaging the wounds. Human flesh was so fragile. The same flesh that built towering cupolas, exploratory space crafts, and even bombs, that same flesh damaged easily, sometimes beyond repair. It seemed this was the case for a five-year old boy who lay motionless on the floor. The thing about the "worst of times" was that it even applied to little boys.

Someone placed a blanket over the boy to prevent shock, and he lay beneath it breathing small, quivering moth breaths. Then suddenly his body shuddered and gave out a last, almost sorrowful sigh, as though in despair of never being able to build any of those cupolas or space crafts. The boy's mother, who was kneeling over him, saw this and began screaming hysterically. "Oh my God! My baby is dead! My baby is dead!"

The nurses did not stop. They had already classified the boy as fatally wounded and were too busy with those they could help.

The mother continued screaming for several minutes before anyone paid attention. Finally, a middle-aged man walked over. "You may not believe this now lady, but you're lucky. He was hurt real bad. I could see that right off." The man gestured to the small, lifeless child cradled in the woman's arms. "Same thing happened to my niece, about three months ago. Only it was a car bomb. The poor little kid, she never did nothing to nobody. She was just minding her business, walking home from school. Wrong place at the wrong time, that's all. She was hurt real bad too. Trouble is she didn't die. She's just a vegetable now. Poor little kid."

The mother's tear stained face looked up at the man. Her expression told him she had not understood a word he said.

"My baby...my baby... ."

"Yeah. Poor little kid. I'm sorry...real sorry," the man said, and walked away.

Joshua Chapman had been watching the woman with her son. "The Jihad!" he hissed between his teeth as though it was a curse.

The elderly nurse nodded and continued to wind the sterile

gauze around Chapman's arm. She had just put a butterfly over a nasty gash on his biceps and gotten the bleeding under control. But it would need more attention than she could give. Swab and bandage, swab and bandage, that's all she could do. But for many of them lying all over the floor, it won't be enough.

"The Jihad!" Chapman repeated caustically.

"It's the times, son," the nurse said wearily. "A person isn't safe anywhere anymore. So much violence! Makes you wonder what life is all about. I tell you son, I see it every day. It makes you wonder."

Joshua watched the team of paramedics place the lifeless five-year old boy on a stretcher and cover his face with the blanket. "Yes," he returned, "it makes you wonder."

Hours later, the blond Chapman was still wondering as he sat with three friends in a dimly lit diner. "What I'm asking myself," he said, "is why aren't we doing anything? Innocent people are dying every day at the hands of these butchers. Why aren't we with the Underground?"

When his three friends mumbled their agreement, his anger only increased. "All we do is sit around and *talk* about joining. It's always the same. We talk, we agree, but we never *do*."

"Then let's do it," David Rosen said, looking wide eyed and serious. Anyone who didn't know him would never guess he was partially blind. It happened in junior high. Five skin-heads, assuming the role of instructor, wanted to teach him the finer points of anti-Semitism. He was badly beaten and almost lost his left eye in the process. But David did learn his "lesson." He learned that hate was a mindless, unreasonable monster with a power all its own. He would never forget that day. It was the day he lost not only his sight, but his belief in the goodness of man. "Let's just do it," David repeated.

"Yes," added the other two friends.

Chapman eyed his companions skeptically and shook his

head. For as long as he could remember they had talked of joining the Zionist Underground. The Underground was an illegal organization formed by Jews to combat the terrorist tactics of the Islamic Jihad. Officially, it was condemned internationally. Unofficially, it was encouraged by the Israeli government. As an illegal organization, it was impervious to UN sanctions and censure. Its hands were not tied by legality or world opinion. It had the will and resolve to strike hard at terrorists, and did. The ramifications of joining such an organization were considerable. In most cases, it meant separation from family and friends. As Americans, Chapman and his companions would not be protected by their government, if caught. They would be outcasts and outlaws. It was a hard road they all had talked of taking, but Chapman wondered if they would ever actually take it.

"I'm sick of empty talk," he finally said.

"It's not empty, Joshua," Solomon Roth returned. "I'm ready to go the distance."

"So am I," said Benjamin Cohen, the third in the group of Joshua's friends. He was the young District Attorney who had taken City Hall by storm with his tough, aggressive tactics. His adversaries said he was more cop than lawyer and that suited Benjamin just fine. He had always wanted to be a cop. His family prevented it. If law enforcement was his path, then he must be a lawyer. He was told no self-respecting Cohen would settle for less. Since coming to America, three generations of Cohens had produced two medical doctors, one psychiatrist, two lawyers, one judge, and two college professors. Benjamin's fate had been sealed by the family line.

"I'm in," repeated Benjamin, thinking that a division of armed terrorists was going to be easier to face than his own family when he gave them this news. But this time *he* was going to win. This time no compromising because of family pride. "If the Jihad isn't stopped, there's not going to be much left anyway," he added.

"Yeah, our leaders are 'old women,'" Solomon returned. "They have lost their will to fight and win. They worry too much about what other nations will say."

Benjamin nodded. "Only Israel has any determination left. But she's constantly pressured by her allies not to make waves. Oh, when will she learn that for the Jew the world is still an oven!"

"That's right. We have to take care of ourselves," David said. "Look how many times we've been betrayed."

Benjamin's clenched fist hit the table. "When push comes to shove a Jew can only count on another Jew. America, Britain, the rest of Europe, they have all let us down. They have all betrayed us at one time or another. What's more, they could do it again. Look at the British and their White Paper."

The others nodded soberly. This was one of Benjamin's favorite topics. They had listened to his dissertation on the British for years.

In 1917 the British issued the Balfour Declaration, which favored establishment of a Jewish homeland in Palestine. It was entered into the canon of international law, and aside from the Arabs, was recognized by the entire world. But in 1920, when oil was discovered in the Persian Gulf, Britain's already waning commitment to a Jewish Palestine waned even further. Finally, with the pressures of a world war to contend with, Britain issued their White Paper in 1939 which completely renounced their obligation outlined in the Balfour Declaration. The White Paper called for a phasing out of all Jewish immigration to Palestine and an end to land sales. It froze the size of the existing Jewish population, having in mind an independent Palestine in the future, with an Arab majority. The White Paper was politically expedient for Britain. They foresaw their involvement in a world war. Jewish opposition to the Nazi regime was certain. But Arab good-will had to be purchased. The White Paper was the price of that good will.

"Yes, Jewish history has been marked by betrayal," Joshua responded, "But this is different. Kamal has declared a Holy War on the entire world, on all nonbelievers, not just Jews. We're dealing with complex issues here. It's not cut and dry."

"Yes, yes," agreed Solomon impatiently, not noticing the

soda spilling over the side of his glass as he poured from the pitcher. "We all know the obvious causes in this 'cause and effect' scenario."

It was well-known that Russia had fanned the fires of Islamic zeal and hatred for years. Before the collapse of Communism, they repeatedly used the terrorist activities of the PLO and other groups for their own purposes. After the collapse, Russia became a federal republic. Five of the fifteen republics were predominantly Moslem. Fearing an Iranian backed Moslem insurrection in these five republics, Boris Yeltsin made a covenant with Iran. Iran would keep hands off. In return, Russia would back Iran in any future military operations. Additionally, Yeltsin installed nuclear plants in Iran and helped train Iranians in nuclear technology. Such encouragement and support emboldened Iran and produced a subsequent increase in global terrorism. It was also no secret that Kamal had trained at Lumumba University in Moscow.

Kamal emerged from a squalid Palestinian refugee camp. When he was seven, he joined the *fedayeen*, the Palestinian freedom fighters. He learned to read and write in the fedayeen school. There he also learned the Koran; mostly those Surahs or chapters that showed the necessity of hating all infidels, especially the Jews. But Surah sixteen guided him most. It told him how the Jews had corrupted themselves by turning from Islam, and how Moslems are correct in heaping punishment on them. By ten, he had slit the throat of his first "corrupt" Jew.

Throughout those violent and rebellious early years, Kamal began envisioning himself a leader of more than just a few ragged Palestinians. When he entered Lumumba University in Russia, it was in search of this higher destiny.

At that time, Lumumba was the collection area for Third World students. Here, they received, in addition to their University curriculum, heavy doses of Communist indoctrination. The brightest and most loyal of these continued training as members of the KGB. The cream of the crop was then trained by Department V, the KGB's Assassination and Sabotage Squad. Kamal proved a very apt pupil. He graduated from Department V at the top of his class.

From there, he joined the Hamas, a Palestinian resistance group that patrolled the occupied territories. Most of his arms, as well as his directives, came from Moscow. Most of his funding came from PLO Headquarters in Tunis. When the Soviet Union ceased to exist, Kamal found himself without a sponsor. When PLO Chairman Yasir Arafat and Israeli Prime Minister Yitzhak Rabin reached their historic agreement of reconciliation, PLO funds dried by and consequently Kamal's funds with it.

But his years in the fedayeen had taught Kamal to be quick on his feet. Taking the most extreme fringe of the Hamas with him, he splintered off into another group that was even more militant. He then wasted no time in making alliances with various elements in Iran, Syria, and Libya. Within a relatively short time, Kamal became the world's most notorious international terrorist.

At first, the dream to capture Jerusalem was the adhesive that held his group together. After the assassination of Rabin and the election of Benjamin Netanyahu and his Likud hard-liners, it was a natural rallying point. Jerusalem stirs the heart like no other city. Palestinians as well as Israelis consider it their capitol. But Jerusalem went by the wayside as Kamal broadened his horizons. The entire world was the target, all nonbelievers the enemy. One thing did not change, however. Jews were still hated, above all others.

"We know the obvious causes," Solomon repeated. "We needn't rehash them again. And we all know there will never be peace, not until Islam stops teaching its children, 'today Friday, tomorrow Saturday, then Sunday.'"

The group nodded glumly. The Moslem saying, taught to their children like a nursery rhyme, had sinister implications. Friday was the day of worship for the Moslem, Saturday for the Jews and Sunday for the Christian. The meaning was first the Jews were to be subjugated, then the Christians, until all the world was Islam.

"There will never be peace," repeated Solomon, "until Messiah comes."

"You can kill a debate faster than anyone I know. You sure

you're Jewish?" David quipped. Of Joshua's friends, David had the best sense of humor and was usually not as glum as the other two.

Solomon's forehead folded into annoyed little wrinkles. "Always with the jokes. Our friend Joshua can tell you how funny it is. Just ask him. He almost got his arm blown off this morning!"

Unconsciously, Joshua fingered his upper arm. After the bombing, he spent several hours in the emergency room. He had needed twenty stitches, in all. Joshua's own brother, Dr. Daniel Chapman, sutured the wound. And while he stitched, he joked about finally getting even with Joshua for losing his favorite Spalding mitt when they were boys.

But Joshua had seen his brother's concern, as well as the profound relief that it had not been he on that stretcher with a blanket over his face.

"Lighten up, Sol," Joshua said, as he put his hand on his friend's shoulder.

Solomon's fingers shook as he ran them through his blond, curly hair. "I don't know what gets into me...I'm sorry."

"Sure Sol, forget it," David returned.

For a brief while the four sat in silence. They were used to Solomon's outbursts and tried to let them pass without incident, like steam from a safety valve. Eight months ago, Solomon's mother and sister, along with two friends, were machine-gunned to death outside their synagogue. The Moslem Jihad took credit. Sol and his father had been there, seen the entire massacre, but were helpless to do anything. Outwardly, Solomon had not sustained any injuries. Inwardly, he had been severely marred; left with a wound that oozed continually, sometimes in anger, as now; sometimes in quiet, weeping grief.

"All I know," Solomon said, slowly picking up his napkin and using it as a blotter. He finally noticed the puddle of soda around his glass. "All I know," he repeated, "is that when a bully shows up at your door, you don't open it and present him your head to club. You roll up your sleeves and fight."

Years ago, Solomon was told he was destined to become a

Rabbi. He believed it. He had always had a deep, abiding love for God. He spent hours at a time studying the Torah. They seemed to him but minutes, such was his love for scripture. But after the massacre, Solomon knew this dream would never be realized. A man of God should not have bloody hands. Circumstances had altered destiny and placed him on a new path. His weapon would not be the Word of God. It would be something that could kill and maim. It would be the weapon of a "blood avenger."

"So, do we fight?" he asked impatiently.

The friends all nodded their agreement.

"Yes," said Benjamin, finally verbalizing their decision. "It's high time we join."

"Then...to the Underground," returned Solomon, his tone passionate, his hand lifting his glass in the air, as though it was the very torch of Liberty.

"To the Underground!" responded the others in a chorus, as their glasses clicked together.

Two

Tisha moved uncomfortably in her chair as she watched the man in front of her. It was coming over her again, that feeling of standing precariously on the shore while the tide pulled at her ankles. What was it about him that unsettled her? He was good looking, but she had known better. He was personable, but not as dynamic as some. What was it then? An unknown, complex factor that defied language? Or...was it rather simple after all, nothing more than a case of common desire? Instinctively, she touched the large, white cross that hung near her throat. Lately, she found herself doing this often in his presence, this act of restoration, this grasping for the land. She did not know the sea. It frightened her. The land was strong, dependable. It was loving. She believed in it. She had spent the entire thirty years of her life rooted in it. And those roots of middy blouses and pleated skirts, prayer books and incense filled churches went deep. But what could take root in the sea? What could anchor in unpredictable, formless liquid? These questions she asked herself over and over because *he* lived in the sea. During the past months, the quest for these answers had led her ever closer, until she found herself on the very edge where land and sea met.

She had been standing there too long, balancing between them, all the while feeling very unbalanced. It was his eyes; yes, it was his eyes that unsettled her, Tisha thought, as she briefly closed her own.

"Am I keeping you up, O'Brien!" snapped a deep, masculine voice.

Instantly her lids opened, and she stared blankly into a smiling face. The face contradicted the voice. Tisha was not surprised. It often happened. She had learned that about him. There were other things too; how he moved his mouth to one side in a half smile when something pleased him, or how he chewed the end of a pencil when he was deep in thought, or the clumsy way his powerful body would react when forced to handle a tiny or fragile object like the toy model of the P1 airplane that sat on his desk. She did not like noticing these things. It seemed too intimate, almost improper, as though it was like knowing what deodorant he used, or how often he bathed. Knowing these things seemed to bring her closer to that shore.

"Looks like your boys did their usual thorough job of mutilation," barked the voice again, while a large, powerful finger jabbed a pile of papers. Both the voice and the jabbing finger belonged to Michael Patterson, president of Patterson Aviation. "The active controls performed well, actually better than expected."

Tisha nodded thoughtfully. Their structural engineer had just completed the wind tunnel testing on a sample wing of the Patterson Two or P2; loading, twisting, vibrating it until it fell apart. Of primary concern were the active controls that automatically adjusted the control surfaces. These controls had distributed the stress more evenly along the wing, and results of all phases of testing were, as Mike Patterson just stated, "better than expected."

"Yes," returned Tisha. "I'm pleased."

Mike studied the beautiful engineer's face. The wing design of the P2 was years ahead of their competition. The wing could move from the conventional position at subsonic speed, then fold backward into an arrow shaped configuration at Mach 2.7 and up. It had been a heavily contested subject between them. She had fought hard for the sweep wing. He discovered something about her then: she made an outspoken dissenter. In the end she had won him over not only with her rhetoric, but with her barrage of specs and diagrams.

"What you mean to say, O'Brien, is that you're pleased you talked me into it."

Light laughter, like a string of musical notes, curled around Tisha's mouth. Two years ago she had come to Patterson Aviation, or PA, as head of their Research and Development Department. She had an impressive resume: a degree in physics and aeronautical engineering, two years of nuclear fusion research at Princeton University, and four years of working at one of the "Big Three."

She came to PA because she had grown tired of working on someone else's innovative ideas and wanted a chance to work on some of her own. Mike Patterson gave her that chance. And while Tisha was grateful, her gratitude never deterred her from open confrontation when she believed it necessary. In fact, the entire P2 project had begun in confrontation. She was doodling, she claimed, and came up with a sketch she'd like him to see; a really innovative idea. He had called her innovative idea "crazy." That was the beginning of the P2. Inch by inch, he contested it. Inch by inch, she had to earn the right to build it. That was how it was with them.

"You must admit you were rather difficult," Tisha sighed in remembrance.

"Mule headed?" questioned Mike with a smile as he tilted backward in the brown leather chair. His large, muscular frame looked strangely out of place behind the desk. His tie was missing, having been discarded within an hour or two after arriving at the office. It was what he did daily, almost compulsively, as though something in his body rebelled at its confinement. It was a powerful, athletic body. One that seemed to press angrily against his herringbone suit. His slightly open shirt exposed a few hairs which curled over one another like miniature tangled black springs, the number of which increased further down his chest. It was a body that always appeared tense; not a tenseness brought about by nerves, but rather one brought about by constant anticipation of being called into some action. It was the mark of a passionate nature; a nature which made it impossible to sever a part from the whole. It was a nature Tisha found unsettling.

"I may have been a little mule headed," Mike repeated.

"Possibly."

"You're being kind."

"Possibly."

The pair laughed together.

"Of course," Mike continued, "you displayed your share of unbecoming qualities."

"Such as?"

"A barbed tongue, for one."

"Barbed tongues do have their value."

"And what value is that?"

"They have a way of pricking one out of his complacency."

"Ouch," Mike laughed as he picked up a pencil and began nibbling absently on the end. "How's the molded graphite?"

Tisha's milk chocolate eyes widened, melting in an almost childlike excitement. She loved her work. "It's incredible," she said, "unbelievably strong and light. It's going to reduce wing panel and fuselage weight by thirty to forty percent."

The pencil landed with a plop on the soft desk blotter. The blotter covered most of the top, but around the three bare edges, rich dark maple showed beneath a heavy layer of polish. Like everything else in the room, the desk was well maintained, being regularly waxed with the same wood polish used on the lighter oak paneling. From so much care, the room always held a faint odor, like freshly saddle soaped boots. "Well, that at least is good news," he said, his tone indicating little excitement.

Tisha eyed the man in front of her. She knew her employer well enough to understand that something troubled him, and they had yet to touch upon the real reason he called her into his office.

Finally he spoke. "I've been going over the report on the

fusion reactor. It's been through seventy-five simulated flights, and in each flight there's increasing evidence of casing deterioration."

"Yes," Tisha returned, understanding all too well the gravity of this information. The problem was cooling the hot ionized plasma which reached over sixty million degrees during fusion, and was contained inside a webbing of magnetic fields, very much like Jell-O being held by a net of rubber bands. Failure to solve the cooling problems could jeopardize the entire P2 project.

She could hear his impatience well up in his mouth like a gaseous bubble. He was impatient, and she was always telling him so. Nothing seemed to come fast enough. The P2 and the nuclear power reactors would catapult Patterson Aviation to the prominence of the "Big Three." The prospect was like sugar in his mouth, and almost impossible not to swallow whole.

"We've got a problem with the cooling system, and we can't count on improving it," Tisha said, her face thoughtful and serious, "not without ramifications."

A subtle shaft of light, like a moonbeam passing over a pond, flickered across Mike's large dark eyes as he watched her.

"Nolan, Audra, and I agree we have only two choices," Tisha continued, unaware of the effect she was having on him. Nolan Ramsdale was R&D's nuclear engineer, and Mike knew Tisha relied heavily upon him in matters concerning the nuclear power reactor, the NPR910. "Nolan favors increasing the magnetic field. I'm opposed because the heavier shielding and additional vacuum pumps will increase gross weight and decrease pay-load. It's impossible, at this point, to know just how much. But we both agree it would mean portions of the P2 would have to be altered."

Mike again picked up the pencil lying on the blotter and brought the eraser end to his mouth. The greatness of the NPR910 was not in the fact that nuclear fusion was possible, but that it was possible in a reactor the size of a Rolls Royce RB11 engine, the famous engine that powered Lockheed's TriStar L1011.

"And the second choice?" he asked.

"Create a casing made from a totally new substance."

"What are you aiming for O'Brien, a new world's record of 'firsts'?" His voice was curt, but his face said he was interested.

Tisha laughed. "Not exactly."

"But you have something in mind?"

"I do. You've heard of titanium carbide, the composite... ."

"That's still in the experimental stage."

"Yes, but... ."

"Why titanium carbide?" It was his habit to shoot questions in rapid fire when something appealed to him.

"Well, a material's ability to withstand corrosion at high temperatures is directly related to the hardness of that thin protective film which stands between a metal surface and a potentially destructive environment. Titanium carbide deposited... ."

"Get to the punch line."

"deposited in the range .3 to .5 has less structural imperfection, and the hardness of the films are second in hardness only to diamonds. The processes of surface and bulk diffusion are thermally activated. The major... ."

"I don't need a dissertation, O'Brien."

"Convince me, you say, then you narrow the tunnel and force me to act as a battering ram to widen it again. No wonder I have migraines."

The burly executive chuckled. "Alright, batter away."

"Where was I? Oh, yes. The major variables in determining the microstructure of deposited films are the melting temperature of the substrate onto which deposition is being made."

"T/Tm ratio."

Tisha smiled in admiration, surprise and pleasure both reflected in her face. It was hard not to respect this man who shared so many of her interests. It was infinitely harder not to be drawn to him. "Yes," she returned, "and based on this T/Tm ratio, a sixty to sixty-five million degree temperature would naturally change the .3-.5 deposition. But it wasn't titanium carbide that I had in mind."

"Then what in blazes have you been talking about?"

"Something *like* titanium carbide."

"Which is?"

"Titanium X."

"Titanium X? Sounds straight out of Buck Rogers. Okay, O'Brien, what's this all about?"

"It's about a substance that will make titanium carbide look like tissue paper."

Laughter, locked in shiny golden Braille, inscribed his face. Mike Patterson was progressive and well informed. He knew titanium X was nonexistent. It was his business to know such things. He also knew his head engineer well enough to realize that she was up to something.

"And what did Nolan say about this?" he asked, trying hard not to smile openly.

"Inconclusive data for formulating an accurate hypothesis."

"Are those his very words?" The smile squeezed past his determination.

"His very words," Tisha answered, returning the smile.

"You are, I take it, an expert on this titanium X?"

"No, Audra is. She's done a lot of work with titanium carbide, and in the process came up with titanium X. I've gone over her notes. More work needs to be done, but I see enough potential to want to pursue it."

Mike looked doubtful. Airframe manufacturers did not, as a rule, build their own propulsion system. Mike's inexperience in this area made him all the more nervous. "Assuming we go with Nolan's choice, what major change do you foresee in the actual design of the P2?"

"For starters, reduction of passenger space from six hundred to maybe five hundred seats."

Mike whistled softly. The P2 had been on the board for two years. That represented thousands of man hours. Wind tunnel testing on various parts was well advanced, and plans for a full scale mock-up were being developed. A change in the size of the NPR910 would mean scrapping a great deal of what had already been accomplished. That would mean a loss of time and money. And money, especially, was a critical factor. If, on the other hand, they were to go ahead with their current project in the hope that a new casing material would be found, the loss in dollars would be even greater if this discovery was not realized. The dilemma was awesome. Should he go with Nolan's suggestion, where much of the P2 would have to be altered? Or should he go, as Audra and Tisha suggested, where success was uncertain, but if achieved, would leave the P2 intact? The question was really a matter of risk. How great was the chance he should take?

As a businessman, Mike was no stranger to speculation. He believed it was the only way to keep his business from stagnating. Two years ago this belief prompted him to begin Tisha's project. He gambled on her judgment because he saw value in it. Since then, he had come to value her judgment even more, and was usually sorry when he failed to rely on it. She had tried to warn him about the reactor casing. But his impatience made him sweep these warnings into a corner, like unsightly dust balls. The sperm of financial and expediential concerns constantly fertilized his impatience and sometimes crowded out good judgment.

"How close is Audra?" he asked, his voice surprisingly free of tension. This fact told Tisha he had already made his decision.

She smiled at him, a soft glowing smile, and folded her arms contentedly across the front of her slim body. Her thick, black hair swept outward from her face in loose waves. It looked like a lion's mane and hung over her shoulders, making her appear wild and tempestuous. It was a sharp contrast to the three-piece suit she wore.

"Very close."

"Okay, O'Brien...we'll go for it."

"Thank you," she said sweetly. She understood his permission to go ahead with titanium X was based largely on his confidence in her.

"For what?" he shot back, keenly aware of the hair, the folded arms, and the slim body. "We've had our differences, but that doesn't mean I don't know what a fine job you're doing."

She inclined her head slightly in acknowledgment of his compliment, then rose from her chair.

"One more thing," Mike said, causing Tisha to sit back down. "It's our interim financing. Since we're badly overextended, the banks have turned us down. That means I have to go through the board."

Tisha moved uncomfortably in her chair. Lack of funds was the familiar shadow that constantly cast itself upon the project.

"I had really hoped to avoid it," Mike continued, "or at least postpone it, but this morning I got some news that makes it impossible. The ten C101's we've recently built have lost their buyer. The freight company that placed the order filed bankruptcy."

Tisha groaned and slumped backward in her chair. "So much for D&B reports." Tisha knew the freight company's credit history had been investigated and the company got a satisfactory rating from Dun & Bradstreet. But the Jihad, with all its accompanying carcinomas, was killing free enterprise at an astonishing rate. This unexpected set-back severely heightened PA's own financial problems. "Why not try the airlines? See if they'll defray some of our R&D cost." It was not unusual in the industry for airlines to pick up some of the development costs. It was this very practice that enabled the Anglo-French development of the Concord SST.

"No good. The airlines are barely recovering from their investment in Concord. And, in addition to R&D fees, the airlines forked over eighty million dollars for each SST purchased. I don't know if they're going to shout for joy when they realize that our P2 will make the Concord look like a dinosaur. Once it's developed, though, they'll buy if they want to be competitive. But it's not easy putting an eighty million dollar dinosaur in moth balls."

"Ninety-two million," Tisha interjected, "and rising. We're in an inflationary market, remember?"

Michael Patterson grunted. His head engineer had an uncanny memory for facts and figures that both pleased and irritated him. "In addition, there's the popular thirty-five million dollar DC10," he returned, ignoring her remark.

"It's ludicrous to compare the DC10 to the P2. That's like comparing a parakeet to an eagle."

"The issues here are not parakeets or eagles, but money and politics. Would you rather pay thirty-five million or one hundred million for the P2? Money, it always boils down to money."

Tisha's fingers drummed absently on the arm of the chair. "I guess you have a point. I imagine you'll need a briefing for the Board along with specs."

Mike nodded. "Minimal specs, showing barest details. I want as much secrecy maintained as possible." Although Mike had controlling interest of PA, fifty-one percent, his father, in the last years of his life, had badly mismanaged the company. Ever since then, it teetered precariously between the black and red world of profit and loss. This situation repeatedly drove Mike to the Board. When he couldn't go through the banks, Mike went to the Board for loans; loans secured through influential contacts. Yet, he didn't fully trust them. The Board members were of various backgrounds and loyalties. The politics of business could make enemies out of friends. "Just *minimal* specs," he repeated.

"I know," Tisha answered. Mike had expressed his fears on this matter before. "There are security... ."

"measures." Mike finished the phrase as he darkened beneath Tisha O'Brien's smug manner. "It's primarily Gunther I'm concerned about," Patterson said, almost sullenly.

Robert Gunther worked for Tafco Oil, one of the largest oil companies in the West. The company was headed by Alexander Harner, a man linked to more than one shady deal. Once Harner was even brought up on misconduct and conflict of interest charges. The charges were eventually dropped due to insufficient evidence. Tafco also operated numerous oil fields in Syria, an avowed Jihad supporter. This fact did not sit well with many businessmen, most notably those who had, at some point, been targets of terrorism. Nor was this sentiment lessened any by the fact that Tafco, both here and abroad, had never been harassed by terrorists themselves.

Gunther had sat on the Board under the elder Patterson and

when Mike took control, he considered ousting the Tafco executive, then thought better of it. Gunther had powerful connections in Washington, and that included both the Federal Aviation Administration and the NTSB, the National Transportation Safety Board. In addition, Tafco's influence spanned the continents. Although Mike retained Gunther, he had no illusions. Under normal conditions, Gunther could be a tremendous asset. Should a conflict of interest arise, however, he could be a dangerous liability. This was all common knowledge and facts Michael Patterson had related to Tisha more than once. "Gunther worries me," he repeated.

The engineer nodded thoughtfully, but remained silent. This angered the handsome executive even more, and he began cursing softly under his breath.

"Just what does it take to get a rise out of you, O'Brien?" he finally said.

"What reaction were you expecting?" Tisha returned with a surprised look on her face. "I understand your concern. We've gone over this before. And I also understand we're living in dangerous times, but sometimes I think you're just a wee bit paranoid."

"Paranoid?" The handsome executive shook his head. "O'Brien, in this sick world you've got to be smarter and tougher than the next guy or you won't survive."

"Yes, but... ."

"But nothing. I had a friend like you; bright, honest, unworldly. He was an engineer who loved cars. Three years ago he invented an engine that could take a car one hundred miles on one gallon of gasoline. He actually believed the world would applaud his achievement and decided to go out and tell everyone about it. Before he could even get an appointment with any of the major car manufacturers, a committee of sorts, claiming to represent the oil companies, came to see him and offered to buy the engine.

"He wasn't sure how they found out about it. But he manage to glean from their conversation that the reason they wanted the engine was to stop it from ever being produced. He was a moralist and in his best self-righteous tone, told them to 'flake off.'

"From that moment on, he was continually harassed. All his efforts to see anyone in the auto industry were mysteriously thwarted. Finally one night, he came to me, frightened and confused. He said he was certain someone was trying to kill him. He had several freakish things happen: car brakes failing, a sudden fire in one of the back rooms of his house, a speeding motorist nearly running him over. When I asked him who was trying to kill him, he said he didn't know exactly, but he was sure it was someone from that 'committee.'

"I thought it sounded like a pretty bad 'B' picture, and told him to go home and get some rest. The next day he was dead, a boating accident. Somehow he fell out of a rowboat while fishing, hit his head on the side and drowned. That was the official story anyway. But I knew better. You see, my friend was an avid fisherman, but he was terrified of the water and wouldn't go on a boat. He always fished off the bank. Only once was I ever able to get him on a boat, and that wasn't until I had plied him with half a bottle of Scotch. According to the coroner, there was no trace of alcohol in his blood stream.

"Another curious thing, that engine and all information pertaining to it disappeared, and with them the motive for murder. Why would anyone want to kill him for an engine that didn't exist? I knew he was murdered, but I'd never be able to prove it.

"Now do you understand why I don't want to give the Board too much information? When three of the five members represent major oil companies. Fifty percent of all fuel used in this country each year is used for transportation. Just one Boeing 747 can guzzle over three thousand gallons per hour. You multiply that by days, then weeks, months, years. How much money do you think that represents? Enough to take a life...maybe several lives? Now take it a step further. If an airplane can operate without gas, why not a car, why not homes, industry? You see how expensive this is becoming? It's expensive enough to wipe out this entire factory and every living soul in it!"

Tisha blinked hard into the somber face of Mike Patterson.

"You're right. It does sound like a bad 'B' picture," she said weakly, her face white and brittle as a potato chip.

"Perhaps you think I'm making this up. Well, I can assure you Cliff Davis is very dead."

The chip broke into a frown. "Clifford Davis? He's the man you were talking about?" Tisha knew of Cliff Davis. As the highly successful owner of a research and development corporation, he had been renowned for his honesty and integrity. At one time, she had hoped to work for him. But before she could, he had died in some freak accident, the details of which only now came tumbling loose, like so much change, from the secret pockets of her memory. But no where in her memory of this was the word "murder" stored.

"Why would the oil companies want to kill him?" she asked, her voice laced with disbelief. "OPEC hates us. The Mid-East situation has worsened. For heaven's sake, there's an energy crises. It just doesn't make sense."

The Holy War or Jihad had gripped the fancies of even those Arab countries once friendly to the US. Though their governments still outwardly professed loyalty, inwardly the pressure was so fierce that it spilled into every aspect of relations and trade. None was so far reaching as the oil situation. OPEC, forced to unite under the banner of Islamic zeal, devised a scheme of striking at the Achilles' heel of every Western nation. An oil crisis suddenly developed. Oil wells all over the Middle East began mysteriously "drying up." As the wells dried up, the price of a barrel of oil continued to rise, reaching sixty dollars. The industrial free world remained gasping for air under this strangle hold. Unable to afford the fuel or energy they needed to operate, many businesses closed overnight. As common as the stories of terrorism, were the stories of suicide by defunct entrepreneurs and ex-factory owners who had lost everything. Unlike the distraught businessmen who, during the stock market crash of 1929, leaped to their deaths from high-rise office buildings, their modern counterparts went home, and without mess or fanfare, overdosed on sleeping pills or other drugs.

"It doesn't make sense because you're confusing the issue,"

Michael Patterson returned. "We're dealing with economics here. Alive, Cliff Davis posed a financial threat. And if he was a threat, imagine the lethal position we hold? The 'committee' stands to lose a great deal in the event of nuclear fusion, especially when there's enough deuterium for plasma available in the oceans to meet present rates of power consumption for at least a million years. What was it you told me about one cubic foot of 'free' ocean water? Didn't you say it represented two million BTU's or close to two thousand gallons of number six oil?"

Tisha, looking rather glum, nodded her head. He was using the same argument she had used two years ago when she first tried to sell him on the merits of nuclear fusion. "Okay, okay, you've got a rise out of me."

"Maybe I'll get another one," Mike continued, "because there's something else...something I don't want discussed outside this room. Two nights ago, someone tried to break-in. One of the security guards stopped it, but the intruder escaped."

Like most large companies, Patterson Aviation had doubled its security staff because of the Jihad. Armed men patrolled PA twenty-four hours a day. PA's heavy security was well known, and in light of this knowledge, Mike found an attempted break-in all the more alarming.

"He was trying to get into the R&D building," Mike said with great emphasis. The R&D building had been a restricted area even before the Jihad. "And...it's the second attempt this month. I want you to be careful, O'Brien. Observe maximum security measures, and that goes during your off-duty hours as well. If anyone suspicious starts hanging around your apartment, if you get unusual phone calls or mail, I want to know about it. Understand?"

Again, Tisha nodded. She understood. The last few years had seen the death of naiveté. Previous decades witnessed Michael Bommi Baumann, a West German working class youth who helped organize one of West Germany's most terrifying guerrilla forces, and "Carlos the Killer," or Carlos "The Jackal" Sanchez, a South American millionaire and notorious political assassin. Now there was an even more hideous killer-assassin, "Kamal the Butcher."

"Carlos the Jackal" once said, "Violence is the one language the Western democracies can understand." "Kamal the Butcher" altered it, "Violence is the one language the infidel can understand." And everyone outside the Kamal philosophy was an "infidel."

The most vicious attacks were made on the West. Here, everyone was a target. Especially hard hit were American businesses. After almost two years of Jihad, many businesses employed their own anti-terrorist protection. Armed guards were common place, as well as complexes protected by barbed wire and sophisticated electronic surveillance devices.

Because terrorist attacks had become so frequent in the United States, and because there was often confusion over which authorities had jurisdiction, local, state, or federal; clear, concise reactions were often too slow in coming. The solution was an emergence of another branch on the Bureaucratic Tree, the Internal Security Service or ISS.

The ISS had special commando groups, hostage bargaining teams, swat teams, and bomb squads. They employed paramilitary tactics when necessary, and were not opposed to meeting violence with violence.

Every company or corporation of any stature was listed by ISS as possible terrorist targets. Every corporation that performed a critical function or a function of national defense was listed on a separate "red" sheet. Companies on the "red" sheet were visited frequently by an ISS official who would assess each organization's risk, then advise how to beef up security.

Patterson Aviation, because of it's work in nuclear fusion, was on the ISS "red" list. And Peter Myers, the ISS representative, was a frequent visitor to the plant. Evacuation drills for possible bomb threats were repeated over and over. Bullet proof glass was installed in all ground level windows, and extra security guards were hired. All employees knew about the "red" list. It was something everyone grew to live with, to accept. They could choose to leave any time, yet no one ever did.

No, naiveté had been destroyed, if not by the world at large, then by "Kamal the Butcher," who, in a very real sense, exposed the core of every human heart. After all, wasn't the heart of man "deceitful above all things and desperately wicked?" Who could know it? Except of course...God. The world was mad. It had run amuck. It had run from the things of God. Really, there were only two ways: the ways of God and the ways of the world. And the two were completely and absolutely opposed to one another.

"I want you to be careful," Mike repeated. "And I plan to keep tabs on you. Do you understand, O'Brien?"

"Yes, I understand," Tisha answered.

"Okay, that's it then."

The slim engineer rose and walked across the room. Her long hair hung like a cape of ebony silk over the suit jacket.

"O'Brien." The hair swished through the air, a shiny black streak, as she turned toward the voice. "This is one situation where that big white cross of yours isn't going to do you much good."

Instinctively, her fingers felt for the cross that hung just below her throat. Most people thought it was ivory because of its creamy white color and highly polished surface. Instead, it was buffalo horn, fashioned by her mother years ago as a gift. Her mother was knowledgeable in the Cheyenne art of crafting jewelry and this was very different from anything she had ever made. In the "old days," long before her mother was born, the Cheyenne made necklaces of fish vertebrae or deer and elk teeth. The buffalo horn was used for essentials like spoons or ladles. Tisha knew her mother chose the horn for the cross because she believed in its necessity.

"If you notice," Tisha returned sweetly, "I'm not the one who's afraid." The full, black hair fell lightly over her cheek. She didn't have the dark coloring of her mother, nor her bold square features. Rather, Tisha's face was softer, creamier; a very striking blend of two nationalities, Irish and American Indian. Even her hair, though thick and luxurious, was not straight but naturally wavy. Absently she brushed it aside.

A broad smile split the rugged face, embedding splinters of wrinkles around the mouth and eyes. He knew how seriously she took that jewel. Although most times, as now, it amused him, there were moments when it baffled him to the point of exasperation. "Well...just be careful, O'Brien."

Mike Patterson stared at the door long after Tisha was gone. There was something very satisfying about her, he thought; something that seemed to both relax and tense that huge frame of his. It was a feeling he had never experienced with anyone else. And...there were times like now, when he felt very close to her. Only, why couldn't she look more like the head of a Research Department and less like someone who should be sipping Martini and Rossi in a negligee, and saying "yes" he thought angrily, even though he had never even asked the question. "Business and pleasure don't mix," he muttered as he stabbed the intercom a little too roughly with his finger. "Have Buck come to my office!" he barked. But minutes later, even before there was a rap on the door, Michael Patterson knew that someday he would ask.

The tan, leathery face of Buck McNight wrinkled into a smile as the square body folded itself into a chair. Massive legs and arms made the chair appear undersized, and only after carefully scrutinizing the rest of the furniture, did one realize it was not the chair that was undersized but that the man in it was quite oversized. He was a man in his early sixties, with an easy, unhurried manner, developed by years of living a life without time pieces or schedules.

But his hands, whose folds and creases were deeply stained by the oil of machines, gave away his real occupation. They were hands adept at ministering to the cogs and wheels of complexity. And herein lay the paradox to an otherwise simple life. Patiently, he sat and watched the man behind the desk chew on the end of a pencil. He loved this office with its clean, friendly smell. He also loved the man behind the desk.

Presently, Patterson rose from his chair and began pacing

like someone trying to work out a cramp. From time to time he would stop, glance casually over at Buck, then resume pacing. Neither spoke, but their silence was the comfortable silence of two people who knew each other well and had nothing to prove.

Buck was more than an employee. He was "family." As a test pilot and mechanic for Patterson Aviation for over thirty-five years, he had been a friend to the elder Patterson. He was also a friend to the son. It was Buck who took young Michael fishing on those hot, lazy summer afternoons. From Buck, Mike had learned how to pitch a pup tent, how to ride a horse. It was Buck who had taken Mike up for his first flying lesson. And it was to Buck Mike would go when burdened with problems, first about failing grades, then failing romances, and now failing projects and companies. He was one of the few people Mike trusted completely.

"How much do you know about deuterium?" Mike finally said, breaking the silence.

Buck expelled a slow, easy chuckle, like a sage rolling lazily in the breeze. "Not much. A heavy isotope of hydrogen; you're using it as the plasma in your reactor. Why?" Buck seldom wasted words or time hedging.

"I'm going to need some. O'Brien's having a problem with the reactor casing. It's breaking down. Her solution is typical; wants to develop a new compost material." Here he paused and laughed. "Imagine!" The word was hurled like a hard ball, gyrating in mockery of the whole idea. Only his tone revealed how much he believed in it.

"What all this means," Mike continued, "is that the seventy-five tests we've done with the reactor will have to be repeated. I don't want to go to our present supplier of deuterium. It would raise too many questions and add to whatever suspicions already exists about us on the outside. I want as few people as possible to know what's going on here. That's why I've sent for you. How would you like to go into the 'mining' business? How would you like to 'mine' deuterium?"

The large oil-stained hands hung limply over each arm of

the chair like two taxidermic trophies. Even this immobility could not belie the power that surged within them. "I don't know as though I'd be too good at it. Seems to me you'd do better with a physicist," he said, eyeing Mike with interest. Not for one moment had he taken Mike literally. Buck knew there was something more.

"You'll have a physicist with you, Nolan Ramsdale. I want you to purchase the land, building materials, equipment, everything Nolan needs. And he'll advise you on this. But I want it done apart from Patterson Aviation. There can't be any connection. Not yet, anyway. At the right time, our attorney will take care of the legalities and annex it to the corporation. But until then, Buck, I want maximum security. No one who doesn't absolutely need to know, must know. When you've set up shop, contact me."

It was as Buck suspected. Unlike Tisha, he never questioned Mike's decisions or motives. Buck knew about Cliff Davis and the two break-in attempts. He also knew about the human heart. "When do you want me to start?"

"Right away. I'll arrange a meeting between you and Nolan later this afternoon. And Buck, I don't want Nolan to know anymore than he has to either."

The motionless paw-like hands suddenly came to life as they slapped against the dungareed thighs. "Okay, Mike. You can count on me."

"I know. Some things don't have to be said."

Three

Audra Shields dabbed her mouth with lipstick like a skilled artisan dabbing her canvas. When she finished, she stepped back. The glass-reflected portrait showed red, well-defined lips, a flawless peach complexion, bouncy, shiny blond hair. She was beautiful in a clean, Ivy League sort of way, though she hated the comparison. Somehow Ivy League seemed rather tame, so packaged and plastic, so Barbie Doll-like.

Still, she valued her good looks, and at twenty-nine had no trouble in turning her share of heads. Yet the thought of becoming thirty disturbed her. She did not know why exactly. Perhaps because it *sounded* so grownup, so mature, as though she should be further along that road of "having it all together" than she actually was. She remembered how as a young girl she had looked into another mirror, had studied this face and wondered if she would grow up to be a "real" person. Somehow the notion had been planted in her mind that people were "real" by thirty. But that was only a few months away, and Audra still felt very much like that young girl.

She pinched her cheek lightly and giggled. "I guess I'm real enough," she said, as she tossed the lipstick onto the vanity. Then she poked around the clutter until she found the mascara under a box of tissues. "Tomorrow I'll tidy this up," she promised herself. But deep down she knew she wouldn't. Domestic chores bored her. And they were more deadly to a woman than toxic shock. She had seen friends grow old under their whip: cooking, scrubbing, chauffeuring children and pets in station wagons.

Once Audra had come close to this same fate herself with Tom Halleron, a college beau. They were in love. He wanted to get married. In their senior year he had proposed. But Tom was studying to be a marine biologist and already had a job offer in the South, while Audra's prospects had all come from the East and West. She was not a romantic. Her career goals came before love. And marriage was, after all, a dying institution. It would probably be just a few years before she and Tom divorced anyway.

When Audra was two, her mother and father divorced after only a few years of marriage. Hadn't Audra heard all her life that the only good thing her mother got out of that marriage was her daughter? Her mother had kept her married name of Shields, however, and while she had many and frequent lovers, she never remarried. Her favorite advice to friends having marital difficulties was "throw the bum out!" She never tired of telling Audra stories of famous feminists, and weaned her on the exploits of Lucy Stone, Susan B. Anthony, Gloria Steinem. "Women don't need men," she would say. "It's the other way around."

Mrs. Shields' job as an RN provided Audra with a comfortable, though not luxurious life. When the elder Shields was not working, she was picketing or protesting on behalf of some feminist cause. Audra's memories of family life were meals shared with two or three of her mother's friends, discussing the evils of marriage. "A farce that has outlived its usefulness," Mrs. Shields would say.

Of her father, Audra knew little except those sparse details furnished reluctantly by her mother. She had only the most shadowy recollection of the man who had visited her every weekend until she was five years old. "He's not coming anymore," her mother had told her one dreary Saturday afternoon. "He's dead.

Died in a car crash." Her mother's explanation had been curt, without emotion.

After that, Mrs. Shields seldom spoke of Audra's father, but when she did, the adjectives were always the same: weak, lazy, selfish. And Audra, who had no reason to doubt her, grew up applying these same adjectives to most men. She had also grown to view Saturdays in the bleakest and dreariest of terms. She did not like spending them alone.

But the absence of male balance, along with her mother's attitudes had, in the end, proven very unbalancing for Audra. Love was only a myth, she concluded. And didn't fathers go and die on their five year old daughters? *She* was not going to get caught up in any foolishness. So Tom Halleron came and went, as all temptations come and go. And she had never come that close again. No obsolete middle class values for her. She was progressive. She had been raised a humanist. That's what her mother had called their creed anyway.

"What are the rules?" Audra once asked her.

"Oh, just try not to hurt anyone," was the reply.

"And...what else?"

"The rest you make up as you go," her mother had answered laughingly. "Isn't it wonderful? Freedom. Freedom to do anything you want."

Ever since then Audra had lived by that creed. And while her life, for the most part, pleased her, something had begun to happen. And it seemed to continue with alarming acceleration the nearer she came to her thirtieth birthday. She had begun experiencing a deep, inner loneliness that was not easily dispelled by her lovers or lifestyle, but only gnawed more voraciously as time progressed. This loneliness had begun to make her careless. She had no girl friends. Over the years she gradually lost touch with her college chums. Most of them married right after graduation and already had one or more children. Audra did not relate well to midnight feedings, diaper rashes, and baby-sitter problems. At work she was surrounded by men, except for Tisha O'Brien. But

Audra did not especially like her. Tisha seemed far too ordered for her taste. Too rooted in that obsolete middle class morality. Audra could not imagine her boss bellied up to a bar and ordering a Black Label on the rocks; or using four letter words; or bringing strange men home to enjoy for the night.

The blond metallurgist applied the mascara with a frown as she recalled the last man she had brought home. He had had a disgusting habit of sucking air through his teeth, and in the morning had stolen all the money out of her wallet. Yes, she was getting careless. She'd have to be more wary she thought, as she raced out the door to Grobens Tavern. But not too wary, she reasoned. After all, this was Saturday night. No, she needn't be *too* careful. She wasn't going to worry about anything; not her thirtieth birthday, or her lovers, or...dreary Saturdays.

Grobens was a large, homey pub, frequented by people over twenty-five. It was not as wild or loud as the clubs of the younger set. Here, the juke box favorites were Kenny Rogers, Lionel Richie, Barbara Streisand. And, once a month, a live band would come on a Saturday night to play an assortment of pop, contemporary, and country western music. The clientele was as varied as the music, ranging from executives to construction workers. They were generally a subdued lot, and fighting was rare. It was Audra's favorite hangout. She was instantly recognized as she pressed against the bar in her tight designer jeans and silk blouse. The blond, lustrous hair bobbed precociously against her cheeks.

"The usual," she said.

The bartender studied her through squinty jackal eyes, then poured out a Black Label.

"Here you go, cutie," returned Ace Corbet, the dark, burley man behind the bar.

Audra gave him a wink, then pushed a twenty-dollar bill towards him. "Anyone interesting?" she asked, scanning the tavern.

"Na. You can dress them in six hundred dollar Blass suits

or put them in jeans, it don't matter. Most of them are jerks. Not the kind a girl like you should bother with. You need someone with class. And I know just the guy who can deliver."

"Yeah, I bet you do."

"No...seriously. I got more class in this here pinkie than these jerks got in their combined bodies. Why don't you wait for me after work and I'll prove it?"

The well-defined mouth arched into a sneer. He was always coming on to her with one pitch or another. "No thanks, Ace. You're just not my type."

"Really?" snapped Corbet, as the burley chest swelled with indignation. "From what I've seen you're not always that particular." Then the chest deflated and the massive shoulders squeezed out a shrug. "Okay. Suit yourself. Your loss. There's plenty more where you come from."

Audra inched slowly toward the juke box. People could be so touchy, she thought, as she paused to sip her Scotch. But minutes later, as she scanned the song titles, Ace Corbet's remark continued irritating her like a small pebble that had worked its way into her shoe.

What should she play? she thought, suddenly feeling depressed and very much alone in the midst of the crowd. Maybe something by Frank Sinatra, she mused, trying hard to recapture those heady emotions she had experienced when she first arrived.

"You plan on playing something or are you just window shopping?" The voice belonged to an attractive redhead in tight leather pants. The T-shirt she wore was wrapped like Saran over her breasts. And red felt letters proclaimed that **BEAUTICIANS DO IT BETTER.**

Audra managed one of those toothy, insincere smiles she used to more or less keep from certain confrontation. "I don't know what I want. You go ahead."

The woman with the red letters squeezed by. "Honey," she said, dropping some coins into the machine and punching several buttons which she seemed to know by heart, "if you don't know what you want by now, you better get help." Then she disappeared.

Audra's brooding depression was instantly pushed aside by anger. How could anyone be so brassy, so tasteless! She had an overwhelming impulse to peal off those disgusting red letters and repaste them on that face. The thought seemed at once so ridiculous that in spite of her anger, Audra giggled softly. Well, it *would* serve her right, she thought, as she half heartedly resumed scanning the LP listings.

"Hey momma! You going to move over and let someone else at this juke? You've been here a while. Tell you what, why don't you let me play a few for you?"

Audra stared into a handsome, grinning face. "Well...I... ."

"I bet you're the Sinatra type, right?" The lean, muscular man bent over the juke box.

"Yes, I like Sinatra," Audra replied. She had never seen him before. There was something strangely attractive about him. A smile split across her face like a popped zip-locked bag, releasing both her anger and depression.

"Well...what do you say?" he asked, tapping the juke box impatiently.

"Go ahead stranger." There was flirtation in her voice.

The man laughed a coarse, insolent laugh. "Not stranger for long, I hope. The name is Bubba, Bubba Hanagan. "And as he slipped a few coins into the slot, he let his left leg casually brush against her.

The sun shone brightly as the warm air swirled through the open car window and playfully rearranged Tisha's hair. Gliding over the road as though it was a ribbon of glass, smooth and swift, the car seemed to be moving ten miles an hour rather than one hundred. Through this section of the desert, the highway was open and wide, and sparsely traveled. To most people, it was a road of little significance, not leading to any major city or town except that town of sorts, the Cheyenne reservation.

The tape deck blasted out a favorite song and Tisha sang jubilantly with it. "'Jesus, Jesus. He's as close as the mention of His name.'" Her spirits seemed to soar, to accelerate like the speedometer, and periodically she had to forcibly bring both herself and the speed down. God was *so* wonderful she thought. She couldn't imagine life without Him. Her mother had taught her about Jesus when she was very young, and Tisha could not remember a time when she didn't love Him. He was the center of her life, the very reason for her existence. How could she be anything but joyful? Hadn't she "eaten the fat" and "drunk the sweet" that the pastor spoke about in church this morning? And wasn't the "joy of the Lord her strength"? Yes, God was good.

But as she pulled into the Cheyenne reservation, her joy began to ebb somewhat. As she drove down the dusty, dreary streets whose sides were dotted with broken-down shanties, it slumped even more. And when she finally pulled in front of her mother's house, it had shriveled into a tiny lump which lodged in her throat.

"'He's as close as the mention of His name,'" she sang again, trying to dislodge it. It was a battle she fought every other Sunday, when she came to visit her mother.

Tisha tried to think about the pastor's sermon as she got out of the car. In front of the one-room shack sat a disheveled woman in a rocker. It was true many of the homes on the reservation were lovely, well kept. Some even had gardens of vegetables or flowers. Others had a neatly fenced corral in back. But not here. Here the stench of rotting garbage hung heavy in the air. Dogs, whose skin sagged over protruding ribs and whose empty bellies cringed against the dirt, foraged among the debris. One could almost hear the melancholy sound of a lone flute echoing among the sandy hills.

Eight years ago, after Tisha's father died, her mother retreated to the reservation. Tisha could not understand this or why her mother continued to live here. Once during a visit, Tisha found all the uncashed weekly checks she had sent her, stuffed into a rusty coffee can. "I don't need anything," was her mother's explanation.

Even her love for tribal customs and history had vanished. She once delighted in retelling the brave exploits of a great tribe, the Tsis-tsis-tas, the "human beings," as the Cheyenne called themselves. In fact, it was from Tsis-tsis-tas that Tisha got her name. Her mother had shortened it to Tsista when it came time to name her only child. But Tisha's father, feeling too embarrassed to give his daughter such a foreign sounding name, and too kindhearted to disappoint his wife, had changed the spelling from Tsista to Tisha, claiming that in English it meant the same. If her mother had been aware of the deception, she never voiced it, and, in fact, always seemed proud of her daughter's name. In contrast, this retreating to the Cheyenne reservation seemed to Tisha so...so cowardly.

Muffling a sigh, she bent over her mother and kissed her. A smile appeared on the elderly woman's face, and gnarled hands patted Tisha's cheeks. Then the catatonic rocking resumed.

Without a word, Tisha returned to the car and began unloading the packages she had brought with her; bags of food, a pair of new curtains, cleaning supplies, a new broom. It was always like this. She would greet her mother with a kiss, bring packages into the house, then clean what she could before preparing a nice, hot Sunday dinner. Then she and her mother would eat together. After the dishes, Tisha would bring out a metal folding chair, place it alongside her mother's rocker and the two would sit silently. There was never much conversation. Talking seemed to upset the elder O'Brien.

Today, the first thing Tisha did when she got into the house was pull a can of Raid from one of the grocery bags and begin spraying underneath the sink. Roaches. She had seen them last time scurrying over the area. With one hand she sprayed the pipes. With the other, she shielded her nose and mouth from the fumes. Only after the pipes were thoroughly coated was Tisha satisfied and put the can away. That done, she slipped on rubber gloves, and with a sponge and diluted solution of ammonia, began wiping down a scarred four-by-four wooden table and two metal chairs. Next, she washed the two short, metal cabinets and Formica tops which were butted together and served as the only kitchen counter in the shanty. These stood between a badly chipped, white electric stove that looked at least thirty years old, and a stainless steel sink held up by a crude two-by-four wood frame. On the other side of the sink was an old, white GE refrigerator which seemed, in its battered and chipped appearance, to be the mate of the stove. Tisha washed everything down, taking special pains to avoid the pipes where she had just sprayed.

To the other half of the shack, she applied the new broom, sweeping grains of sand into little ant hill-like piles. On this half was a single lumpy bed, a night stand, one ripped green vinyl straight-back chair, and a large, wooden cabinet that served as a closet.

When her mother first came here, Tisha brought furniture; a bedroom set, a dinette, but these things were either given away or stolen. An old woman alone was an easy target for the drugged and liquored men who prowled the area. That was why Tisha sent checks instead of cash, and why she had set up a bank account for her mother in the small nearby town. The account was rarely used. Instead, Mrs. O'Brien actually seemed to prefer her condition of poverty, as though it reflected an inner life that was deficient and poor. And the only things that managed to stay in the shanty were these odd and broken pieces of furniture.

Tisha washed the only window, hung the new curtains, then stepped back. The perky floral fabric draped the glass valiantly. But its courageous effort to cheer was not sufficient to overcome the general bleakness. It was as a cotton swab trying to erase a giant blackboard. With a heavy heart, Tisha turned from the window and began seasoning the roast beef and praying silently.

As the elder O'Brien rocked, Tisha sat quietly in a metal folding chair next to her. The cool evening breeze was a refreshing change from the heat laden shanty. Tisha tilted her head backward to catch the wind. From time to time she reached over and lovingly squeezed her mother's hand. Mrs. O'Brien would smile in response and nod her head as though answering some question when in actuality no word had passed between them this entire visit, not even over dinner. Her mother had been extremely quiet today and seemed more preoccupied than usual. There were always at least a few words about the weather, what they were eating, perhaps even a sentence or two about Tisha's job.

Little wrinkles of worry creased Tisha's face as she squeezed her mother's hand again. She felt so inadequate. What could she say or do to help? She loved her mother very much, and it hurt to see her this way. Her mother was the kindest person Tisha had ever known. She had never heard her say a mean thing about anyone in her life. She just seemed to love everyone. When Tisha was young, her mother taught her about Jesus. Tisha found it easy to understand God's love. She saw it in the elder O'Brien daily.

Her mother had always been there for Tisha; had provided a happy, peaceful home in which to grow up. Tisha knew there were times when her mother went without in order to put braces on her teeth, or give her that new school wardrobe, or that class trip or some other thing that kids were always needing. Yet while Tisha felt her mother had always been there for her, she had not always been there for her mother. There was a time, in junior high, when Tisha was ashamed of her; when she began apologizing to her friends for the way her mother dressed, talked, acted. She continued to bring her friends home, but it was always a little painful to watch them stare with amazement at something her mother did or listen to them giggle at some mispronounced word her mother said. Tisha didn't understand until later that her friends were simply fascinated by her mother's uniqueness and girlishly tickled by her often funny way of saying things.

This angst over her heritage started when she began hearing the word "half-breed" float past her in the school halls, and hearing it seep from snickering lips like poisonous gas behind her in class. Her youthful insecurity cried for acceptance. She did not want to be different or stand out.

That only lasted about a year; a year when learning and

growing, tears and joy all folded together in awkward adolescence like a jelly roll. Looking back she could see the striation of both the bitter and sweet. The sweetness of her mother's face was still vivid in Tisha's mind the day she had come over and sat so solemnly next to her on the couch. Tisha could see she had something on her mind. The elder O'Brien had taken her hand, much like the way Tisha had now taken her mother's. Love had shown from her mother's eyes like a flashlight into Tisha's dark heart that day. "Never allow anyone to make you ashamed of who you are," she had said. "Remember, God has made you. Do not insult Him by your shame." *She had known. All that time her mother had known how she felt!*

It was a bitter revelation. Tisha felt ashamed of her feelings and ashamed of her cowardice. Everyone wanted to be loved. Everyone wanted to be accepted. But she had paid a price too high. Mrs. O'Brien had not been angry. Instead, she had looked compassionately at her daughter. She understood how a little soul clings, like a fledgling, to security and safety, even the security and safety of negative conformity. Mothers were amazing. How did they know such things? Who taught them?

"You must soar like an eagle," her mother had said, "and you must not be afraid." They had hugged each other and cried that day. And then for a very long time after, they sat holding hands and talked. Tisha had never felt so close to her. Now, holding her mother's hand, Tisha wished they could talk that way again.

"Mom, it's almost time for me to go. Wouldn't you like to talk a little?" There was a pleading note in her voice.

To Tisha's surprise, her mother answered, "Yes." And tears rose up like a fountain in the old, tired eyes.

This reaction frightened Tisha. "Mom? What's wrong? What is it!"

Mrs. O'Brien shook her head. "No, no. Don't worry. I am fine. I...Tisha, I saw Jesus last night."

The beautiful engineer's mouth dropped open like a draw bridge. "Oh...that's really wonderful," she said, trying to hide her misgivings. Her mother was not prone to hysterics or fanciful visions. She had no reason to doubt her. Still, it was hard to believe. "Are you *sure*?"

Her mother ignored the skepticism. "He told me I had let my heart wax cold."

That one sentence, at once so simple and yet so profound, removed Tisha's misgivings. She could see that God had reached into the inner recesses of her mother's heart and exposed it as only He could, by the light of both truth and love. She tried to push back the tears that now began welling up in her own eyes. Oh Praise God, her mind said over and over again, while with her mouth she said nothing. She was completely overcome with joy.

"He said my heart had waxed cold because...because I was angry with Him." The elder O'Brien had difficulty speaking. Her voice broke several times and at one point dwindled to a near whisper. She was unaccustomed to forming so many words at one time and this veritable address was not without its price. The words came slowly, clumsily, like the faltering steps of a toddler. But the weight of her message was such that in spite of the clumsiness, Mrs. O'Brien seemed determined to relay it in its entirety.

"He said," she continued, "I blamed Him for...for Paddy's death." At this point the elderly woman could no longer contain herself and burst into tears. "It's true," she sobbed. "I hated God for taking my Paddy...my darling... ."

Like a safety net, Tisha's arms encircled her mother, and the heaving body simply fell into them. "I know. I know."

"His words made me sad. All I could do was cry as I am now. But...it is over. It's finished."

"Then you must come home with me. You'll live with me now. I'll take care of you."

"No!" The forceful reply so stunned Tisha that for a moment she sat in confused silence just staring at her mother.

"Then...what are you going to do?" she finally asked.

"I will stay here, with my people. There are things needing to be done. Do not worry about me any longer my Tisha...my little human being." There was a tenderness in her mother's voice that Tisha had not heard in many years. "Things will be different now. But this one thing does not change, I love you, my daughter."

Tisha's arms tightened around the aging woman. Her face was wet with tears. "I love you too." And as she held her mother, Tisha had an inner knowledge that she would be all right.

Audra could not believe it was Sunday night and *he* was still here. She looked over at the large body sprawled across her bed, clad only in BVDs. The handsome square face was studying its new object of lust, a sizable Granny apple. After a few bites, the face wrinkled.

"It's sour," said the voice, while a powerful hand flipped it with disgust onto the floor. The apple was soon forgotten, however, as attention was transferred to the massive biceps. They quivered in brief, isometric jerks. He was into body building and possessed the powerful physique of an avid weight lifter. Indeed, aside from women, lifting weights was his only passion.

Audra had scoffed at what she considered a rather ignoble pursuit, and had asked what he saw in it. "Power," had been the reply. He then provided an immediate demonstration by twisting her arm.

Audra looked at the discarded apple. "Bubba! I don't know where you come from, but here we don't throw food on the floor."

The blond, blue-eyed man rippled his quadriceps and chuckled good naturedly. "Sorry Audra, just one of my bad bachelor habits." He made no attempt to pick it up. "What's on TV?" he asked, sounding bored.

"Look for yourself," Audra answered with an irritation in her voice that she made no effort to conceal. She tossed the TV Guide onto the bed, just a bit out of reach, so that Bubba had to pull himself over in order to get it.

"You broads are all alike."

Audra walked over to the partially eaten apple, debated for

a second whether to pick it up or make an issue, then finally bent over. "And you men are all alike," she snapped. But even as she walked into the kitchen, carrying both the apple and her anger, something told her she wouldn't ask him to leave tonight, just as she had not asked him to leave the night before. In fact, she might not ask him to leave for quite sometime. He was crude, brutish, possibly even dangerous, and these things she didn't like. But there was something about him. He was sexually satisfying and a companion to fill that lonely space that seemed to gnaw at her more and more. He was also so deliciously selfish and self-centered; the type with whom you never form an attachment.

When Audra was in her early teens she discovered D.H. Lawrence's *Lady Chatterly's Lover*. It immediately became her favorite book, and remained so for years. In all, she read it fifteen times. To Audra, Lady Chatterly was the embodiment of the truly perfect woman; liberated but not forsaking breeding, intellect, or femininity. She seemed a sharp contrast to Audra's mother who often appeared crude and uneducated; and a contrast to many of her mother's girl friends who had forsaken all vestiges of femininity in their hard hats, fading dungarees, and leather work boots.

Audra had also adopted much of the philosophy which D.H. Lawrence had so liberally woven throughout the fabric of his novel. Some she even committed to memory and applied to her own life as a personal "golden rule." One of these "golden rules" had been: "Unless you had some emotion or sympathy in common with a man, you would not sleep with him." She had substituted man in place of the word, woman, which appeared in the Lawrence novel. And for years she lived by this rule.

While many of her girl friends judged their sexual experiences as so many collected scalps, more being better, Audra opted for higher standards. There always had to be "some emotion or sympathy in common." But as Audra got older, she began to view this "golden rule" as too idealistic, too romantic. Her friends had been right all along. Nothing meaningful need pass between either party. And in most cases, this void actually proved to be best. No sloppy sentimental attachment could be formed with someone like Bubba; no jealousy over other flirtations, no possessiveness when things got too serious—things would never get too serious. Certainly there would be no talk of marriage, no temptation to walk down the aisle and drive station wagons in suburbia.

"Hey momma! Get me a brew while you're up, will you?"

Audra smiled to herself as she opened the refrigerator. Men. "Can't live with them and can't live without them." Women's Lib had yet to solve the real issue between the sexes, perhaps between humanity itself. Basically, everyone was incompatible. And how do you solve that? The blond metallurgist shrugged. Let those who dared, try to figure that one out. As she reached for a bottle of Miller Lite, Audra chuckled sardonically. For all their accomplishments, she doubted if the Women's Movement had, or could ever have, any impact on the likes of Bubba Hanagan.

Tisha bent over several large sheets of paper that cluttered the long metal table. With her pencil, she made a notation here and there, with her eraser, a few corrections. Then she stopped and smiled, a loving, parental sort of smile, for to Tisha the P2 was much like a child. She loved her grace, her promise. Self-indulgently, Tisha scanned the specs, not with her usual critical eye, but with the eye of love that sees nothing critically. Suddenly, she felt something touch her fingers and the intimacy of the moment, between parent and offspring, was broken. This annoyed her until she turned and saw a large, powerful hand covering her own.

"Mind if I sit down?" asked a male voice.

"Why not, you're the chief," Tisha returned, smiling.

Gingerly, Michael Patterson stepped over the bench and eased his body next to hers. His presence did not surprise Tisha. He came often. He claimed it was his favorite room. Yet it wasn't much to look at; a giant cafeteria type room with large metal tables and benches set up here and there. Against the far wall, partitions separated the space into cubicles containing small metal desks.

Each cubicle belonged to a different employee of R&D; a place where their books and notes were kept, a place to go for quiet thought when not in one of the busier rooms containing the reactor or the wind tunnel or the computers that displayed a different spec on a screen at the touch of a finger. It was in this drab room that seeds of excitement and innovation were sown. This is what made it special for Mike.

"How are you doing on that briefing?" he said absently.

Tisha thumbed through some papers on the table, and after finding the right ones, slid them close to him.

His eyes quickly raced over several pages. "Not bad. But you'll have to complete the rest without Nolan. He's out of town...on special assignment."

"Alright, no problem," she returned with a smile, her curiosity aroused. But she did not question him. She knew his passion for secrecy.

"Good," said Mike. "I guess that's about it. Except... ."

"Yes?"

"Thanks for not asking about Nolan."

"Oh, you're welcome, J. Edgar."

"J. Edgar?"

"Yes, as in J. Edgar Hoover."

"The former FBI Director?"

"Yes."

Mike chuckled. "Oh, I get it. The obvious comparison, the secrecy, the 'cloak and dagger.'"

"Could be twins."

"That so? From what I hear, he was pretty tough on his boys."

"He was," Tisha replied.

"Well, keep that in mind, O'Brien."

"What?"

"That you're just one of the boys."

***

The flickering candle sent a thin ribbon of smoke curling up the sides of its glass enclosure. It had an herbal scent, but remained undetectable over the aroma of the bouillabaisse on Tisha's plate and the huge Maine lobster that lay open before the skilled hands of Dr. Daniel Chapman. His long, slender fingers held a thin, silver, pick-like object which he used dexterously in probing the lobster's left claw.

"Why do I feel as though I'm still in the operating room?" he laughed, his shining, blue eyes providing stiff competition for the candle.

Tisha looked over at him and even in the dim light could see the indentation of a dimple. He was more charming than handsome, and had rather ordinary features. He was extremely good natured, and this fact was reflected in his face. He always appeared to be smiling. Tisha watched the dimple deepen as she licked her fingers. "Messy," she said as she picked up her napkin. "A definite Emily Post no-no."

Daniel laughed and continued picking at his lobster claw. "I've never known anyone who enjoys food as much as you, except possibly me." Daniel Chapman's tall, lean body was the deceiving receptacle that held the heart of a true Epicurean. He loved food. Yet he was of that small but fortunate breed that could consume great quantities of it without ever sacrificing his waistline. At thirty-five, he still retained the sleek, muscular frame of his youth.

"That's why I love taking you out. You're fun to watch. Most people are inhibited when they go to a restaurant," he continued. "Think they have to be so perfect. Napkin just so on the lap. Having the proper salad fork, cake fork and so on. Never getting a morsel of food on the table or on your face, like food isn't supposed to be *messy*. In ancient times everyone ate with their fingers."

"Well, isn't that why God made hands?"

Daniel chuckled. "I had a date once who insisted on eating her chicken leg with a knife and fork. Insisted, mind you, as though the entire canon of etiquette would come crashing down if she did otherwise. That's one of my pet peeves, you know."

"What is?"

"People eating chicken with a knife and fork. Just too much bother to suit me."

"Well, don't let it get out, doc. People won't have much faith in a surgeon who couldn't skillfully use his knife on one poor little chicken leg." Tisha's chocolate eyes softened with affection. She often teased him about his work, but always underlying her words was a tone that reflected both respect and pride.

The supple, almost boyish lines of his face folded into a smile. "You could always use it as blackmail."

"I don't need blackmail."

"No, Tisha," he said, his tone soft as cotton bunting. "I'm afraid I'm as defenseless as a chicken leg in your hands."

"You mean these messy things?" she said, smiling.

"You know I'm crazy about you, don't you?" he said, looking a bit too earnest.

Tisha laughed softly, almost girlishly, as though she was used to hearing sincere men say they were crazy about her, when the opposite was true. During her last two years in high school, she had more than her share of dates. Saint Joseph's was medium sized and went from first grade all the way through high school. Socially, it was years behind the mainstream. Here there was no need for metal detectors to expose hidden arsenals under jackets. Dances still brought out the crowds, and a date with a guy didn't mean an automatic trip to the back seat of a car. For the most part, Saint Joseph's boys were eager, hopeful, but not very demanding.

At first, Tisha enjoyed the attention and found it flattering to be sought after. But by graduation, she had become bored with the whole scene, and tired of thwarting clumsy and unwelcome advances. In college it was another matter all together. It was as if she had stepped from a child's fairy tale into the glaring, vulgar "real world." Here the boys or would-be-men were often arrogant, crude, and very demanding. All too many believed the price of a beer entitled them to a cornucopia of liberties. Dating became as appealing to Tisha as mud wrestling, and she stopped it altogether. Because of her aloofness, she was dubbed "Ice Queen" by the jock fraternities.

After college, she dated sporadically, but found that it was just more of the same, with a sophisticated twist. Her dating adventures became just dreary little blips on the sonar of her free time. The tension and pressure on each date seemed to build-up then break-up over the same reoccurring subject, *sex*. She had once heard it said that "men play at love to get sex and women play at sex to get love."

She had seen her share of men playing at love and then drop her when she wouldn't play at sex. She had heard all the lines expressing feigned ardor, then all the unflattering adjectives when she did not buy the lie. "Frigid, old-fashioned, out of touch with her sexuality," were some of the milder descriptions. Others were obscene, and still others were creative but ludicrous like the warning that stifling sexual urges caused cancer by triggering abnormal chemical reactions in the body. She had laughed outright over that one. She just couldn't help herself.

But the "frigidity" tag was the one that made her smile on the inside. She knew better than anyone how untrue that was. She was as thawable as the next girl, maybe even more than some. Her passions were easily aroused. That's why she had to keep such a tight lid on things. And that was the joke; that was what the guys never understood. She had to protect herself from *herself*. That's why she had to be so careful.

It all made dating too dreary and she was about to swear off it forever, when she met Dr. Daniel Chapman. He came like a breath of fresh air. Not an octopus, but a gentleman with a sense of humor and a brain. She enjoyed his company immensely. They had been going out a year now and she was terribly fond of him. But try as she may, the "thunderbolt" would not strike, and deep down Tisha knew she really didn't love him. A friend of Tisha's once told her that she was not the type to fall in and out of love, but when she fell, it would be very very hard. But Tisha was beginning to wonder if she was ever going to "fall" at all.

"Did I tell you how gorgeous you are tonight?" Daniel added, looking sheepish and sweet at the same time.

"Only about ten times, but thank you. I think you're just grateful to see a woman who isn't wearing white."

Daniel shook his head as he eyed Tisha appreciatively. Her hair was pulled back into a French braid, and pearls, the shape of large tear drops hanging from each lobe, glistened in the dim lighting. She looked like she stepped out of a fashion magazine: stylish, sophisticated, beautiful. His heart melted like the candle in the center of the table. "You're the most sensational looking woman I know."

"Makes me wonder just how few you actually must know."

"I know plenty, thank you. And believe me, there's plenty more who'd like to know me. Not that I'm Mr. Wonderful or anything. It's just that 'Doctor' still has a magic ring for the ladies. Believe it or not, as liberated as women say they are, they still want their daughters to marry a doctor. I *know*. I've had enough mothers try to set me up with their little beauties. Funny, isn't it?"

"Well, my mother kept telling me to *be* a doctor. She never said anything about marrying one."

Daniel laughed. "You're still the most sensational looking woman, but you must know that."

"I don't know any such thing. Besides, I thought it was my mind you liked," Tisha said as she finished wiping her fingers on the napkin. "Now I find you have a thing for women who love to make little piggies of themselves." She dipped a small corner portion of the napkin into her water glass and began rubbing a splatter on her dress. "Sorry, but if I don't get this out now, that's the end of the outfit. They can send a man to the moon, but they can't invent something to guarantee removal of grease stains from a dress." Tisha busily rubbed the green silk bodice. Finally, she looked up and smiled. "I normally wouldn't fuss, but it's new."

Daniel eyed the flounce dress with long sleeves that buttoned around the wrists. It was delicate and flowing, and looked like green mist covering her body. He couldn't take his eyes off her. "I hope you bought it just for me."

Tisha wrinkled her nose. "Speaking of clean... ."

"Was that the topic? I thought it was you and me."

"No, I believe we were talking about messy food, little piggies, and the like."

Daniel sighed. "Not too romantic, but okay, okay, what about 'clean'?"

"Well, it reminds me of something your brother wrote."

"Has he given you more of his poetry?"

"Yes."

"You read them of course."

"Of course."

"You're very kind. And that's another thing I *love* about you."

Tisha laughed, ignoring the ardent look on his face. Things seemed to be taking a turn in their relationship. He was beginning to look at her too intensely, too longingly. Just too much of everything she wasn't ready for. "I read Joshua's poetry because I like him and because I like his poetry. Some of it is quite good."

Daniel Chapman grunted disagreeably, but there was pride on his face. He loved his brother very much. "And what did my brother write that just reminded you of clean?"

"He called it, 'Clean Out Your Ears.' It was about Q-tips and how people never listen to each other."

"Sounds terrible!"

"Don't be so jealous, just because you haven't got one poetic bone in your body," she teased. "Besides, he has talent. Someday he'll be famous."

"Maybe...if he lives that long." Daniel Chapman's face suddenly tightened. "He's...he's doing it you know. He's finally doing it. He's joining the Zionist Underground."

Tisha pushed her plate away. Suddenly she wasn't hungry.

"He's been talking about it for so long. Still...I had hoped he wouldn't," Daniel mused.

"I'm surprised he didn't do it sooner," Tisha responded. "His passion for Israel is too great. Your father has made a zealot out of him."

Daniel nodded. As a result of Britain's waning commitment to a Jewish Palestine in the twenties, frustrated Jews formed a semiunderground, semi-illegal Jewish army, the Haganah. By the thirties the Haganah was active in smuggling Jews into Palestine. After World War II, they openly engaged British soldiers and blockades to help surviving European Jews enter Palestine. Daniel's father, David Chapman, fought in the Haganah under Ben-Gurion.

David Chapman was part of the attack on a British concentration camp at Athlit where over two hundred illegal Jews were liberated and later dispersed into the kibbutzim. After the Haganah made a truce with Britain in 1946, Chapman joined the Yishuv and fought with Menachem Begin. Chapman was convinced that the Jews would get nothing except what they were willing to fight for. Even after Israel was declared a state on May 14, 1948, David Chapman remained in the Yishuv. Israel's emergence as a state had so enraged the Moslem world that their armies immediately crossed the Palestine borders in an effort to forcibly nullify the partition resolution. Israel, more than ever, needed her fighting men.

Years later, when David Chapman moved to America, he continued fighting for Israel, though in a different capacity. He formed a small, knowledgeable group, Supporters of Israel, to lobby Congress and influence matters which concerned that nation. One of the most zealous of the group was his own son, Joshua.

"Yes, Joshua is committed," Daniel said, almost sadly.

Tisha reached over and took Daniel's hand. "It's what he wants. It's what he lives for. There's nothing you can do to stop him."

"I know."

"So quit blaming yourself."

Daniel's eyes narrowed as he studied his date. "How did you get to be so smart?"

"I'm not that smart. I just know you. And I know that

50

you're tearing yourself apart."

"I'm the older brother, remember? I promised Dad I would look out for him."

"And you have. You've been a good brother, Daniel."

The lean surgeon squeezed Tisha's hand. "Thanks for that."

"You don't have to thank me for speaking the truth."

Daniel shrugged and began looking broodingly at the flickering candle.

"So when does he leave?"

"Next week," Daniel said, rubbing his hands over his face as though he were tired. "You know, all I kept thinking while I was stitching up his arm after the airport explosion was that he could have been killed. Tisha, if he joins the Underground, I may never see him again." Each word was so thickly coated with fear they sounded foreign in his mouth.

"It's a horrible thought, and it will torment you unless you put Joshua in God's hands," Tisha said softly.

"You're right, but it's not easy," he replied, still looking downcast. "If it was your brother, you'd be able to do it. You have such a sense of God, so much faith. How I envy you! I'm afraid mine is pale in comparison, but yes, I know that's the answer."

They sat holding hands across the table for awhile and by degrees, Daniel Chapman's face began to brighten. "You know, you were right about something else," he continued, trying to lighten things up. "People don't listen to each other."

"That's Joshua's line."

"Well, then he's right, at least about some of us."

"Oh?"

"Yes. I listen to you. You don't listen to me," he teased.

"When? When didn't I listen?" Tisha responded in mock indignation, pleased to see the smile reappear on Daniel's face.

"Today on the phone, when I called you."

"I heard every word you said."

"Okay, repeat them."

"Well, you said, 'Hello' and... ."

"Funny, very funny! Tell me the part after I asked you out."

"I said I love going out with you, that we have fun together," Tisha continued.

"Go on."

"Then you said we should get married. And my comment was that that was a rather silly reason for getting married. And you said people have gotten married for sillier reasons."

"Well?"

"Well what?"

"Well, you weren't listening. I *was* asking you to marry me."

"Because we have fun together?"

"Because I love you!"

Tisha brought the crystal water glass to her lips and sipped slowly. She felt the same emotions as when, in the fourth grade, she caught Johnny Lawson stuffing a love letter into her school bag. She would never forget that biting look of humiliation on his face. How its vicious teeth ripped into her heart! It was painful to feel what other's felt, to feel their hurts and disappointments. She had tried hating him for his adoration, for transmitting that pain to her like a contagious disease. But she never could. Now, twenty-one years later, she saw that same look of humiliation bite into Daniel's face as he realized the extent of her surprise.

In the past year of dating, marriage was never discussed. Tisha greatly admired Daniel. He was one of the finest men she had ever known. And marriage was something Tisha viewed as desirable and worthwhile. She had been the product of a successful marriage and she remembered how after over twenty-five years of marriage, her parents still held hands; still, with heads together, whispered their inner-most secrets; still laughed and had fun; and how every once in a while they would even steal a kiss on the couch. But she couldn't force her feelings, fabricate something that wasn't there. Her feelings were just not that strong for him. Not like her feelings for... . She stopped. She had no business thinking about her boss. He was a married man. A future with him was unthinkable. A relationship was impossible. But try as she may, it did effect her feelings towards other men.

Slowly, she swallowed another mouthful of water, letting it soothe her throat, hoping it could somehow soothe the words that would come from it.

"You're right. I don't listen," she finally said. "Daniel, you know I love you but not in *that* way. I'm terribly flattered...but... ."

The deeply etched dimple yielded to the blow of disappointment. For a moment he looked like someone who had just been kicked in the stomach. As he covered his mouth, Tisha feared he would lose his lobster dinner all over the table, but when he removed his hand she saw the dimple cave deep into his cheek in a fake smile. "I suppose I'll have to adjust to the concept of just being friends with you. We can be friends, can't we?"

"Yes," she returned gratefully.

"Who knows, maybe in time you'll change your mind. I'd like to hold out that hope. Do you mind?"

Tisha shifted uncomfortable in the chair. "I don't know, Daniel. I can't make you any promises," she said, all the while thinking how much she really did love him, how easy he was to love. He was kind, gentle, compassionate, easy to talk to. Oh, why couldn't she love him the way she loved...Tisha's thoughts became frozen and seemed to dangle unfinished in front of her like icicles. Slowly, they melted, forming a puddle in which she clearly saw the truth for the first time. The "thunderbolt" *had* struck. And the realization that it was Michael Patterson she loved made her feel sick.

Daniel's eyes squinted as he scanned the road. It was unusually dark outside; the quarter moon being obscured by clouds. Even the stars were difficult to define. They too were obscured. The entire sky looked like it was draped in gray gauze. And along this section of the road most of the street lights had been destroyed by vandals. It made the gloomy neighborhood even gloomier. It had not always been this way. In recent years the city had experienced a boom. With it came a mixed bag of poverty and prosperity. In its eastern sector, the beginnings of a slum had grown, like an ugly wart on an otherwise blemish-free face. It was into the heart of this wart that they were now driving.

Finally, the car stopped in front of an old apartment house. When they stepped out of the Cadillac, the stench of rotting garbage assaulted them. Dim lights shining through grease-smudged windows cast an eerie glow around the entrance way and by this light Tisha could see the faint outlines of battered galvanized pails along both sides of the stoop, some overflowing, others overturned.

Tisha and Daniel had said little to one another since leaving the restaurant. They were silent now as they climbed the crumbling concrete steps. Tisha had wanted to say "good-bye" to Joshua. Daniel was happy to oblige. Being alone with Tisha after her rejection was proving awkward. He would need time to get over it.

Finally, they reached the massive wooden front door of the apartment house. It was heavy oak with elaborate scroll work along the sides and deeply etched designs in the middle. It had been beautiful once. Now, much of the scroll work was chipped away, and the elaborate etchings were disfigured by pen knife drawings and monograms. "Cindy loves Hank" and a crude carving of a large heart was sprawled carelessly across the width of the door. In another five years, it would probably disappear completely, perhaps to be used as firewood or someone's bed in the alley.

Slowly, the pair climbed another flight of stairs. They had come here often together. For Daniel it was always a bitter climb. He was perpetually protective of Joshua, who was eleven years his junior, and hated to see his brother live in such squalor. But the idealistic young poet was bent on making it by himself and while he was selling his poetry at a most satisfying rate, his financial state never changed. Every extra dollar went into his Zionist activities.

They finally reached the familiar gnarled door and knocked. Seconds later, a pleasant boyish face beamed at them. "Hey! Come on in. It's good to see you!" He gave Daniel a hug, and kissed Tisha affectionately on the cheek. "Look who's here!" he yelled to his three friends who sat huddled together, embroiled in a heated discussion. The friends nodded politely as the pair entered but beyond politeness showed little interest.

"We're going to Israel together," Joshua announced. There was pride in his voice.

"So I hear." Tisha, touched his arm lightly. "How is it?"

Joshua looked down at his bandaged biceps. "Almost like new. My brother does good work."

Daniel screwed his face into a frown. "A child could have taken care of that. Maybe next time you wouldn't be so lucky, especially where you're going."

Joshua threw his uninjured arm around his brother's shoulders. "You worry too much."

"That's because I have to do it for both of us. You don't have enough sense to worry! Haven't you heard that Kamal has sworn by Allah that he will annihilate the Zionist Underground?"

"Kamal is an egotistical maniac," returned Joshua as he ushered his guests to two folding chairs. Tisha smiled to herself. The chairs looked much like her mother's at the reservation.

"And you?" asked Daniel.

"I am a zealot."

"Some call Kamal a zealot," Daniel persisted.

Impatiently, Joshua brushed the comparison aside. "We've been through all this. Give it up, brother. There is nothing you can say to change my mind. We are all sick of terrorism. And you, Daniel, in your profession, have ample opportunity to see its fruits. Surely you are weary of picking up the bloody pieces. Somebody *must* take a stand."

"Yes, certainly the US isn't going to do it," said Solomon Roth. "We continue to make blunders. We meddled and pressured where we shouldn't. We've cut our defenses. We've even disbanded the Strategic Air Command. Talk about an open invitation!"

"Yeah, there're eleven countries that have nuclear capability and twenty-two Third-World countries building intercontinental ballistic missiles. Sometimes you wonder who's minding the store in Washington," returned David Rosen.

"Russia alone has over twenty-nine thousand nuclear warheads, some of which are being sold on the black market," added Benjamin Cohen. "If Kamal ever got hold of one of them, he'd... ."

"Iran's been gobbling up some of these Russian missiles and you know Iran is Kamal's biggest supporter," interrupted Solomon, a fire rising up from the depths of his being to flush his face. "It doesn't take a rocket scientist to figure out that the Jihad would love to add a nuclear war head to their chemical and biological arsenal. It's no secret that Iran has been conducting amphibious training exercises under contaminated conditions. Not too difficult to figure out what they've got in mind."

"You're going to try to sell us on your theory that they plan to hit Saudi Arabia. Forget it, Sol, I don't buy it," returned David Rosen, equally fired up.

"You just don't get it, do you? This whole thing is a *spiritual* battle. Rafsanjani wants Mecca and Medina, the holy sites, and he'll commit all of Iran's resources to get it, you mark my words," said Solomon. "And he may even use Kamal to get the ball rolling."

"Moslem is not going to go against Moslem," said Cohen.

"Why not, they've been doing it for years. Besides, to Iran, the Saudis are traitors. They've gotten too chummy with the Great Satan, and... ."

"Sounds like we're about to have our own war right here," said Joshua from the kitchen. Metal and stoneware clanked as he finished preparing instant coffee and peanut butter smeared crackers for his guests. "The point is, we're finally willing to do something about all this," he said, as he carried in a tray made from a cut down cardboard box. He placed it on a small wooden table in the midst of them.

"You make things sound rather dismal," said Dr. Chapman, finally breaking his silence. "I mean, nuclear war heads, Kamal, Iran, Russia. Just what do you hope to accomplish, the four of you? You're just little grasshoppers in comparison."

"And King David was only a little shepherd when he killed the giant, Goliath," returned Joshua with a smile.

There was a general noise of consensus among Joshua's three friends. Daniel Chapman gave them a dirty look.

"It's time for the grasshoppers of the world to unit and take the offensive. It's time for David to meet Goliath," Joshua said.

"Here, here!" chimed his friends.

Daniel Chapman threw up his arms in exasperation. "Alright, alright, so we have four heroes with sling shots. Heroes never listen to anyone, so I won't even try to talk you out of it. But just be careful, Joshua. *Be careful.*"

Joshua winked at Tisha as he handed her a cup of coffee. "Tell my brother that there is just as much danger in Everman City as anywhere else in the world."

"That's true," said Tisha, smiling at the younger Chapman. "We live in perilous times. And if I were a man...well, slay a giant for me, Joshua."

Audra lay nude beneath pink pastel sheets. Next to her was Ace Corbet. "That tickles," she giggled, as he traced her face with his finger.

"You *are* cute, cutie," said Ace grinning, as he stared at her from his propped position.

"And you do have class," Audra returned in a mocking tone which Ace failed to decipher.

"I told you you wouldn't be disappointed."

"No, I wasn't disappointed, Ace," she lied, sinking deeper into her pillow, thinking about the past hour with Corbet. She had been feeling especially lonely. Bubba Hanagan had more or less moved in, and against Audra's better judgment, she had given him a key to the apartment. He had also given her a key to his, a return gesture of sorts, but something she had no intention of using. It seemed a satisfactory arrangement: both went their separate ways, no explanations necessary.

But Bubba had not been to the apartment for three days, and it was Saturday night. That gnawing ache inside had taken her to Grobens. Five Black Labels on the rocks had only deepened the void, and when Ace Corbet made his usual advances, Audra did not retreat. Now she was filled with mild disgust, coupled with boredom, and she wished Ace would leave. But he didn't seem to be in a hurry. She was thinking of how to get rid of him when suddenly she heard a voice.

"Hey momma! Looks like you're having quite a party for yourself. Don't mind me. I just came for a pair of shoes I forgot."

Abruptly, the couple sat up. Ace clenched his fists in anticipation of having to fight an irate lover and was dumbfounded when he saw the muscular Hanagan leaning calmly against the door frame. His arms were folded over his chest like a cigar store Indian, and a big, toothy grin was plastered across his face.

Audra was white with rage. "You could have knocked or something! You could have shown some common decency!" Her anger was fanned by the sickening knowledge that Ace Corbet would not have to use those clenched fists.

Bubba laughed mockingly. "I won't take long. You two keep doing whatever it was you were doing." With that, Hanagan entered the bedroom, rummaged through the closet until he found a pair of tan work boots, tied the laces together, and slung them over his shoulder. Flashing his teeth again, he waved. "Catch you later, momma." And suddenly he was gone.

In one swift motion, Audra jumped out of bed, and not even bothering to put anything on, ran nude to where Corbet's clothes lay piled on a chair. "Get out! Get out!" she shrieked, as she threw his clothes at him. "Just get out of here!"

Four

A udra's honey blond hair folded into perky curls around her face. Every curl merged perfectly with the next, like an army of precision springs that bounced together as she walked beside Tisha O'Brien.

"You'll be spending most of your time in here," Tisha said, her arm sweeping the premises as though she was showing off the Taj Mahal rather than a drab, unimpressive looking room. The room, situated next to the one housing the reactor, was previously used for storage. It was clean now. Audra would use it for her titanium X experiments.

The entire R&D Department was injected with renewed enthusiasm. The department had worked feverishly for two years on the reactor and P2. It had become a labor of love. When they discovered that the metal of the reactor casing was beginning to deteriorate, their disappointment went beyond that of employees facing a set back. Each one of them had invested a part of himself into the project; had infused it with his life. The eight member staff knew the purpose of Audra's undertaking and they would follow her progress with more than casual interest.

Audra's sparkling, blue eyes flared when she saw her new

work room. "I'm nervous and excited all at the same time."

"So am I," Tisha returned, as she led Audra down the hall toward the reactor. Nuclear fusion had always intrigued her. Prior to her employment at PA, Tisha had worked at Princeton with the tokamack. The tokamack or Princeton Large Torus was a doughnut shaped nuclear fusion test machine. It used deuterium in four neutral beam heating devices to achieve near fusion threshold. However, fusion was never achieved because of insufficient plasma densities and confinement time. During her employment at PA, Tisha's department had solved these problems. One such problem was eliminating impurities from the hot plasma held at the core of the magnetic doughnut. These impurities would cool the plasma and therefore retard fusion. When the plasma bombarded the stainless steel wall of the vacuum chamber, these impurities, especially iron nuclei, would sputter into the chamber. The solution was using sputter resistant titanium.

Audra looked pensive. "Are you going with a back-up plan? I mean, while I'm doing this, will Nolan be doing preliminary work on the shielding and vacuum pumps?"

Tisha shook her head. "Afraid not. Mike wants to put all the eggs in your basket."

The metallurgist sighed. "Rather risky, isn't it? I have faith in titanium X, but just suppose... ."

Tisha lightly touched the blond's shoulder. "It's a lot of pressure, Audra, I know. But try not to think about it. Just concentrate on your experiments. You're not responsible for what the executive office decides. You can only do your best and that's all I ask."

"It's a little tough when it's the last inning and the balance of the game rests on you," Audra said in a gasp as though the weight of this responsibility had suddenly squeezed the very air out of her.

The two women stopped in front of the closed door, and Tisha turned the knob. There was no need for a key. The rooms of the Research Department were locked only at night. Patterson

Aviation's eight-building complex laid sprawled, like a sleeping lizard, about ten miles south of Everman City. The smallest of these, Building Six, more or less, formed the tail, and belonged exclusively to R&D. The back entrance of the building was always locked. The front entrance was protected by a gun-toting security guard with explicit instructions to use his weapon on any intruder.

"We're all here for you," Tisha said as she threw open the door. "We have a good team in R&D. I've instructed everyone to give your needs top priority. Just remember, you're not alone in this. Don't try to assume all the pressure and burden. When you're stressed or have problems, come to me."

Inside, the room was small, drab, and looked much like a concrete bunker. A large, glass window partitioned off the room and gave a clear view of what looked like a jet engine in a type of sling device. The special glass, the concrete walls, were just precautions, perhaps overdone, as essentially no radioactive waste was produced by deuterium. In front of the glass an array of buttons and switches dotted a panel, like miniature cookies on a platter. The "engine" was controlled from outside.

Tisha pressed against the glass like a mother viewing her new born through the nursery window. She knew every inch of the structure by heart. She and the R&D team had agonized and sweated over every nut and bolt. They had all done their best. Now it rested primarily on Audra to solve perhaps one of the most difficult problems of all.

"I have confidence in your titanium X," Tisha said, taking her eyes off the NPR910 and looking squarely into Audra's face.

The blond turned away. She knew it was largely due to Tisha's influence that her titanium X project, rather than Nolan's, was chosen by Michael Patterson. But Audra had stamped out all feelings of gratitude as you would a smoldering fire. She didn't like Tisha O'Brien. They were light years apart.

Tisha sensed Audra's antagonism, but accepted it without rancor. She had experienced this before, being disliked without cause. Tisha herself had a genuine fondness for people. At one time such unwarranted hostility hurt. It had also puzzled her. Finally, in high school, she had asked her father about it. "Tisha," he said in his customary good-natured way, "you must not expect to be liked by everyone." She had stared at him for a few minutes, then answered, "But *I* like everyone." Her father had laughed and given her a big hug. "You will learn lass, that people who like themselves tend to like everyone else as well." She had to think about that for some time, and after much observation, came to believe what her father said was true. Now, she no longer took rejection personally. And being disliked by someone never prevented Tisha from liking them just the same. As Tisha turned to face the nuclear reactor, she smiled. "Audra, I have confidence in your titanium X," she repeated. "And I have confidence in you."

The pile of papers hit the desk top with a dull thud. "Here you go, chief," said Tisha. "Your briefing as ordered."

The handsome executive bared his teeth in a smile. Long ago he had asked Tisha to call him Mike, but for some reason she never would. Instead, she had called him Mr. Patterson, which he hated and told her so. In response, she rarely called him by any name at all. However, once in a while, she would call him "chief." It began as a joke, with Tisha explaining that the chief of a Cheyenne tribe was a democratic ruler. Actually, among the Cheyenne there were forty-four chiefs; four principal chiefs and four from each of the ten bands that made up the total tribe. The chiefs were elected to this office based upon their courage, wisdom, and kindness. If they failed in these areas they could be removed. Their primary job was to implement the will of the tribe as a whole, to keep peace, and to care for any widows or orphans. Their authority originated from the people. It was a sharp contrast to "boss" which implied authority over the people. And Tisha often delighted in making that distinction. Once when he had asked her in what category she belonged, she had promptly identified herself as one of the four principal chiefs. It was a jest he thoroughly enjoyed, because although Tisha was head strong and often fought him on a point, she never did so as a show of power, but because she truly believed in the issue of debate. She had no desire to overstep her authority or to test his. With her, the question was always one of principle.

"I've prepared a short outline for you, encapsulating the entire report, and made six sets of the report, one for each Board member."

Mike picked up the edge of the papers with his thumb and let them flip like a deck of cards. "Did you go to secretarial school too?"

The large, brown eyes seemed to overflow with laughter like a percolating coffee pot. "No praise. I accept cash or credit cards only."

Mike leaned back in his chair. "By heaven, you do deserve a raise," he said. She was always surprising him, usually pleasantly. In the past two years he rarely felt as though he knew exactly what to expect from her. There was warmth and admiration in his voice. "Thanks, O'Brien."

"You're welcome," Tisha returned. And for a moment his dark, searing eyes bore into her own. She could feel their heat as they began to boil away the coffee. If she let him, he would dehydrate them, leaving only two empty holes through which he would see her vulnerability. She turned away.

Michael Patterson said nothing but picked up a pencil and absently nibbled the end. Suddenly he flung it wildly on his desk as though he had just remembered something. "By the way, O'Brien, we're having a party Friday night. And before you say 'no,' let me add, you can't refuse. It was originally for my wife's political friends, but I'm combining it with business, much to her distaste." He paused to chuckle as though picturing his wife's anger and finding it humorous. "Our Sales Director has two very rich, very influential cattlemen who have just bought two EX4s apiece, and he's hoping to sell them part of that C101 order we got stuck with."

Tisha visualized the corpulent Sales Director with his pleasant, red face. "We're going to try to sell them on the idea of transporting their livestock by air," Mike continued. "If we're successful, some of the other cattlemen may follow suit. It could mean big money for PA."

"But I know nothing about the cattle industry. What exactly am I supposed to talk about?"

"Talk? Who said I wanted you to talk? I need you as window dressing. Wear something sexy."

"There are dirty names for women like that." The supple red lips blossomed into a flowering smile.

"Hmmm...true... ."

"I thought I was just 'one of the boys'?"

"Well... ."

"Of course I'll expect a raise."

"I know, cash or credit cards only."

"See, you are temperate. I don't know why anyone would call you unreasonable."

"Someone called *me* unreasonable?"

"It doesn't matter."

"Who said it?"

"You shouldn't take these things personally."

"Who, O'Brien?"

"Well, I have called you that once or twice."

Deep, throaty laughter filled the room. "Alright, O'Brien, would you mind coming and giving our Sales Director a hand?"

"I'd be happy to. I assume your invitation includes my date?"

"Your date? Well...I suppose so... . It would be mostly shop talk, boring...but yes, fine, bring a date."

The black, flowing hair hung like an ebony cloud around Tisha's face and shoulders. She brushed it off her cheek as she thought of Daniel Chapman. She would bring him. Daniel would provide a buffer between her and Michael Patterson. She did not want to go to the party alone; especially now that she had identified her feelings, now that the ugly truth had crawled out into the open. She had never felt such a strong need to protect herself.

"Then we'll be there," she said as she moved towards the door, opened it, and paused. "Regarding the Board meeting."

"Yes."

"Just remember what Lincoln said." She turned to face him. "'You may fool all of the people some of the time...but you can't fool all of the people all of the time.'"

The athletic body rose from its chair like a mountain rising out of the sea. Its action was startling, even electrifying, and Tisha felt paralyzed. "It's obvious Lincoln did not benefit from Despreauz's wisdom," Mike said, reaching the engineer in only a few strides. Unconsciously, he put his hand on the door next to hers. "'Greatest fools are oft most satisfied.' Now beat it, O'Brien, before I qualify you for unemployment. You've got a racket around here. Too much easy living has made you imprudent."

Tisha iced a swelling smile and quietly closed the door behind her.

Mike returned to his desk and sat down. The massive hands folded over each other into a beige knot. They were hairless, smooth hands with large, square, well-manicured nails. But they were also strong, sinewy, with knuckles like walnuts. They were hands not only at home on the top of a desk, but on the throttle of a four hundred ton machine. Mike had wanted to place them on her, to feel the silkiness of her hair, the velvet of her cheek, to feel her substance. But he could not. Instead, he had fabricated his own substance, a tissue paper story so flimsy a child could see through it. Yet he had to bring her there, to his home, to draw her close, to somehow possess her substance without ever really touching her.

He had done this twice before. "Compulsory business parties," he had called them. But this desire to bring her close always stopped short of any real intimacy. And it had nothing to do with mixing business with pleasure. It had to do with fear. If one touched, then one could be touched. It was the kind of risk Mike had unconsciously avoided all his life. He could sense the threat like a hunter can sense the lion in the bush. Even a tamed circus lion was unpredictable, dangerous. This time he had come a little too close. He had felt an inexplicable jealousy because of her desire to bring a date. Even now it gnawed at him, not like a large, starving mongrel; but like a small termite, insidiously, slowly, hidden.

Until now, jealousy was alien to him. In ten years of marriage, he had never once felt jealous. And that was odd, or some of his friends seemed to think, since he and his wife, Renee, had an "arrangement." Simply put, they saw other people. Even when one of Renee's lovers turned out to be Mike's friend, it was never Mike who felt awkward, but the friend. "How can you stand it?" a friend once asked. "How can you stand knowing that this guy or that guy is making it with your wife?" Mike had felt a mixture of surprise and amusement because the truth was it never bothered him. Not once had he felt the slightest twinge over Renee's lovers. The termite gnawed a little more. So how could he feel jealousy over a woman he had never as much as touched above the wrist?

Swiftly his hands moved across the desk and picked up the outline. There was comfort in the crisp white paper, in the bold black lettering, in its...inertia; to be moved only at his pleasure, at his will. It could be controlled. It seemed to make him forget the termite. Presently his lips parted and he began to read out loud. "Page One. Patterson II. Aerodynamic Control Surfaces... ."

"Page Four. Patterson II. Subassemblies. Please note that in spite of the wide body and considerable passenger capacity, gross take-off weight is only eight hundred fifty thousand pounds. Now if you flip to the last page, you will find the estimated cost for total development of our SST. One hundred million, the bottom line, gentlemen." Mike paused to allow the five men sitting at the large rectangular table time to digest all he had said. He knew it had been a sweet fare until the last page. One did not chew bitter herbs readily.

The pinstriped suits clustered together like a gray lotus. Pages turned with a crisp, crackling noise, and heads bent together. Yet the page most frequently studied was that final page which showed the nine figure number and seemed to dwarf all else.

Michael Patterson paced quietly behind his seat at the table, as though marking time. After a seemingly designated number of paces, he again addressed the group. "You're all aware we have not been able to replenish our R&D fund since it was severely depleted during the creation of the EX4, even though that aircraft has been leading the industry in the executive craft category for over a year. We've gone over most of the reasons for this before, and I see no reason to rehash them now. The problem I want to focus on is how to get the money we need to complete the P2. Once before, when we were first developing the fusion reactor, I asked you to procure loans for its development, using your influence and prestige to attract investors. I again make that same request. Of course stock warrants will be issued, same as last time."

Mike searched the faces of his audience and found favorable signs on all save one. It was as he had anticipated. This was no new adversary. The dissenter, a thin, sickly looking man, was Robert Gunther. He was one of three Board members affiliated with an oil company, and of the three, the most powerful. Mike needed his support. "Your reaction, Bob?" he asked, zeroing in on his antagonist.

The soft, pasty lids, like folds of dough, blinked over two dull eyes. It was as if he had not heard the question. But Mike knew better than to underestimate Robert Gunther. What he lacked in stature and strength, he possessed in knowledge and cunning.

"Well Mike," came a calm, authoritative voice, "I can't say I'm impressed. It looks like a stretch version of the Concord SST to me," he said, thumbing the papers in front of him, the blue veins pulsating visibly beneath the thin tissue-like skin of his hand. "As for the NPR910, why are there no progress reports? Where are the test results? We have already stuck our collective necks out far enough. I think before you ask us to stick them out any further you should back your request with more substantial performance data. Just *what* have you done so far?"

"The performance data on the NRP910 is highly sensitive

material," Mike returned. "We're keeping it under wraps. Only a handful of people have access to it. To start letting it whirl around the typing pool and Xerox machines at this time is, in my opinion, an unnecessary risk. I need not remind you that in our business 'industrial spies' are not uncommon. As for the P2, its greatness lies in its engine. Still, it is a remarkable aircraft in its own right. If there's a resemblance between the P2 and the Concord, it's only visual. In all other areas the P2 excels. As for why you should stick your necks out again, there's a very practical reason; to guarantee the return of the money your investors have already made in the NRP910. After all, what good is the engine without the plane? The plane, in this case, gentlemen, is built around the engine." To Mike's puzzlement Gunther appeared uncharacteristically flustered. There had been nothing in his rebuttal that had been particularly dynamic. He had much more to say, more ammunition to utilize.

"And if the P2 fails," said Gunther, the voice still calm, but noticeably less authoritative, "not only have we lost our investors' capital but our credibility."

Mike Patterson frowned. "That's true, but if you don't back me now, the project has no chance at all. Without further funding we can't continue. We've been counting on future sales of the P2 to bring us solvency. If the P2 cannot progress beyond the drawing board, then we'll undoubtedly be faced with bankruptcy. And what, gentlemen, would that do to your credibility?"

Four of the executives went into an immediate huddle. Only Mike and Gunther remained facing each other, both knowing by the look of panic on the other faces, who was emerging victoriously.

"Alright," said Gunther, breaking up the huddle. "I believe you've made your point, Mike. I'm certain no one here wants to see either Patterson Aviation or the project fail. However, at present PA is considerably over extended. Perhaps if you brought this matter up in six months or a year, and at that time backed it with more performance data on the NPR910s... ."

"Six months! A year! In less than six months I could produce a full scale mock-up. In a year the P2 could be rolling off the assembly line," interrupted Mike, his face flushed with anger.

"The reactors...you're that close?" asked Gunther, stunned.

"We're that close."

"And the mock-up? Six months or less?"

"That's right," Mike answered as he looked at the other four faces. They again seemed to bloom with favorable signs and Mike knew this time he had them. He searched out the blank eyes of Robert Gunther and smiled into them. Men of cunning always understood each other.

The full length mirror reflected the image of a tall man adjusting his tie. The image appeared symmetrically perfect and from a distance looked like the reflection of a male model. But closer inspection would reveal the physique was much too powerful; the face too rugged and chiseled, not "pretty" as those on the fashion pages. Large, square shoulders jutted out over a narrow torso, all held up by strong, muscular legs. It was the body of a Spartan; a body that was not enhanced by clothes but restricted by them. It was a body that was keenly tactile, and both evoked and responded to all that was physical.

Mike was aware of his good looks as one is aware that day is light and night is dark. It was a fact not dwelt upon but accepted. If he had been less handsome, he might have been preoccupied by physical beauty as it is with people preoccupied by things they do not have. But being so endowed, he gave it little thought, and had over the years even developed a philosophy that men really didn't need good looks to make a deal, a woman, or anything else for that matter.

To Mike, good looks counted only when found in the possession of a female, and in this area he was quite preoccupied. It had been one of the reasons he married Renee. Instead of love, Mike had sought more realistic and practical grounds for marriage; good looks, money, social status. And he found them all in his wife. For the bulk of his ten-year marriage, the choice had seemed satisfactory enough. Renee was an eye pleaser, wealthy in her own right, a gracious hostess, and had, on numerous occasions, used her social influence for the benefit of his company.

Lately though, Mike had become increasingly restless, discontented, and perhaps worst of all...bored. Several years ago Renee had found out she could never have children. She feigned disappointment, but Mike knew she was actually pleased. It seemed to settle the issue of future unwanted responsibility. He had not minded...at the time. But now, more and more he was feeling a need for something; some warmth that would touch his life, make it glow like a well-heated coal in his later years. He was thirty-five and had suddenly begun to think about those years. It was a change, for apart from his business he seldom thought beyond the next week. Renee had teased him, told him he was going through a premature aging crisis. He had tried to stave off that crisis by speaking of adopting a child. A son would stoke those fires, rekindle that dying coal. But Renee, who was in many ways so like a child herself, had flatly refused. At the time he claimed he understood. Yet the discontentment grew, making him increasingly aware of Renee's petty, selfish ways. Things that never bothered him began to irritate him more and more. She whined and pouted like a child when she didn't get her way. She was excessive, overindulgent with money, and she could be cruel and biting when angered. He had always dealt with these things by never trying to deal with them. Now the strain of his new frustration was beginning to be felt by Renee and a tension had begun to grow between them. What was wrong with his life, he wondered as he knotted his tie before the mirror.

"Michael, hurry up! The guests are beginning to arrive." Mike watched Renee's reflection in the mirror as she approached, and noticed, with amusement, that she wore a black, floor-length, silk jersey with a neckline that plunged to her waist. The wide V exposed more than half of the soft, ample mounds of each breast, and accentuated even further the thinness of her waist. No doubt she was out to impress someone tonight, Mike mused. It would be difficult to remain unimpressed. She had a superb figure, the best Mike had ever seen on any woman, and she could never resist showing it off. Renee had always been overtly sexual, and it was this very fact that had sparked his interest in the first place. Now, looking at her through the mirror, he felt a sudden impulse to hug her affectionately. As he did, without quite knowing why, he whispered, "Won't you reconsider adoption? You have all the servants you need and we could get a nurse, two nurses, a dozen nurses... ."

"Are you going to start *that* again!" she said, pushing him away. "I thought we agreed, Michael, no kids. You know I'm not the motherly type. Besides, I thought you liked things as they were. Haven't we already got everything?" she said, as they descended the winding staircase that led into a huge room which had been entirely rearranged for this party. "You've been a little cranky lately. What you need is a vacation...or a good fling."

"Open those doors!" Mike barked at a passing butler, indicating the double louvered patio doors. Yes, he was cranky. But how could he explain it to Renee? How could he explain it was a culmination of ten years of him not caring enough; ten years of her not caring enough; ten years of unstoked fires, of chilblain, of cold...ten years of drafty emptiness?

When the doors were opened, music filled the room. "You've hired a band!" he protested in ill humor.

Renee smiled demurely. Her eyes, green cat eyes, watched him, stalked him. She could be charming when she chose to be, when it was to her advantage. She did not want Mike annoyed with her, not now when she was having people she wanted to impress. He might be irritable, even rude, and she did not want the Senator exposed to that.

"You know how I hate the idea of dancing with all those plump, gray-haired wives," Mike continued, bombarding her with his frustration as if the last ten years had been all her fault. "Especially tonight. I've business to discuss."

Renee leaned over and kissed him on the cheek. "You'll survive darling. I want my party to be a success and women love to dance. They expect to when they bother getting all dressed up."

Mike gave her a sharp look. "Well then, *you* dance with them!" he snapped and walked off.

Renee watched him for a moment and then with a sigh she too went off. In spite of his ill humor this was going to be a great party. It was full of all the right people. Plus, she had spent the better part of two weeks preparing for it; had all the woodwork re-painted, the rugs shampooed, even had some "Spanish" touches added. The artesonado ceiling with elaborate boxed out squares of wood, one foot by one foot, and centers filled with grille work was new. So was the parabolic archway at the main entrance of the room. This was all done for Senator Garby who had spent several years as Ambassador to Brazil. Since meeting the Senator and his wife at a government party eight weeks ago, Renee had seized every opportunity to be in their company. And that involved such tactics as inviting herself to functions where they would be present and using her influence to extract an invitation when an uninvited appearance would seem too gauche.

There were reasons for her behavior. Her father, a cattle baron, had rarely traveled. When he did, he never took her. Al-though he pampered and spoiled Renee, he had tried to keep her insulated from the sophistication of the larger world outside the ranch. Up until the day she married, she had never traveled more than one hundred miles away from home. This cloistered life had not made her innocent or reticent, but rather petty and often cruel; for her life-style had fostered a personality that saw nothing larger than itself. After her marriage she made a few trips, but none out-side the States. Once, Mike begged her to go on a European vaca-tion, but she had refused, feigning ill health. The truth was that her vanity would not allow her lack of sophistication to be exposed. Shortly after that, she began aligning herself with the government crowd. In Everman, this consisted mainly of petty bureaucrats. But they had given Renee exposure to what she believed was cosmo-politan life, and she hungered for more.

The Garbys, however, provided Renee with her first taste of

real sophistication, and like a shark in a feeding frenzy, she pursued them. They were very powerful and influential in Washington. This impressed Renee greatly. For her, Washington had become the Mecca of proper living, of all that was desirable. The important people of the world traveled through its gates, and for some reason, she was beginning to envision herself as one of them.

But Mike did not share her aspirations. In some ways he even seemed to deliberately thwart them. He had annoyed her when he told her of his plans to turn the party into a business meeting. He had enraged her when he disclosed that his business "associates" would be cattlemen. "Cattlemen," she had told Mike, "were coarse and low." He had just laughed in his customary way, and she returned by screaming how they better not bring in any cow manure on their boots.

Now, Renee looked with disgust at two men in Western garb. "Cattlemen!" she said under her breath just as the doorman entered to announce a new arrival. Quickly, she moved toward the large mosaic vestibule. Her face glowed like a full moon when she saw the tall, dark man and his wife. "Oh, Senator and Mrs. Garby! How wonderful to see you again!"

The Senator made a slight bow of the head and the fragile looking woman beside him smiled weakly. "Mrs. Patterson... ."

"Renee."

"Renee," continued Senator Garby, "allow me to introduce you to a good friend of mine, Mr. Alexander Harner, president of Tafco Oil."

"Alex to my friends," interjected the robust executive. Until now, Renee had not noticed him nor had she noticed the delighted expression on his face as he viewed her wide plunging V.

"I hope you don't mind, but I insisted that Alex accompany us here." The senator laughed rather nervously.

Renee eyed Alex Harner. She viewed oil men with the same disdain as cattlemen. However, Harner was not the only oil man at her party. Politics often necessitated dealing with unpleasant people. What oil men lacked in breeding, they had in money. A trip to Mecca was expensive. "Don't be silly, Senator. Your friends are my friends. Mr. Harner...Alex is welcome... ."

Suddenly, the tune of the Mexican Hat Dance came blaring from the patio. Renee giggled nervously. "Don't you just love Spanish music?" She failed to see the sneering look that passed between the Senator and his wife. Then, instead of making proper introductions, Renee took them to a long rectangular table covered with food. To one side were platters of lobster tails, chateaubriand, crystal bowls of caviar, oysters Rockerfeller, shrimp, and dozens of salads and vegetables. To the other, tureens of *gazpacho* on top of a bed of ice, platters of *tostadas* and *enrollados,* steaming mounds of *albondigas* and *empanadas,* a large tongue in almond sauce, *paella, pollo escabeche,* and *garbanzo salad.* Renee did not believe in passing around cheese and crackers. At her parties, food was served all night.

"I hope you find something here to your liking," Renee said rather boastfully, stopping next to the gazpacho. "Just tell them what you want and they'll take care of you." She gestured toward the staff of servants who stood mutely about in white starched uniforms like plaster statues. The couple smiled politely but showed no interest in the food.

"Perhaps a drink then," she said, a little sullenly, and even while Renee spoke, she signaled to the man behind the rolling bar. "Dewers and water, Bubba."

Bubba Hanagan made the drink as ordered and handed it to Renee, then looked at the other three quizzically. "The usual Hanagan," returned Alex Harner. "And how's it going?"

"Fine, Mr. Harner," answered Bubba as he mixed a Scotch and soda.

"Still lifting weights?"

"Of course, sir," replied the muscular blond.

"Oh, you know each other?" questioned Renee. Hanagan ignored her as he handed the oil man his drink. Renee shot a glance at Alex Harner.

"Hanagan used to be my body guard," volunteered Harner.

"Small world as they say," replied Renee in a bored tone. She had completely lost interest in the matter and was intently watching the Senator and his wife, so intently in fact, that she failed to notice the bartender slipping a piece of paper into Alex Harner's suit pocket. It was a brief note that read:

Will continue surveillance. May have something for you soon.

"Nice party," said a beautiful woman in a silk, oriental looking dress that nearly touched the floor. Slits on both sides of the skirt reached to the knees, revealing long, shapely legs. Around her throat arched a stiff collar, and passing between her breasts, a long row of tiny silk covered buttons. The severe line of her gown was sharply contrasted by the casual manner in which her hair was piled on her head. Soft, black wisps framed the sides of her face like a picture.

The robust Sales Director of Patterson Aviation smiled broadly. "Tisha, you look wonderful!" He took her hands and pressed them between the chubby palms of his own. "I swear, if I weren't a happily married man you would be in constant danger of my advances." She gave him an affectionate kiss on the cheek, then he hastily introduced her to the two cattlemen next to him.

"My friends were just telling me," said the Sales Director, "how this Jihad madness has effected their industry. They've had some of their trucks bombed or hijacked. And the energy crisis is taking its toll. It's inflating beef prices across the country. I was telling them that a good alternative to trucking their cattle East would be transporting them in a fleet of cargo carriers. It's quicker. Less chance of having something go wrong. No stops on the way." The director paused and chuckled softly. "Actually, Tisha, I was about to seduce them into buying our C101's. That is, until you came and otherwise seduced us."

Tisha smiled at the salesman who blushed with pleasure. "I'm afraid real seduction is your department."

"You're certainly right there, Miss O'Brien," offered one of the cattlemen, slapping the director on the back. "And he's been doing one heck of a job."

Someone's plump, gray-haired wife had managed to corner Michael Patterson before he was able to reach his Sales Director. But he stood near enough to observe the three men, while periodically bobbing his head politely up and down for the benefit of the matronly woman before him. Shortly after Tisha joined the group, however, Mike ceased bobbing and excused himself rather curtly.

"May I have this dance, Miss O'Brien?" he said, when he reached her, his voice low and husky. Before Tisha could respond, he pulled her out to the patio where he began leading her through motions resembling a slow two-step.

"You look good, O'Brien. Although I've seen sexier dresses on ten year olds. Still...you look good," he said, trying hard to subdue the high he was feeling.

"Thank you," she returned, ignoring his sarcasm, thinking how good he also looked, and hating herself for enjoying the feel of his strong arm around her.

For a while they just danced quietly, a bit awkwardly. "How was the board meeting?" Tisha finally asked, trying to ease the tension.

"Gunther wasn't happy. He wanted more data on the NPR."

"Did he buy your double-talk?"

Michael Patterson nodded his head.

"Really? What happened?"

"He gave in. He had to because the others went my way."

"They usually follow him. How did you manage to get them on your side?"

"By promising them the P2 mock-up within six months."

"What! That's crazy! What if Audra can't come up with the new casing and we have to enlarge the shielding?"

Mike ignored her. "I want you and a few others to join

Nolan. I want it done in complete secrecy. I've already purchased two hangers a couple of hundred miles from here. It's an isolated spot, the remnants of a private airstrip that belonged to an eccentric old geezer who always wanted to take off over the sea... ."

"It's near the ocean?"

"except that the strip wasn't long enough for take off, and you could say that the project never really got off the ground."

"Very clever," Tisha said sarcastically. Mike's eyes twinkled as he watched her. "Okay, you have two old hangars by the ocean, is that suppose to mean something?"

"Deuterium," he said, as if that explained it all. And to Tisha it did.

"So, that's what you've had Nolan doing. You *are* clever. But are you clever enough to convince the Board to finance the P2 if the casing fails?"

"In a few weeks I'll give the orders to begin tooling-up."

"Why do you keep ignoring my questions?" Tisha asked crossly.

"In the mean time you'll start building the engineering mock-up."

"You can't build an airplane like this. It's backwards. Besides, how can you expect only a handful to accomplish such a mammoth task?"

"I expect you to get it rolling and when the time is right, I'll assign others. No one said it would be easy."

"I don't expect easy. But how about sensible?"

"Was it sensible when you came to me two years ago *begging* me for a chance to build the first fusion powered aircraft?"

"I didn't beg."

"Oh...then what do you call groveling on all fours?"

"Exaggeration," Tisha returned, and the pair laughed.

"By the way, what happened to your date?" The sudden realization that Tisha had come alone pleased him.

"Something came up." At the last minute Daniel had called from the hospital telling her there was an emergency and he couldn't get away. "He's a doctor. Things like this happen," she added almost defensively.

"You were stood up."

"No I wasn't."

"Later you should have a drink, get your mind off it."

"My mind is not on it."

"I know, O'Brien. You're thirty, unmarried, and even though you pretend you don't care, deep down in your left ventricle you're afraid that some day you'll wake up and find yourself an old maid. But don't worry. You've still got your looks. There's still a few good years left."

"You're ridiculous."

"I understand. Believe me I understand. That's why I feel so guilty about having to isolate you, to remove you from your puny but nevertheless existent social life, and send you to a God forsaken spot by the sea."

"I think I'll live."

"I want you out there in three days. I've booked a room for you at a local hotel; although we'll be working such long hours you won't get much chance to use it."

"You made no mention that you'd be there." Tension traveled up her back like a fast moving train.

"Oh...didn't I?"

"No. Is...this...wise?" Tisha stammered, trying to control her panic. There was no way she wanted to go to some secluded spot with this man. "I mean...you shouldn't start anything until after we've developed the casting. Why are you jeopardizing your entire company?"

Mike smiled. The faint flush of embarrassment on her face delighted him. "Why, O'Brien, you look like you're blushing. Can't imagine why. I haven't said anything off-color. I wouldn't dare, you know, not with someone who wears a cross all the time."

Tisha had left the first four buttons of her dress undone and although it didn't make much of an opening, it was enough that almost half of her ivory-colored cross could be seen. "Did anyone ever tell you you were infuriating?" she returned with a frown.

The handsome executive chuckled. "No, only you. That's why I like you, O'Brien. You're not afraid of me. I know I'm taking a chance but sometimes you need to take chances. This is one of those times. Everything I have, everything I care about, is riding on it. And I'm counting on you to help me. So, what I need, O'Brien, is for you not to tell me I'm crazy, but to say you're with me."

Tisha looked at him sideways. "Very touching little speech, chief. But you already know I'm with you. You're not going to silence me that easily. Make me into a yes-man. This approach is crazy and you know it. But I'll work the skin right off my fingers trying to make it succeed."

Suddenly his large hands tightened around her. "Is it always going to be a battle with us? Will you never say 'yes' like a lamb?"

Tisha shifted uncomfortable. Somehow she felt he was asking a question unrelated to business. She avoided his eyes.

"Well?"

"Well what?"

"Shall we call a truce? No more battling?"

Tisha pushed him away, just as the music stopped. "Isn't that what the big bad wolf said to one of the little pigs just before he ate him?"

The broad chest expanded with blasts of laughter, strong, vibrating, like thunder, and even after Tisha left him amid the Mariachi Band and lamp posts strung with red and orange streamers, she could still hear it.

"Tisha. Tisha how divine you look."

The engineer turned toward the silky voice.

"Thank you, Renee," she responded perfunctorily.

"Marvelous dress, dear," Renee sneered. "So cute with all those little buttons down the front" Immediately everyone's eyes went to Tisha's high buttoned collar and then to Renee's plunging V. Senator and Mrs. Garby appeared somewhat embarrassed, but Alexander Harner was thoroughly enjoying the situation.

"Isn't it terrible about those two British school teachers?" Senator Garby said hurriedly, as though diplomatically trying to break the tension that had suddenly developed. "You know...the two school teachers on vacation in Damascus who were brutally murdered this morning? Kamal himself took responsibility. He said justice had been served because all so-called democratic nations taught lies about the Moslems and the Islamic cause in their schools."

"Serves them right," Renee returned. "After all, you'd think teachers would have more sense than to go to a place like Damascus."

Alex Harner chuckled. "It did show a high degree of stupidity or arrogance."

"Violence and terrorism...that's all you ever hear about anymore," injected Mrs. Garby, her eyes wide and agitated. "When will it all stop?"

"As long as terrorism is big business it'll never stop," returned the barrel chested Alex Harner.

"Big business? What exactly do you mean?" Renee asked. The smugness had suddenly gone from her manner.

Harner smiled. He seemed to enjoy the uneasiness he was creating. "It's a known fact that many Arab oil countries have been financing various liberation groups for years, including the current Jihad. In addition, armed men extract money by force from their own people, like the Palestinians, for example, and even those in refugee camps. Why, Libya's President Gaddafi ordered a six percent reduction from the pay of Palestinian exiles working in that land to help subsidize Yasser Arafat."

Senator Garby nodded solemnly. "Yes, that's true. It's estimated that last year's income of the PLO was equal to that of the nation of Jordan. Terrorist revenue goes into the millions. They have so much money they have begun acting like multinational companies and even make legal investments via the world stock exchanges."

Harner chuckled. "To be sure. The PLO has invested over ninety-five million in London alone."

"Didn't the PLO virtually go bankrupt after Arafat backed Saddam Hussein during the Gulf War?" Tisha asked.

"Yes," returned Alex. "But all is forgiven. Money has been pouring back into that purse for some time, much of it quietly."

"This sounds absolutely horrid!" Renee gasped. "It makes terrorists sound like...well, like...entrepreneurs."

"Exactly," Harner returned. "And their commodity is terror. Why, they even have their own bureaucracy with office staffs of thirty-thousand-dollars-a-month men, complete with secretaries and company cars. In addition, Iran, Syria and Libya fund the different dozen or so terrorist groups that are currently operating world wide. And it's the group that does the most damage that gets the most money. So all the groups, including Kamal's, have to constantly try to outdo each other in order to get the big bucks. It's like an incentive program."

"Come now, we're here to have fun," said Renee. "This conversation is depressing all the ladies. Let's hear no more of it."

"Actually, it's rather fascinating," Tisha said, looking hard at Alexander Harner and Senator Garby. "You both certainly seem to know a lot about it."

Harner studied the beautiful engineer with renewed interest, while the Senator flushed pink.

"You're very observant...Tisha. I heard Renee call you that. It is, Tisha, isn't it?" asked the graying executive. The engineer nodded. "Well, Tisha, neither the Senator nor myself of course uphold violence and terrorism for any reason. We are, however, not unsympathetic towards the Arabs. We believe that they have been maligned and misrepresented to a certain extent. As for our knowledge of any PLO balance sheets...I own and operate one of the largest oil companies in the West."

"I know who you are, Mr. Harner," Tisha said.

"Alex, call me Alex, please." Tisha said nothing, but remained looking at the oil tycoon. Harner shrugged and continued. "You must understand that in my business you have to keep up with these things. With the energy crisis being what it is, and with Middle East hostility being what it is...well, I have to keep informed."

Tisha nodded thoughtfully, as though an idea had just struck her. "Of course," she said slowly. "But this sympathy of yours isn't possibly due to the fact that your company has never experienced any terrorist attacks? Rather startling good fortune, when you consider that no other major oil company can say the same." Tisha's information had come to her via Michael Patterson. His suspicions concerning Gunther and Tafco Oil were suddenly, as though by osmosis, becoming her own.

Alexander Harner shook with laughter. He was not a man easily rattled, and instead of finding Tisha's statements offensive, he found her delightful. "Money, Tisha, money! I pay protection. Simple as that. Are you shocked? Of course, I can see by your face that you are. But you needn't be. Businesses do it everyday. Oh...maybe not in outright payments, but in the form of 'gifts' shall we say. 'Gifts' given to the right people can buy a remarkable amount of friendship."

Tisha stared blankly at Alexander Harner. She had allowed Mike's suspicious nature to momentarily poison her own. Surely she was being overly critical of these two men. It was true, in her estimation Senator Garby was a fool. But this was still a free country, and he had the right to espouse any opinions he pleased. As for Harner, it was not to his discredit that Robert Gunther, a Tafco employee, sat on the Board of Patterson Aviation, or that Gunther frequently gave Mike grief concerning the P2 project. After all, Gunther had a job to do. They all had jobs to do.

She smiled pleasantly. "Well, Mr. Harner, politics is certainly vastly more complex than an SST."

"That's because you're more interested in airplanes," Renee added, anxious to get into the mainstream of both the conversation and the Garbys' attention. "And who cares anyway? The

Middle East is a backward land filled with backward people. They're all fanatical puppets whose strings are pulled by plump, decadent sheiks."

"Kamal is not a sheik," returned Mrs. Garby, finding her hostess' statement rather ignorant. "And I'm afraid that what is happening in the Middle East is effecting the entire world. My God, don't you read the papers!"

The Senator gave his wife a sharp look and she immediately retreated. Then he smiled condescendingly at Renee. "I guess there are still some sheiks who call the shots."

Harner began to laugh. "Yes," he said, patting his robust middle. "Sheiks like us." With that, he winked at Senator Garby and everyone laughed, everyone except Tisha O'Brien.

Hours later, when the party had ended, Renee disrobed slowly, carefully, while her husband pulled off his suit and tossed it across a chair. "You know, I forgot to congratulate Tisha on her achievement."

"Oh? What achievement is that?" Mike asked, trying hard not to sound too interested.

"Getting you to dance so long. It must be a new record. You know how you abhor it. How in the world did she ever manage?" Then a sudden thought struck her, and the rosebud lips curled into an ugly sneer. "Or is she your newest playmate? That isn't like you, Michael, mixing business with pleasure, although I've always thought that rule of yours rather silly. Well, is she...are you two having an affair?"

Mike chuckled softly, "Hardly...not with that one. She's what you'd call a 'goodie-two-shoes.'"

Renee wrinkled her face in disgust. "Still, I sense something between you... ."

"Why the sudden interest?" Mike interrupted. "You've never questioned me about anyone before."

"Well, it's just... ."

"I don't like it, Renee!" He was suddenly very cross. "Tisha is not the type who would have a cheap, little affair with the first guy who asked her."

"Cheap? Not a word you normally use when discussing our 'arrangement.' I don't understand...unless...unless you *did* ask, and she refused. Michael, did she refuse you?" Renee released a cruel, crackling laugh. Her husband just ignored her and continued undressing as though she had said nothing at all.

For a moment Renee appeared confused, uncertain how she should react. Finally she positioned her body into what was supposed to be a seductive pose, except that too much liquor had made her clumsy, and she appeared more comical than seductive. Renee always approached sex rather vampiricaly, as though in draining others she replenished herself. She needed that now, to know that while she meant little to Mike, no one else meant any more. But how could he prove something he wasn't even sure of himself? Silently, he looked at his wife, at the sleek lines of her torso, the soft jutting breasts, the slim waist and round curve of her hips. She was a beautiful, hallow mannequin. And for the first time he felt sorry for her...for himself.

Instinctively Renee reached for her robe as though trying to cover herself from his rejection. She didn't look at him but walked listlessly to the bed and sat down. Staring at her painted toes, she wondered if she needed a pedicure. She would go to the beauty parlor tomorrow where she would be tweezed, brushed, lacquered. These too could replenish. And then of course there were other men, there were always scores of other men.

"Michael," she said mechanically, "the Garbys have invited me to DC for a vacation. I have decided to go."

"Sounds good. I've always said you should travel more. It might help you to realize that people like the Garbys are pretty common after all."

"You don't like them?"

"I really don't know them, but I don't care to either. There's a lot of controversy surrounding the Garbys, and ugly talk."

"Since when do you pay attention to rumors?"

"I don't usually, but I know some of the crowd he hangs with, and well, birds of a feather and all that."

"You mean Alexander Harner?"

"Exactly."

"I take it you don't think much of him either."

"Right."

Renee shrugged her sculptured shoulders. "I don't care for him myself. He's an oil man. But the Garbys...well...they're special. They're the type of people who shape history."

"Really, what type is that?" he asked in a mocking tone.

"Why are you acting so superior? I don't get it, Michael. What exactly did you hear about Senator Garby that makes you so cynical?"

"For one thing, it seems that when Garby was in South America he made friends with some pretty unsavory people...some very dangerous people."

"Like who?"

"Radicals, malcontents."

"You mean *terrorists*?"

"That's what I mean. It's no secret that Garby is sympathetic to the Palestinian cause, and during his first senatorial campaign, it's rumored that some of his finances came from these sources, in a round about way, of course. The money was well laundered, and nothing was ever proven. It's also no secret that he works closely with pro-Arab lobbyists in Washington."

Renee's chin jutted out stubbornly. "Well, that doesn't mean anything. Lots of senators and congressmen are backed by special interest groups. Oh, I refuse to listen to all this malicious gossip. I don't care what anyone says. I like the Garbys. They fascinate me. And...they are powerful."

Renee was right. In spite of the fact that controversy surrounded Senator Garby, his star was rising swiftly. Money poured like Monsoon rains into his second senatorial campaign fund, and virtually overflowed. His publicity was equally abundant. Papers and TV news were fast making the senator a household name. It was almost as though a secret edict had been issued to the various segments of the news media to "puff" Garby. Yet, careful evaluation of his actual record as senator would have revealed a poor performance. His attendance in the senate was spotty, and his voting record exposed inconsistent views and conflicting loyalties. Even so, large segments of the press covered him faithfully: Senator Garby at VA Hospital; Senator Garby calls President too "radical" on terrorism; Senator Garby challenges all nations to disarm nuclear arsenals, and so on. But most of it was superficial rhetoric revealing little or no actual achievements. It was all very curious.

"You don't realize how powerful Senator Garby really is."

"Is that why you've been following after him like a hound?" Her husband's voice was heavy with scorn.

"I haven't been following him, I mean, I have been to some parties and yes, I've asked a few friends to include me. Oh Michael, really, you're impossible. Why am I trying to explain? You just don't understand. Your problem is you associate with too many cattlemen."

"No, I'm afraid that's your problem. Deep down, Renee, you're terrified you'll never get rid of the smell of cow dung. And you're right, you'll never be anything but a small town girl."

"What a hateful thing to say! I could just stab you with one of my nail files right now! Sometimes I loathe you. Do you hear that, I loathe you!"

"Good night." The springs creaked as Mike climbed into bed. Renee did not respond, but lay quietly with her back toward him. Though the space between them on the mattress was only a few inches, they had never been so far apart.

Tisha lounged on the couch reading a CS Lewis novel. From time to time, she placed it on her lap and absently fingered the pages. She had wanted to go right to bed, but the party had left her restless, pensive. How could she work so closely with Mike

Patterson? The question played again and again in her mind like a haunting melody. It frightened her. The strange surroundings, the hotel, perhaps frequent moments alone with him. She was not a very "modern" woman. Although sometimes in a weak moment, as tonight, when Mike had held her very close, she wished she could be. It would be so much easier.

....

Tisha's brown eyes were moist with fear, and she held them downcast as she walked toward her father. Her thick black braids hung, limp as her courage, against her chest. He did not appear to notice her, but sat in his favorite armchair reading the newspaper. He was a large, robust man with a great crop of curly blond hair. She stood silently beside the chair as though it was a formidable mountain she could not scale. Finally, she released a timid little throat-clearing noise that miraculously floated upward to the summit and into the ears of Paddy O'Brien. He looked down at his young daughter. "Oh, Tisha, lass," he said, his brogue thick with warmth and affection. "And what would you be wanting from your father?"

Without a word, Tisha dropped a smashed Milky Way onto his lap. Paddy O'Brien picked up the candy bar which was still in its wrapper, examined it and his daughter's face, and deducted from both that this was not exactly a gift.

"And what is this lass?" he asked, somewhat puzzled.

"I stole it daddy!" Tisha blurted, barely able to hold back the tears. "And now I am going to go to hell!"

Paddy O'Brien picked up his eight year old daughter as easily as if she was a rag doll and placed her on his lap.

"No, no child," he said, trying hard not to chuckle, "you are not."

The little girl sighed with relief and rested her head on her father's chest.

"Why did you do it, Tisha?" Paddy asked with touching tenderness.

"Because of my dream."

"Your dream?"

"Yes... ."

"What was this dream, lass?"

"I...well...oh daddy, *promise* me you won't laugh."

"I promise."

"I dreamt I was Superwoman, and that some of my friends were in trouble. I forgot exactly what trouble...but my friends didn't know I was Superwoman. They thought I was just...me."

"Yes, I understand."

"Well, these friends were in trouble so I...that is Superwoman wanted to help. But I had on my uniform, you know, my St. Joseph's uniform... ."

"Yes, I know."

"And when I took it off, I didn't have on that wonderful red and blue suit with the beautiful cape and big 'S' on it."

"No? What did you have on?"

Large, shimmering tears welled up in Tisha's eyes. "Oh, daddy, it was awful! I had on this ugly lace pinafore with these tiny letters in the front—'gts.' And when my friends saw it, they all laughed and said 'oh, it's just goodie-two-shoes!'"

After saying this Tisha collapsed sobbing against her father. He patted her back gently until he was able to quiet her.

"Do your friends tease you much?" he finally asked. The young child's head bobbed up and down.

"And that's why you stole the candy bar? To show your friends you were not such a 'goodie-two-shoes' after all?"

Again the head bobbed. "Do you think God is disappointed in me, daddy?" Tisha managed to say between sniffles.

Paddy O'Brien lifted his daughter from his lap and walked to where the large family Bible was kept. He picked up the worn, familiar book and returned with it to his chair. Placing the Bible on one knee and his daughter on the other, he began thumbing through the pages until he came upon the book of Romans. "No, sweet lass, God is not disappointed," he said. With his finger he followed the words. "As it is written, 'There is none righteous, no not one.' You see, Tisha, God knows we are weak. He knows we do wrong sometimes. That's why we need Jesus. He paid for all our sins. All we have to do is accept Him and trust in Him."

Tisha nodded in understanding. "Oh, daddy I do, but does Jesus still...love me?"

Paddy O'Brien squeezed his daughter with one hand, and with the other hand, tapped lightly on the large book before him. "Darlin' lass, this says that Jesus will never leave you or forsake you, and that He loves you with an everlasting love. Now, that means forever, Tisha. And that means no matter what."

Tisha's face lit up like a sunrise. "Oh, daddy, that's so wonderful!"

"Yes it is."

"And daddy, do you know what!"

"What?"

"If that's true, then I don't care if anyone calls me 'goodie two-shoes' ever again!"

....

Audra Shields sat slumped over the small white Formica desk in her bedroom. She had been there for hours pouring over her notes on titanium X. Suddenly a voice from seemingly out of nowhere startled her.

"Hey, momma. You still working at this hour? All work and no play, you know, makes little Audra a dull girl."

Audra's eyes shot towards the voice and rested on the muscular frame of Bubba Hanagan. Then they darted to the small digital clock on her desk. It was three in the morning. She had no idea it was so late.

"Where have you been!" she shot fiercely. The words were barely out when Audra realized that was not what she wanted to say at all. In reality she cared little where he had been. His comings and goings had never mattered before. They mattered even less now. Ever since Bubba had walked in on her and Ace Corbet, Audra had become increasingly cranky and annoyed with him. After several weeks of living together Audra knew their relationship was rapidly drawing to a close. It had not been an especially good relationship. She knew little more about him now than when they first met. She didn't know, for instance, that Hanagan had just come from Michael Patterson's house or that he had served as bartender during the party. No, he was a stranger, and what Audra had meant to say to this stranger but didn't was, "How dare you walk into my apartment at this hour!"

Hanagan ignored Audra's angry question and walked over to the desk. "What are you doing?" he asked casually as he peered at the papers that cluttered the top.

Immediately, Audra scooped her notes into a pile, as a hen would scoop her chicks into safety, and shoved them into the bottom drawer of her desk. It was here that she kept a duplicate copy of all her papers. With a stiff, angry motion, she locked it.

Audra never discussed her work with her lovers, and she resented Bubba's sudden interest, however superficial. "It's none of your business what I'm doing," she snapped.

"Okay, okay. You don't have to bite," he said, trying to sound cheerful, but the look on his face became hard. "What's the matter? Got the rag on?"

"I hate that expression!" She was beginning to yell. "Only you stupid men would use it!" She was standing up now, beside the desk.

"Just who are you calling stupid?" Bubba asked between clenched teeth.

"There are only two of us here," returned Audra, glaring at him; all the hatred and frustration of her life pouring from her. "And I'm not the one who resembles Magilla Gorilla."

"Why you...," Bubba Hanagan sputtered between the hard lines of his lips. "I don't take that from any broad." One big hand reached over to the night stand and lifting the lamp that was on it high in the air, ripped its cord from the socket. He poised the lamp, like a weapon, over her head, and for one sickening second, Audra believed he would smash her skull with it. But slowly the angry lines on Hanagan's face dissolved, and finally he threw the lamp on the bed.

"You broads are all alike," he said with disgust. "You want to play in the big league, but you don't have the stomach for it."

Audra's rage was so great it made her remarkably bold. "And you men are all alike," she spat. "You have more brawn than brains. I want my key back, and I never want to see you again!"

Hanagan's lips curled into a mocking sneer as he dug into his pants' pocket and pulled out the apartment key. With a gesture that was both arrogant and threatening, he flung it onto the floor by her feet. "And good riddens," he growled.

Long after the apartment door slammed shut and Bubba Hanagan was gone, the pretty blond sat hugging her knees and shaking in the middle of the bed. She knew she had come within inches of serious injury, perhaps even...death. "Oh God!" she cried loudly, as the realization peaked, and vivid pictures of her smashed, bloody skull filled her imagination. "Oh God!" she cried out again. She just had to get a grip on her life. It was spinning out of control. She began shaking her head from side to side. She knew her supplication was useless. "'No deity will save us, we must save ourselves,'" she said out loud, quoting the memorized line from the Humanist Manifesto. Her mother had quoted that line a hundred, perhaps a thousand times. Audra had accepted it. It was part of her now. But there was one question her mother had never been able to answer, and that was *how? How* did one save himself?

Five

The blustery wind filled Tisha's sweatshirt and blew it out like a sail. Now and then she would tug at it trying to flatten it over her blue jeans. "It's really beautiful here," she said.

"Yeah, sort of gets into your blood," returned Buck, grinning beside her. "Look, look over there, Tisha, how the strip leads to the very edge of the cliff and then nothing. Boy, if a plane isn't airborne by the time it gets there, that's it, it's all over."

They had been walking along the unkept airstrip for a considerable distance. Tisha looked ahead in the direction of Buck's pointing finger where the strip continued for about a quarter of a mile more and then ended abruptly as the land ended abruptly. She couldn't see the boulders and jagged rocks that helped form the sharp drop into the sea. You had to be at the edge of the cliff to see that. But she could hear the muffled sounds of the pounding surf.

"Seems like there's plenty of strip for a safe STOL," she said, her eyes scanning the total strip in measurement as the two turned around and headed back toward the direction of the hangar.

"The P2 won't have any trouble taking off here, not with the power she's got. But for conventional aircraft it would be risky. The winds are strong, unpredictable. And there's no way to enlarge the run-way, except by leveling that mountain on the opposite side." As he spoke, Buck pointed to the area behind the hanger.

Tisha looked at the cliff that rose high in the air like some great stone monolith. Nestled beside it was a hangar, which in comparison to the size of the mountain looked rather like a metal doll house. Yet, when viewed alone, it was gigantic in its own right. Earlier, when Tisha parked her car, she noticed that the hangar's midsection was new, its corrugated metal still shiny and unscarred.

"I see you joined the two hangars," she said as they continued their walk.

Buck nodded. "You've got about four hundred thirty-five thousand square feet of work space. Enough room to build one heck of an airplane."

The dark haired engineer smiled and slipped her arm through Buck's. Already she was beginning to feel better about things. Being here might not be so bad after all. "Do you really think we can do it?" she asked.

"Kelly Johnson and his 'Skunk Works' crew at Lockheed designed, wind tunnel tested, and completely built a ready-to-fly XP-80, in just one hundred and eighty days. We have been working on the P2 for two years."

"I know, but I still think we should do more testing, especially on the wing. Then of course there's the casing problem... ."

"Relax, Tisha. I know we have problems. But everything will work out fine. You'll see." Although his voice was optimistic, Tisha knew Buck didn't really believe Kelly Johnson himself would build an airplane under these conditions. "And good news," he continued. "I spoke to Mike yesterday and he's decided to send a small hand-picked crew of mechanics and shop workers tomorrow."

"Well, that's a step in the right direction," said Tisha as they passed through a small side entrance. Immediately two men in overalls stopped, waved, then resumed opening large crates housing equipment and machinery.

"What a mess," she whispered to Buck while viewing the maze of boxes that cluttered the hangar.

"Yep. It's going to take a lot of work to make it happen."

"It is exciting though, isn't it? I mean, we have a chance to make history right here."

"I suppose we have. I really don't think about it much. I guess my interests are a little narrower, more selfish."

"You love him, don't you?"

"Mike? Yeah. We go way back. In some ways, I raised him as much as his father did."

"I know, I've heard."

"I guess that means I have to take credit for the bad as well as the good."

"What does that mean?"

"It means that I love Michael Patterson like a son, but I know he has faults."

"Are you trying to tell me something?"

The leathery man chuckled. "I really do like you, Tisha. I liked you right off, when you first came to PA. You looked to me like a scrawny, wide-eyed kid then, but when you opened your mouth and started talking about airplanes, you didn't seem like such a kid anymore."

The beautiful engineer squeezed his arm gently. "I like you too, Buck."

"Then you won't mind me talking to you like a father?"

"I'd be flattered."

"Okay, what I want to say is that Mike's not the kind of man I'd want my daughter to get involved with, if I had a daughter that is."

"Buck, I...I don't know what to say," Tisha responded, stunned to the core.

"Mike's favorite toy was always the one he couldn't have. Do you understand what I'm saying?"

"Perfectly, but surely you don't think I'm interested, that I...I mean he's married," Tisha stammered, humiliated by his honesty, yet unable to return his honesty with a lie of denial. "For heaven's sake, he's a married man," Tisha repeated.

"Exactly. And you're what my generation called a 'nice girl.' And nice girls and married men aren't combinations that add up to a happy ending."

"I should feel insulted that you could think such a thing, but I don't, Buck. I only wonder how you guessed. I didn't even know myself until recently that I...that I had feelings...for him. I suppose I'm not insulted because I'm too ashamed."

Buck put his arm around her and gave her a hug. "We can't always help how we feel, can we? We can only help what we do with those feelings."

"I wasn't planning on doing anything with mine," Tisha returned. She felt utterly depressed.

"I didn't expect you would. But you see, I also know Mike, and he's...well, he's attracted to you. Don't ask me how I know, it's little things that wouldn't mean anything to you. And I think he'll, well, *he* may act on his feelings. We're a long way from home, and people get lonely and sometimes do things they normally won't do otherwise."

Tisha's face darkened. "You're very blunt."

"I'm sorry if I've overstepped, it's just that I like you and I know Michael."

"But you really don't know me. I'm not a school girl. I can take care of myself."

Buck let out a deep sigh. "I've offended you. I'm sorry. But I think Mike's working himself up to making a good old-fashioned pass. I've seen him work himself up before."

"You sound a little disloyal. Aren't the 'guys' supposed to stick together? You don't seem to be looking out for his interests."

"Oh, but I am. Aside from liking you, Tisha, I don't want to see Mike get involved with you, for his own sake."

"And why is that?"

"Because you're too dangerous."

"Dangerous?"

"Yes, you're the type he'd fall in love with. You're the kind who could break his heart."

Tisha's color drained. "This sounds like sleazy gossip," she finally said. "Is this what's going around the PA lunchroom?"

The powerful arm drew her closer to him. "I doubt if anyone in the world knows how you feel, including Mike. I'm not much of a talker, Tisha. I do more watching and listening. And I saw it coming over Mike, just as I saw it come over you, like a slow growing cancer."

"Cancer? I guess that pretty well describes it. I'd laugh if I wasn't so thoroughly miserable."

"You're tough, Tisha. You can get over this. Not all cancers are incurable. But Mike, he's the one I'm really worried about. He's never been in love before."

"You make him sound like some innocent school boy, when you know the opposite is true."

"He's far from innocent, but he's vulnerable, more vulnerable than he even knows."

"Buck, you're one of the nerviest people I've ever met."

"Yeah, I like you too, Tisha. But I already told you that. If you're ever feeling low or want to talk, just remember, I'm here."

"Well, thanks for that anyway. And thank you for wanting to be my conscience."

"I don't need to do that. You've already got one. I was thinking more along the line of being a 'friend.'"

"I think I'm going to need one out here."

"In return, can I count on you for something?" Buck said with a smile as he looked at an organized section in the back, full of bottles and holding tanks. A man in a white shirt and khaki pants stood, by what appeared to be a large pump, busily writing something on a pad.

"What's Nolan up to?" Tisha said, following his gaze.

The strong burley man beside her chuckled. "Well, that's the thing I am counting on you for. I was hoping you could tell me. I can never understand what he's saying."

Tisha's somber face finally broke into a smile. "He's brilliant, you know." She waved to Nolan. The neat, lanky man waved back in recognition. Then she gave Buck a little squeeze. "I'm *very* glad we're going to be working together," she said and walked away.

"Nolan, hello! I heard about your 'special project.' How's it coming?" Tisha said as she approached the tall, thin man.

Nolan had a serious but comely, almost girlish face. He rarely smiled and was, in fact, generally pessimistic. Now his face knotted into little bows of consternation. "Actually," he said, "considering the circumstances under which I am forced to labor," here he paused, allowing Tisha to observe his makeshift lab, then continued, "I suppose I am doing quite well."

Tisha grinned sardonically. "Seems like we're all going to be working under adverse conditions," she said, thinking of her conversation with Buck.

"Yes, I was advised of operations moving here." He looked wretchedly at the disorder around him. "Well, I think this entire adventure is ludicrous. What type of mentality would conceive of building an aircraft mock-up without first perfecting its propulsion system?"

"I'm afraid, Nolan, that often times politics fails to employ even the lowest IQ."

The physicist grunted bad-temperedly. "Of all people, I thought that you, at least, would try to prevent this."

"I did try," Tisha returned calmly, while picking up his note pad. "What's this? 0.0042869?"

"Oh, I was just going over some of the notes I brought from PA. That's the mass change of the deuterium nuclei. Using the relativity relation $E=MC^2$, this gives 4.5 X 10^{13} calories per gram atom of deuterium. Thus, about 0.1% of the mass is converted to heat energy. Naturally, the greater the heat energy, the greater the destruction of the casing by the plasma. We know there was no evidence of breakdown in the first thirty-five tests. I propose to find the exact point at which our metal began to break down. Based on what I've done so far, I think maybe if we use one more water cooled vacuum switch tube with its capacity to control another twenty-five million watts, plus additional shielding in each... ."

"The tubes alone are three hundred and twenty pounds a piece; times that by four reactors on one P2 that's 1,280 additional pounds, just for starters, without even getting into the metal shields or additional vacuum chambers," interrupted Tisha.

"True, but the alteration of the P2 may not be as drastic as originally anticipated. If we pursue this course, maybe in six months we can begin the mock-up."

"In six months we must complete the mock-up."

Nolan's girlish face warped in panic. "I...I am a scientist; a logical being who deals in facts and then proceeds in careful, pre-cise action. You are also a scientist, Tisha. I have always held you in the highest esteem. How...how can you submit to such chaos? How can you submit your staff to this chaos?"

Tisha understood Nolan's frustration. A person didn't ex-pend his energy, his blood, his very life into building something fine and wonderful, and then casually accept the possibility of it being towed into a scrap-metal lot. Sympathetically, she looked at the lovely brows, the small perfect nose, the rosebud lips. He was so fine, so delicate, like a porcelain bust.

"Nolan, I understand your feelings. But there are things in-volved here that neither you nor I have any control over. What happens here, though, will control the future of PA. This makes our work even more vital than ever. We have to pull together regard-less of our personal feelings. I need you, Nolan. And I need to know I can count on you one hundred percent."

With a sigh Nolan picked up his pad, "Tisha, you know the answer to that."

"Looks like you need a break, O'Brien," said a voice that seemed to fill the hangar with a gusty breeze of its own. Brushing the dust off her blue jeans, Tisha turned toward the sound. There were smudges of dirt across her cheeks and stray wisps of hair framed her face like a little lace cap. For several hours now she had been helping to rig one of the large mobile platforms.

The tall, muscular man smiled broadly, thinking how pretty the face was and feeling unusually pleased at seeing it. Gently, he guided her through the maze of disorder and to the rear of the hangar where a dented metal pot sat on an old, paint chipped table. "Come on, I'll buy you a cup of coffee."

"I accept," she answered, hoping she didn't seem too pleased at his sudden appearance.

"Looks like you're moving along fine."

"Well, I suppose we've progressed from total chaos to semi-chaos. Progress is being made, as they say."

Mike poured them both coffee, then handed Tisha hers. He remained silent for a long time, his brown eyes staring at the steaming liquid in his cup as though it held some great mystery or perhaps some great answer. When he looked up he was smiling, but his eyes were intent, serious. "Do you realize that neither one of us has ever called the other by his first name? I think it's time we started."

"Why?"

"Because after two years of working together, I think we should be friends. And friends are on a first name basis."

Tisha laughed, thinking this was the second offer of friendship she had received that day. The first offer she had accepted readily. This offer was quite another matter. She didn't want to be, nor was she capable of being friends with Michael Patterson. Under the circumstances, she wanted as little to do with him as possible. She needed to keep her distance. "Yes, I suppose you're right," she finally said, forcing a smile. "After all, I am one of the boys."

This time Patterson laughed. "Seriously, Tisha, you're the first woman I've ever been able to speak to as if you were a man."

"I'll take that as a compliment."

"It's meant that way," Mike returned.

"To friendship then," Tisha said in a hollow voice as she sipped her coffee.

"To friendship," Patterson responded, he also drinking from

his cup. But his eyes never left her and he had a strange look on his face.

Tisha's thick, black hair was gathered at the neck by a ribbon, and a faint blush of embarrassment pinked her exposed ear lobes. Mike reached for her hand, his fingers touching her lightly. "Tisha...I wish... ." Abruptly, he removed his hand and jerked backward. "I wish we had all the money in the world so we could build this airplane properly." With that, the tall, handsome executive disappeared among the maze of boxes.

A deep, cauterizing fear burned inside Tisha, causing her to drive herself ruthlessly, almost frantically for several hours as though that would extinguish the fire. But after completion of the huge mobile platforms and ladders which resembled scaffolding in a shipyard, the only thing she had succeeded in burning out was herself. And when Mike Patterson said, "Okay everyone, let's knock off," she was immensely grateful.

Wearily, she left everything and slipped out the side door. She had no wish to see him. All afternoon she had managed to avoid him. This was an impossible situation. How did this happen to her? How did she suddenly wake up one morning in love with a married man? She felt utterly dejected. Buck had called it a cancer. That's what it was. A slow growing malignancy bent on complete take-over. How was she going to get rid of it? Cancer in the advanced stage could not be cut or burned out with chemo. She must make certain it didn't get that far. But how?

Working so closely with Mike was going to be difficult. If she had any sense she would quit right now. But she just couldn't leave the project. Still...the way he had looked at her! She could hardly bear the memory of it. He said he wanted to be friends, but was there more? Did he know, like Buck did? Had he seen something on her face, heard something in her voice that told him how she felt?

Tisha was aware of Mike Patterson's reputation with women. Suddenly, she imagined his face contorted with laughter, saw her name scrawled over some dirty urinal in some dirty men's room, heard it bantered about in a locker room heavy with male perspiration. It was an ugly vision. It exposed the depth of her desire for him. He had gotten her to the sea. She looked in the direction of the cliff, listened to the muffled sound of pounding surf. A person could die in that she thought, and began walking slowly to her car.

The full moon, like a large lucid bowl of golden crystals, seemed to sprinkle everything with light, making even usual shadowy objects appear remarkably luminous. Some things were best left in shadows, Tisha thought, as she came upon the great gold and white helicopter bearing the lettering Patterson Aviation, and the initials M.P. He was a man used to flying in and out of people's lives, oblivious to all the turmoil and dirt he raised, as if the disorder could be easily tidied-up. How many hearts had he broken, she wondered? How many lives had he disrupted or damaged?

Suddenly, she felt angry. But her anger was at herself, at her weakness. And when she pulled into the Sea Breeze parking lot she was still angry. She had wanted to be alone, so she drove around for a long time before coming to the hotel where the entire Gibs Town staff was lodged. Michael Patterson had rented one wing of the hotel. She stopped her red BMW in front of a marble horse-head post with a large brass ring through its nose. The Sea Breeze Inn was a converted mansion and several touches of the former splendor still remained.

Glumly she got out of the car, walked through the lobby, the hallway, and towards her room. But as she approached the door marked twelve, her heart began to pound.

"Mike...what are you doing here?"

"My room's right next door," he answered casually, but his face was anything but casual. The large eyes were serious, probing.

Tisha stared mutely at her employer, thinking of Buck's caution. And for a few seconds her silence prevailed like a great shield of armor between them. Then the strong, powerful executive took the key from her hand and unlocked the door.

"Look, I'm tired," she said, trying to slip past him behind

the door. Doors could be locked. But she was not fast enough or perhaps Mike was just too fast, for suddenly he had hold of her arm.

"There was something I wanted to tell you, over our coffee earlier." His voice was hushed, throaty.

"What...was it?" Tisha asked hesitantly. By way of answer Mike Patterson simply touched his face to hers. At once Tisha lost all sense of breathing. It was as though he breathed for both of them. As she tasted his mouth, she suddenly felt the pulling of the tide. If it wasn't for the strength of his arms holding her, she would have been swept away. Then, as though someone had deposited her safely on shore, she found herself leaning against the door frame, looking into the face that a moment ago had been so intimately a part of her own.

"Tisha, I can't explain what I'm feeling now. I don't understand it myself. I know that I want you. Maybe I'm just making a fool of myself. I know you're not the type to look twice at a married man. But my feelings are so strong I can't be silent. Is...is there a chance for me?"

Tisha stood propped against the frame unable to speak. All she could do was shake her head.

"I guess I expected that. But I had to try. You know how impetuous and impatient I am." He tried to smile, but gave it up.

Buck had known this was coming. He had warned her. But in her heart, Tisha had not believed that Michael Patterson would really make a pass. Now that it was happening it seemed so silly, like something out of a romance novel, and yet so...frightening.

Mike Patterson gently grazed her cheek with his thumb. His face was only inches from hers. "Don't look so terrified, Tisha. You're not going to have to spend all your time here at Gibs Town fighting me off. I swear I'll never touch you again, unless of course it's by your choice. The door between our rooms locks on both sides. My side will always be unbolted...good night." With that the powerful frame disappeared behind the door marked eleven.

Tisha retreated into her own room, closed the door, and without turning on the light made her way to the bed. Like Jell-O running off a plate, she slid to the floor, the bottom of the bedpost clutched firmly between her hands. She was formless, the full scope of her emotions melting her into a pathetic little puddle. She was on her knees now, holding fast to the bedpost, holding against the rushing tide that was pulling, pulling her body. She wanted to crawl like an animal to the door that separated her from him. Instead, she clung desperately to the post, knowing if she but for a moment let go, the tide would sweep her away, away from her convictions, away from this room and into his.

"Jesus," she whimpered, "this is too hard. I can't do it." She began to weep. "Help me. *Please* help me." Suddenly through her tears, Tisha heard a still, small voice. "I will never leave you or forsake you. I love you with an everlasting love."

Six

Mike briskly toweled his wet body. Around him hung a steamy cobweb-like mist, and when he opened the bathroom door to disperse it, he was surprised to see Renee shuffling about.

"You're up early," he shouted, as thought the steam was a barrier his voice had to penetrate, when in truth it was his feeling of awkwardness, of being around Renee. He had spent few nights at home during the past three months.

It was eight a.m. and early only to someone like Renee who seldom rose before ten. "I have a lot to do," she returned, gathering a pink, satin robe around her shapely body. "It's the trip. I need a whole new wardrobe since the Garbys have seen practically all my clothes, everything decent anyway."

Mike chuckled, "It's as good an excuse as any." He knew of Renee's fondness for shopping. But he was only mildly interested in her upcoming trip to the Garbys. Renee had recently spent two weeks in Washington as the Senator's guest. Her time in DC had been primarily occupied with luncheons and parties. It had been exhilarating, almost overwhelming for her. She had finally eaten from the plate of political life; drank from the cup of notability.

"When are you leaving?" Mike asked as he stood in front of

the mirror shaving, feeling not as refreshed after his shower as he normally did. There was something withering about moving. He felt it every time he transplanted himself from Gibs Town to Everman, and he knew what it was, separation from Tisha. Even though Tisha had yet to open the door between their rooms, Mike had become increasingly close to her. Aside from friendship, he felt a deep stirring love that was at once unexpected, frightening and satisfying. His hopes of getting her to cross from a platonic to carnal relationship pulsed more feebly with each passing day. She was not giving an inch and he was beginning to have serious doubts of succeeding in an arena where he had never had trouble before. While his hopes began to wither, his passion for her grew. He had never wanted any woman as much as he wanted Tisha O'Brien. And he had never cared for anyone like he cared for her. She filled his thoughts as no other woman before her. "So, when are you leaving," Mike repeated, trying to sound interested.

Renee ignored his question. "Michael, the Garbys would like you to come too."

Mike knotted the towel around his waist. "Impossible."

"Why? We haven't gone away together in a long time. A little vacation would do you good."

"You're probably right, but there's too much happening at the plant. I just can't leave town, not now, not for a long time."

"You're just making excuses because it's the Garbys."

"Renee, right now the Pope himself couldn't induce me to leave my company."

Renee laughed. "Poor illustration. You're a Methodist and not a very good one at that." Suddenly her face clouded. "No, it's the Garbys. You've let lies and false rumors poison your opinion. And that's not *fair* Michael." Renee's sensuous mouth puckered like a pouting child's.

"We've been through all that. I'm not going to defend my position. And you're right, I'm not interested in spending time with the Garbys. I am particular about the company I keep. I'm at a point in my life where when I do have free time, I want to spend it with people I like. Can you understand that?"

"Of course I can, Michael. What it boils down to is that we like different people." Renee shrugged. "So be it. But it's a shame. Senator Garby is interested in you and if you made half an effort you could be friends. He can do a lot for you, for both of us, even for Patterson Aviation. At any rate, he asks me about you all the time."

Mike's suspicious nature was piqued at once. "Yeah? Like what? What did he ask?"

"Oh...questions about your company mainly, what you do, the planes you build, that sort of thing."

"And what did you tell him?"

"I told him how secretive you are, and how even I don't know half of what goes on."

Mike's face knotted as his suspicions increased. "Go on."

"That's about it... ."

"What *else*?" There was a startling harshness in his tone.

"Nothing...well, he did ask why you were so secretive. Why are you so secretive?"

"Why is Senator Garby so interested?"

"How should I know? Honestly, Michael, you're so suspicious! You'd think you were hiding some tremendous secret, you'd think... ."

"And what else?" Mike interrupted.

"And nothing!" screamed Renee, but the force of Mike's stare began pulling out the answers like a suction.

"Well...," she stammered, "he did mention once about how he'd like to visit your plant, and then Alex, Alex Harner... ."

"He was there?"

Renee nodded. "Yes, and he told Senator Garby it would be good publicity for his campaign, you know, Senator visits factory, mingles with the common worker and all. Then Alex suggested the Senator enlist you in his campaign."

"Why would he want to do that?"

"Grass roots dear. You're a prominent businessman. He

must think your backing would get him a few votes."

"And what did you say?"

"I said I'd talk to you."

"And that's what this DC invitation is all about?"

"Yes... ."

"You were supposed to set me up, is that it?"

"You don't have to put it like that." The conversation was not going at all as Renee had planned. It was not supposed to be like this. He was supposed to go with her on vacation. Then during their flight to Washington, she would tell him the purpose of the trip, drop seeds that would hopefully germinate by the time her husband met with the Senator. But he was so uncooperative, so...impossible! Now he was going to spoil everything. All her maneuvering, all her scheming, all her plans, he was ready to stuff them down the garbage disposal and grind them into tiny pieces. She never hated anyone as much as she hated her husband at that moment.

"And what exactly were you supposed to get out of this?" Mike asked sarcastically. "An invitation to the 'inner circle'?"

"Well, I...I... ."

"You'd sell my company right out from under me, if you could, just to get a little attention from your precious Senator."

"You're such a boor. Nobody but you cares a bit about your company."

"Then why did they bring it up?"

"They care about you, as a potential vote-getter, and... ."

"Grow up, Renee. These boys don't give anything away, not even their time or attention, unless there's something in it for them."

Renee threw up her hands in exasperation. "Politeness, Michael, it's just out of politeness that they show any interest in you. Maybe you've forgotten such things as manners, I don't know. But believe me, the Senator doesn't give a hoot about your company. The only thing he didn't understand was that I don't either!"

Mike stared at his wife. Even without makeup and with her

auburn hair hanging like limp spaghetti around her face, Renee was beautiful. But her eyes were barren and gritty like a desert, and when you looked into them you knew there was nothing growing there, not love, or kindness or joy, not anything. For a second, Michael felt sorry for her. "It's not your fault, Renee. It's not your fault. It's us. That's what's wrong. It's *us*."

Deep lines of anger contorted Renee's face. "Don't be so condescending! I've never been interested in your company, you know that. Ever since you began running off to that secret workshop of yours, you haven't been the same. Michael, honestly, you can't get so worked up over an airplane!"

"Let's just drop it, Renee," Mike growled. "We've already established that we don't care about what the other does."

"For heaven's sake! What's wrong with you? You have an opportunity here to make something of yourself and... ."

"Make something of myself? I thought I already had."

"I didn't mean it like that. It's just that Senator Garby is very powerful and I don't think it's wise to deliberately offend him. Surely you can't refuse... ."

"I can and I do."

Renee's face reddened. "Well, what am I going to tell the Garbys?" she whined. She could hear the sound of her ground-up dreams being flushed away.

"Tell them to go... ."

A sudden timid rap on the bedroom door brought the conversation to a halt. Impatiently, Mike grabbed the knob and turned. A young, rather mousy looking woman in a starched uniform stood before him. He did not recognize her, but that in itself did not distress him. Renee was always hiring and firing servants on whim, and he was used to being in a house full of strangers.

"Yes!" he said gruffly, annoyed at this delaying his departure and at the thought that she may have been there for some time.

"I...I'm sorry to disturb you, sir. A phone call for you, a Mr. Buck McNight. He said it was urgent."

Mike had not heard the phone because there wasn't one in

the bedroom. Both he and Renee never liked being woken up by the sound of its rude ringing. Immediately, Mike went to the sitting room.

"Yes, Buck, what is it?"

The voice on the other end sounded crackly, like crumbling aluminum foil. "There's been an explosion. The autoclave. Mike, the whole wall is gone! No one was hurt. But if it had blown a little later, when the assembly line began, we'd have a factory full of dead bodies. I came a little early, around seven. Had some work I wanted to clear up. I heard it, the explosion, while I was still in the parking lot. This is the first chance I've had to... ."

Mike cut him off. "I'll be right over," he said, and hung up.

The massive hands hanging limply beside the faded blue jeans belied the tension that laced the leathery face of Buck McNight. "What a morning," he said, almost to himself, shock still in his voice. "It's a miracle it wasn't worse."

Mike nodded. Adhesives, which Lockheed helped develop, had replaced riveting in large fuselage panels. The adhesives were also used to apply titanium straps. Those body parts of the aircraft on which adhesives were used had to be put into the autoclave which bonded the adhesives under tremendous heat and inert gas pressure. The autoclave functioned like a giant pressure cooker, and the heat and inert gas were capable of great destruction.

"I still don't understand how a thing like this could happen. There were safety devices, strict guidelines were observed. What went wrong?"

Buck clicked a boot heel against the leg of his chair and shook his head mutely.

"It couldn't have happened at a worse time."

Buck remained silent as he watched the president of Patterson Aviation pace in front of him. When Mike was stressed, Buck knew the best remedy was to let him talk it through.

"We've had a rough ride these couple of months, and things

don't look like they're getting any better. Of all times for this to happen! We're so backlogged with the EX4 and C101 deals... ." Mike's voice trailed off. PA's Sales Director had been able to sell all ten C101s, plus five more. These five, plus the EX4s he had sold earlier, put production schedules on an overtime basis. The damaged autoclave would cause heavy loss of productive man hours.

"I guess we've survived worse," Mike continued, trying to encourage himself. His face told Buck it was not working.

"We might be able to meet production schedules by increasing OT once the autoclave is operable, but that will raise overhead. And of course, there's the cost of operations at Gibs Town." Patterson Aviation was at present precariously poised beneath the sharp blade of a financial guillotine. "Yeah, that's the way to go. OT. That'll do it. That's the way to pick up the slack." Finally, a smile appeared on Mike's face. "Heck, we've outrun our creditors before. We can do it again. The money from the ten C101's will keep us for awhile. In the mean time, I understand we've got a few interested investors ready to open their wallets. Yes, we're going to do this, Buck. We're going to be fine."

Buck's smiling eyes looked fondly at the man in front of him. "Never doubted it, Mike," he said, the smile finally reaching his lips. "That brings me to something else," he continued. "The rumors are really flying."

"What rumors?"

"That you're building some kind of 'super plane.'"

"I expected that. It was only a matter of time. A thing like this always spawns wild speculation." Aside from the Gibs Town crew and R&D, only a chosen handful knew about the seaside hanger and the nature of the work being done there. But everyone knew something was afoot. It was difficult not to notice when key co-workers failed to show up at PA. Common speculation had it that these key people were elsewhere working on a secret assignment. "Do you think we can keep the lid on?" Mike asked.

"Not much longer," Buck returned. "I got an earful yesterday. There's talk all over the plant." Buck had flown with Mike in the helicopter from Gibs Town. They had been in Everman less than twenty-four hours.

Buck looked solicitously at young Patterson. How unlike the father he was. Where the elder Patterson had been weak, Mike was strong. Where the father had been timid, Mike was bold and not wary of taking risks. Buck had liked the father, but he loved the son, as though Mike was his very own. "Don't worry," he said in a tone he had used so many times with Mike through the years; times when he had to stand in for the busy elder Patterson. "We still have a good chance of pulling it off. By the time anyone knows what's going on at Gibs Town, it'll be too late."

Mike Patterson watched Tisha pace as he talked about the autoclave incident. She had not gone with him to Everman, and until now, no one at Gibs Town knew of the explosion.

He had missed her more than he thought possible during the few days he was absent. He couldn't bear to be apart from her. And aside from desperately wanting to sleep with her, he desperately wanted to get to know her, really know her. He had never felt like that about anyone. He was falling in love. It was a new experience. It both thrilled and frightened him.

"Thank God no one was hurt," Tisha said, black hair flying about her as she paced. "You think it was a malfunction?" she asked, lowering her voice. They were in the small coffee alcove in the hanger and Tisha didn't want to be overhead.

"There's always that chance, but it's pretty slim."

"What does Meyers say?" The Meyers, Tisha mentioned, was Peter Meyers, the ISS agent in charge of Everman security.

"He naturally sees every malfunction as a terrorist attack. But his boys will go over the autoclave with a magnifying glass before he gives his official ruling."

The lovely ivory face shriveled into a frown. "I don't understand. If I were a terrorist, I'd blow up the entire plant, not just the autoclave. It's strange... ."

111

"Terrorists aren't logical. Who knows why they do any of the things they do? You're not dealing with the normal mind."

"Then," Tisha said, thoughtfully, "Patterson Aviation may be the latest target of the Jihad."

"Probably."

Tisha finally stopped pacing and sat on a nearby chair. She thought of Joshua Chapman and his friends. They were somewhere in the Middle East. She wondered if she'd ever see them again. The whole world was like a wound, oozing purulent insanity, and this insanity was beginning to seep under her very doorstep. But it didn't frighten her, it only made her feel very sad. She dropped her face into her hands. Oh Jesus, she thought, why won't the world love You?

Mike was watching her and misread her sadness for fear. "I bet you didn't even miss me," he interjected suddenly, trying to bring her out of it.

Tisha's face formed a puzzled look. A part of her was always on guard when she was with him. Mike had no way of knowing that his presence produced in her a tremendous inner turmoil. He had no way of knowing the number of nights she lay sleeplessly listening to him pace in the room next to her and wishing she was beside him, or the times she cried into her pillow with grief. Over the past three months, he had worked his way into her heart so deeply she was beginning to give up hope of ever getting him out. She had never been so thoroughly miserable. But Mike was ignorant of all this. He only marveled at her reserve, at her ability to be warm and friendly without compromising herself in the slightest.

"You didn't even miss me," he repeated.

"I missed you," she replied without emotion.

"Then why didn't you tell me that when you saw me? 'Mike, I missed you,' why didn't you say that?"

"Mike, I missed you," she said, her voice hollow, pacifying.

The brawny man bent over her. "How I missed you!" The words worked through her hair like a ribbon. "I'm falling in love with you, Tisha. I'm sorry, but I am."

Tisha rose from her chair and walked over to the battered electric percolator. With a slightly shaking hand, she poured each of them a cup of coffee. "I know," she said softly.

"How do you feel about that?"

Tisha took a sip from her cup. He was digging at her more and more, trying to strip her down to the very marrow of her bones, to draw her out, to reveal herself. What did he want from her anyway? Why couldn't he just leave her alone? "Mike, you're married. That's the beginning, the middle and the end of story. And I can't add anything to it."

"Can't or won't?" There was pain on his face as he looked at her.

"Does it really matter?" she returned, sensing his unhappiness for the first time. It never occurred to her that this could be more than a game to him, that his concept of "love" was more than a perverted challenge she presented to his ego. When he had told her he loved her, Tisha knew he meant it, as far as he understood love. Now, she wasn't so sure. Suppose he really was…suppose. Suppose what? Suppose he was really in love with her? Suppose he wasn't in love with the idea of her, not in love with the challenge or idea of conquest? But just *her*? What if he was? What difference did it make? But it did make a difference. It made everything that much harder. Silently, she handed him his coffee.

"You know, Tisha," he said, looking down into the steaming liquid, his voice strangely tender. "I wish we had met ten years ago." And something inside Tisha told her he really meant it.

Audra walked down the hall of Patterson Aviation's R&D Department tightly clutching her pocketbook. Her stomach churned queasily. She had eaten little breakfast. Ever since the autoclave explosion her nerves had been as unruly as a disobedient child. Peter Meyers and his group had swarmed through the plant like a regiment of locusts inspecting everything from fingerprints and locks, to position of furniture and inventory; asking question after question.

The entire company had been in an uproar for days. Everyone knew Meyers was ISS. And he meant trouble. Words bounced from one department to another like a Ping-Pong ball. Sabotage! Jihad! And suddenly everyone began seeing bogie-men. Bushes blown by the wind covered hidden assassins. A tailgating car became a pursuing vehicle of terrorists. The latest gory newspaper stories were traded like baseball cards. Fear can be as contagious as the flu, and PA experienced an epidemic.

Audra had also seen her share of bogie-men. She had thought, but was not sure, that once, someone stood outside her front door. She had thought, but was not sure, she had heard breathing and then the knob turning. She had been sorry she had thrown Bubba Hanagan out. He was a brute, but he was a big, strong brute. And a big, strong man, be he brute or not, was a comfort in times like these. But he wasn't there, so she had to buy her comfort elsewhere. It came in the form of a .25 caliber hand gun; a small blue-black pistol, perfect for a woman's pocketbook. She took it everywhere.

With quick, stiff jerks, Audra moved down the hall, tightly clutching her bag. She did not release her grip until she stepped into the room that was outfitted for her titanium X experiments. Madness, it was all madness. The world was going mad, Audra thought, and she just hoped she wasn't going to go mad with it.

Seven

W hat! Say that again, Audra!" Tisha shouted into the receiver. She could hardly contain herself as she spoke, and bounced slightly up and down as though doing a cheer. She had been waiting and hoping for this news for months. Now that she was getting her heart's desire, she was having trouble believing it was true.

"I think I've found it. I think I've found a way to stabilize titanium X." Audra had worked long, hard hours over the past months. She had spent many nights on the cot in her office. Her colleagues admired her dedication, but Audra had motives that went beyond devotion. It was true that she was deeply committed to the project. But time spent at PA meant time not spent in an empty apartment. PA was heavily guarded. Surveillance was doubled at night. At the apartment, her only protection was the .25 caliber that she kept under her pillow. She had bought a second gun. One never left her purse. The other never left her apartment.

But the two pistols only gave a meager sense of security, and fear dominated her life; fear of being followed home, fear of someone breaking into her apartment, fear of being bombed, fear of *everything*. For the most part, she had even stopped going to

Grobens. Like a hermit, Audra had succeeded in secluding herself from almost everything that did not pertain to her job. Patterson Aviation was the only place where she felt a measure of safety.

A deep sigh spilled from Tisha's lips. "Wonderful! Absolutely wonderful! How did you do it?"

"I've been focusing on the films."

It was the thin protective film that stood between a metal surface and a potentially destructive environment. Tisha already knew it would be Audra's logical point of concentration. "I gathered that," Tisha said, both excited and impatient.

"In the past I concentrated on promoting the formation of a noncrystalline surface through laser glazing," Audra continued, a little breathlessly.

Again she wasn't telling Tisha anything new. A noncrystalline film produced a more effective barrier to corrosion than a crystalline one. "Okay, what's the end result!" Tisha chuckled to herself when she realized she was sounding as impatient as Michael Patterson.

"The laser beam melted the outermost layer of titanium X and then when the beam was removed, the rapid cooling produced a glassy metal coating. But even after this treatment the film wasn't hard enough and couldn't stand up to the corrosive microworld of fusion. That's when I thought of ion implantation."

"Oh...yes, of course!" Tisha's excitement grew.

"I was able to alter the surface of my metal, disorder its atomic structure, and render it glassier. I bombarded the titanium surface with an ion beam in a vacuum chamber, which then drove thousands of atoms into its surface layers. It took me awhile to convert all the variables into a successful formula, but I think I've got it now."

"Oh, Audra! Audra, I'm so happy I hardly know what to say!"

There was silence on the other end, then Audra's voice returned a little less euphoric and a little more nervous. "Don't get too excited. I've had some success, but more testing is needed.

Maybe in three months... ."

"We don't have three months," Tisha interrupted.

"Well...maybe I could cut some time off, I don't know. I'm working sixteen hours a day as it is... ."

"Forget all that. We're going to test it on the reactor itself."

"Test it on the reactor? How?"

"By making a titanium X casing. We're fighting time and we're going to have to take some short cuts."

"Tisha, this is so...irregular."

"I know. It defies all normal procedures."

"Putting it mildly, but...okay. You're the boss."

"I'm sending Nolan tomorrow. Let him go over what you've got. He'll help you from here on in."

"That makes me feel a little better."

"And Audra."

"Yes?"

"You did a spectacular job."

When Tisha told Mike about Audra's news, his first words were, "Tonight we celebrate." And despite all her cautious, almost nervous reminders that Audra's achievement, while a major break-through, was still not a "sure thing," he whistled and hummed through the rest of the day. And that evening, after he sent Tisha to the hotel, he disappeared on a mysterious errand, and returned forty-five minutes later carrying a large, brown paper bag. He knocked briskly on door number twelve and before Tisha could answer, he let himself in.

She had washed and changed immediately after work, and looked like someone who was beginning rather than ending the day. He marveled at how beautiful she looked. "Shouldn't keep your door unlocked," he said. "Never know who's liable to barge in."

"So I see." Her eyes followed him as he placed a package on the coffee table.

"Dinner's on me tonight," Mike said, beaming.

Tisha sat in the small, stuffed armchair watching Mike open the mysterious package, then place little, white paper containers on the round table before her.

"For the lovely miss, there is Wonton delicacies, shrimp toast, and Szechuan scallops. For the handsome gentleman: egg drop soup, spare ribs and Lobster Cantonese."

In spite of herself, he always managed to thrill and surprise her. Unconsciously, Tisha clapped her hands together like a delighted child. "Chinese food! Where in heaven's name did you ever find Chinese food?" Her usual fair was a sandwich or hamburger brought in by the local luncheonette. And sometimes, on rare occasions, she would go to the only decent, nearby restaurant, a steak and seafood place.

"I can not divulge my sources, Madame. But allow me to present my next surprise."

"Yes?" she said with interest.

"Dessert!"

"Dessert too?" She was smiling now.

"Even better than dinner; an old Laurel and Hardy movie on channel three."

He watched the smile fade. "I've invited Buck. He'll be along soon. Hope you don't mind," he added casually.

Tisha's smile returned, warm and grateful. Mike had never been in her room before. Having Buck here would lend propriety and put her at ease, or at least as much ease as was possible for her when she was around him. She blessed him silently for that, and settled comfortably in her chair. She was learning there was more to him than she ever thought possible.

"You want everything yesterday. Look how much we've done already." Tisha waved her hand like a wand over what greatly resembled a giant whale's skeleton whose two rows of bleached ribs curled toward each other.

Mike stood beside the huge rib-like section, the jig, over

which would be assembled the fuselage panels, but he did not look at it. Instead, he looked at the large, overhead crane with special halter used in moving the nose section into position for mating with the mid fuselage. "We should be using that by now," he said dryly.

But Tisha just pointed to another section of the hangar where a group of men was joining the upper and lower assembly of the flight station, and to the left, three more men were completing the radome. "The forward fuselage will be completed by the end of the week. Things aren't all that bad."

"Oh yes they are!" returned a foreboding, masculine voice. The pair turned and saw Buck's strong, pleasant face twisted by some unknown trouble. "Let's go over here," he said quietly, leading the couple to a small, partitioned space somewhat removed from the bustle of the main hangar section. It was the coffee area.

"What is it, Buck?" Mike asked.

The leathery face cracked into a frown. "It's Nolan," he said, not hesitating to talk in front of Tisha. He knew Mike confided heavily in her. "He crashed about twenty miles from here. No identification was found on the body. His papers and wallet were burned. But the police could still make out the company name on the helicopter so they called PA in Everman, and our contact there give our number here. The crash was bad. They said the helicopter is twisted like a broken toy. Nolan's...dead. They're taking him to the morgue and want someone to make a positive ID."

Mike had agreed with Tisha's decision and sent Nolan in the helicopter to PA. But before going ahead and building the titanium casing, he had wanted the physicist's reaction. Nolan was to return this evening with his report. They had all been working late, awaiting his arrival.

"Do you want me to go?" Buck asked.

"No, I want you at the crash site. Check it out. Do you know where it is?"

Buck shook his head. "Not exactly, but I can find out."

"Well, get there as quickly as possible. You probably can't do much in the dark, but stay the night. I don't want it moved or

119

touched until you've had a chance to go over everything, piece by piece."

"What are you thinking? More than an accident?"

Mike's face darkened. "We can't afford to overlook any possibility."

Buck nodded. He understood Mike's caution. The recent autoclave explosion had proven to be deliberate. As a result, security was tightened even more. New computerized ID badges were issued to all employees. The latest sophisticated burglar alarms replaced the old ones. Iron grille-work covered all first floor windows. PA was beginning to look like an armed fortress.

"I know one thing though," continued Mike. "This accident shouldn't have happened either. My helicopter is serviced regularly and Nolan was a good pilot."

Tisha remained quiet in her chair. From where she sat she could see a portion of Nolan's area. He had worked there every day for the past several months. She looked at his equipment; a large, silver pump that forced sea water into a round, metal drum and then from there through small, rubber tubing from which tiny quantities of water were released at regular intervals then subjected to an infrared laser which dissociated the deuterium molecules and deposited them into six-inch long glass vials. The vials were positioned on racks like rows of fine wine. Nolan had used this equipment in a procedure he himself had modified, but had initially borrowed from Sidney Benson's carbon dioxide infrared laser, which irradiated dichlorethane where about one in two thousand molecules of the substance contained an atom of deuterium. Nolan's procedure was faster and cheaper, and solidly demonstrated the ease at which deuterium, as a virtually inexhaustible source of energy, could be obtained. The great pump was silent now. The lab equipment was positioned neatly, the way Nolan had left it, in readiness for his return. His clip board hung on a bent nail.

In the months ahead, Tisha would often look at Nolan's section and feel as she did now, confused, angry, sad.

She instinctively reached out for Buck's hand. Their

friendship had deepened over the past months. With the other staff, Tisha found herself in the roll of either boss or exhorter. With Michael Patterson, she was tense and on guard. But with Buck, she felt comfortable. She could be herself. Consequently, she spent most of her free time with him. They took long walks together, sometimes silently, sometimes full of shop-talk and other chatter. Now he took her outstretched hand and squeezed it gently.

"How frail and vulnerable we are," she said. There were tears in her eyes.

"I've never seen you cry before," he returned awkwardly. He brushed her cheek lightly with his fingers, all the while feeling foolish and inadequate.

Mike looked over at the pair, his face an agony. "What does a person say at a time like this?"

"Nothing," Tisha answered. "There is nothing to say except perhaps, why?"

While Buck went to the crash site and Mike went to ID Nolan's body, Tisha remained in her hotel room. She paced the floor, then tried to sleep but could not and only thrashed around restlessly. Finally, she dressed and left the room. She walked the mile to the hanger, then walked the length of the old cracked runway. Leaning over the edge, she stared down at the rocks and waves. It was already dark, but the full moon made the water glisten as it pounded the shore. She watched the violent action of the sea and thought of the violence that twisted a helicopter and tore a life from its body. Wave after wave rolled over the sand and rocks, first like sprays of madness, hissing and tearing, then calming to resemble the foam of soda in a glass.

She didn't linger, but walked the long strip back to where the hangar was huddled safely and serenely against the mountain. She picked a spot of grass where it was flat enough to be comfortable, and sat down. She didn't know how long she sat, minutes, hours, it all blended together. She watched the stars, she ran her hands through the grass, she felt the smooth bolder against her back. There was no point in returning to her room. She wasn't sleepy. She decided she would stay and watch the sunrise. There was tranquillity here. Finally, the tranquillity began seeping into her shattered emotions. Being so close to nature made Tisha feel close to God. He was so big, so encompassing. Perhaps she would never know why Nolan died, why some evil hand had reached out and robbed him of his life. But she did know that no matter what evil existed in the world, God was still in charge.

The news of Nolan's death traveled through PA like a summer brush fire. And when Peter Meyers and his boys again showed up, the plant virtually sizzled with speculation. Was this just a tragic accident or another terrorist attack? Ever since Meyers confirmed that the autoclave was sabotaged a heightened uneasiness hovered over the plant. And in spite of all the additional security efforts, it would not go away.

Audra, like other PA employees, had trouble coping with this new tension and developed her own cure: two glasses of wine at bedtime. It was the only way she could get to sleep. Even when she spent the night at PA, she needed her wine. She plunged herself into her work. The complexity of her research, the intense interest it held for her, enabled her to escape from her fears for a time, but always they returned. It was worse when she had to leave the company and go to an empty apartment. There, the echoes of her fears would bounce from wall to wall in cruel mockery. Then thoughts of what could happen...all those real or imagined dangers that lurked behind every minute...would parade themselves before her.

Audra took three large gulps of her Dewers as she pressed against the bar. Tonight was not a "two-glasses-of-wine" night. Nor was it a night she could stay alone. She, like others from PA, had left work taking the news of Nolan's death with her. On the way home, her purse had been clutched most tightly under her arm. When she had arrived at her apartment, her arm had ached from so much squeezing, but just as she was about to relax, she had noticed someone had been in her apartment. The intruder's marks were not obvious. He left only subtle clues. The drawers of the dining room hutch were open, a living room chair was slightly shifted as though someone in a hurry had passed and knocked into it. But other than this there was no mess, no furniture overturned, no personal articles strewn about the floor.

Then a fearful thought had hit Audra. Suppose the intruder was still in the apartment. Slowly, with jerky, fear-filled motions, Audra had pulled the gun from her purse. The bedroom was the most logical hiding place. Stiff legged, she had proceeded in that direction, and when she had gotten to the door, her finger had been firmly on the trigger. It was possible that she would have to kill or be killed. Holding her breath, she had flicked on the light with her free hand. There was no one in sight. Carefully, she had searched the room, inch by inch, under every nook and cranny, until she had been satisfied that she was very much alone. It was then that she had noticed it. The bottom drawer of her desk was pulled wide open, the lock obviously forced and broken, the drawer itself completely empty. "Oh no!" she had cried. All of her duplicate research notes were missing.

She had sat for a long time on the edge of the bed, shaking. And that queasiness she had experienced over the autoclave incident returned with such vigor she had begun having dry heaves. Someone had violated her apartment. Someone had robbed her. The more she thought about it, the more in focus that someone became. "Bubba Hanagan!" Audra had said, spitting the name from her mouth.

The apartment had not been broken into. A key must have been used. Bubba could easily have made a duplicate. Nothing else had been disturbed in the bedroom. It was as if someone had come for a specific thing and had known exactly where to find it. But why the hutch drawers? She did keep some expensive silver pieces in it; heirlooms from her grandmother, two candle holders, part of a silver service, a candy dish. They could probably fetch a good penny from a pawn broker. Quickly, Audra had run into the dining room. The drawers were empty. Bubba had stolen her silver. The pig! So...he ripped off her silver, okay. But why the research data? What would a muscle-bound ignoramus want with such highly technical material?

Audra had clutched her stomach and retched. She would have her lock changed tomorrow, but tonight, she could not stay alone. Without even bothering to change her clothes, she had placed her pistol back into her purse and left.

Now, with a shaky hand she swallowed another mouthful of Dewers.

"Whoa cutie!" chuckled Ace Corbet as he began fixing her another drink. "Too much too soon ain't good. It's like other things, if you know what I mean." He winked at Audra from across the bar and for a moment she felt sick again. "Now let Ace here take care of you. I'll set your pace. That way, you'll be able to get up for work tomorrow." He made a pathetic twitching motion with one eye as he winked again and leaned his elbow on the bar.

Audra shuffled nervously. It was Tuesday night. Only a few silhouettes moved in the semidarkness as the twang of a Western song echoed in the near empty tavern. With such meager pickings Ace would be especially attentive. Ever since the time Bubba Hanagan walked in on them, Audra's repulsion for Ace had grown. It was only an acute case of loneliness that had enabled him to entice her the first time. She had vowed there wouldn't be a second. She was about to tell him to twitch his eye somewhere else, but the thought of those empty hutch drawers stopped her. Quickly, she took another large gulp of scotch, then smiled at the bartender.

"That's very generous of you. I think I'll just put myself in your hands," she purred. "And if there's the teeniest possibility of my not getting up tomorrow, why, you could be there and just see to it that I do."

"Sabotage!" Mike boomed. "Are you sure?"

"Yes," Buck answered, as he paced back and forth in

Tisha's room. The three had met there at Buck's request. He had wanted to share this information in private. "Someone tampered with the helicopter."

"What about autorotation?" Autorotation insured that if the power failed and the rotor was disengaged from the engine, it would still continue to turn freely.

"Useless if a jamming device is used."

"Do you have proof?"

"Yes." There was a clinking sound as Buck handed Mike a few pieces of twisted metal.

Mike studied them in silence. It was like a jigsaw puzzle where nothing seemed to fit. Who? How? Why? He jiggled the metal together in his hand. Even so, a clear picture failed to emerge. He squeezed them tightly in anger until finally his large knuckles grew white. Then Mike tossed the pieces onto the coffee table. "Who would have had time or opportunity to do this?" he asked, his voice jagged and sharp as the metal.

"It wouldn't take long for someone who really knew choppers. A few of these wedged in the right places would take only a couple of minutes. I also found traces of acid on the engine wires. By the time the engine failed, the rotor was jammed. Pretty clever. From what I can see, it's a miracle Nolan was able to get as far as he did." Buck watched as Mike's face clouded. "The helicopter was exposed at PA's landing field for almost twelve hours. Even with the increased security it would have been possible for someone with phony ID in a mechanic's uniform to get to it without being stopped."

"That means a professional job," Mike returned.

"There's no doubt of that."

"Then we have to assume it's the Jihad."

"That'd be my first guess. But if that's so, we may have an even more dangerous situation on our hands."

"Meaning?"

Buck frowned. "I think we'd have to consider that it was you they were after."

Tisha listened quietly in a nearby chair. She had had a similar fear. "He may be right, Mike," she finally said. "After all, it was your private helicopter." She was sitting on the edge of her chair now. "Let's just suppose a saboteur had posted a stakeout, knowing that every few days you flew to PA. He could have spotted your helicopter at the Patterson airstrip and not known it was Nolan who flew in, then sabotaged it, expecting you to fly it back here."

Buck nodded his agreement. "It's possible, Mike. We'd be foolish not to consider it."

"Okay," returned the handsome executive without a trace of emotion. "I'll grant that it's possible. But why? Why would any-one want to kill me?"

"Well for starters, a dozen or more overworked employees might be able to answer that," returned Tisha, trying to sound brave, but feeling very frightened. She still hadn't gotten over No-lan's death. She didn't know how she could stand it if something happened to Michael Patterson. "Seriously," she continued, with added tension in her voice, "you yourself said terrorists don't need a reason. Maybe there is no logic here."

Mike Patterson nodded as he studied the concerned look on Tisha's face. "Don't worry, I'm not easy to get rid of. You of all people should know that by now," he said tenderly, his eyes melting into hers in an effort to both comfort and consume her, and know-ing for the first time how utterly she consumed him.

Tisha leaned back into her chair. She had spent many nights on her knees praying, asking God to dig Michael Patterson out of her heart. She had no right to care for him this way, to love him, but she did, and she knew she would spend even more hours asking God to protect him.

Eight

The sun streamed, hot and bright, through the closed window. It was the beginning of summer and though winter never really came to Everman, summers were a fine thing to see. Outside, everything looked golden as though capped by a giant halo. But even though the sun had forced its way through the picture window, it couldn't penetrate the cloud of gloom that hovered over the office. Three men, hunched around a large maple desk, worked to the drone of an air conditioner.

Several manila folders covered the desk top. They were the personnel files of employees hired by PA within the past four months. Meyers hoped the person responsible for both the autoclave explosion and the helicopter crash would be among them. It was possible the terrorists had planted an inside man.

Tall, blond Peter Meyers looked silently at the other two men. Boyishly handsome, but somewhat out of character in his dark gray suit, Meyers resembled someone found in Malibu or Aspen; better suited to bathing trunks or skiing parkas. Although he had that youthful, all-American look, closer observation revealed him as a man in his early or mid forties.

Over the past two years, Meyers had come periodically to

scrutinize the progress of the P2 on behalf of the ISS. What happened at Patterson Aviation could have far reaching effects in defense, and the ISS was especially protective of the company. And the recent death of Nolan Ramsdale caused them great concern.

As a precautionary measure, the Department had ordered the immediate deployment of armed guards around the company grounds. These guards were not the ordinary security type. They were employees of the ISS; well dressed in three-piece suits, polite, clean shaven and cropped, sharpshooters, and proficient in various techniques of self-defense. They were able and willing to execute their one overriding order: to deter if possible, and to kill if necessary, any unauthorized intruder. Yet, in spite of all this, it was ISS policy to interfere as little as possible with the actual running and management of PA.

Peter Meyers absently twisted a paper clip back and forth, bending and unbending it. "My people will start with these right away. I wanted to know from you first if there was anything you could tell me about them."

Michael Patterson pushed away the pile of folders. "You know that we've rarely been here, Pete. Most of the time we're at Gibs Town. I can't even match a face with these names."

"I thought as much," Meyers returned.

"There is one in that pile I've noticed," Buck said. "Nothing concrete, just a gut feeling, and it's nothing that he's done. It's just that he seems out of place here, having a steady job, I mean. I've seen a lot of 'down and outers' in my time, and he, well, he fits the mold."

"Who?" asked both Meyers and Patterson at the same time.

"Ivan Skinner."

Meyers shrugged. "Nothing unusual in his file. But like I said, my boys will check everyone out."

Michael Patterson had more faith in his friend's intuition than Meyers did. "You have a lot here." His hand rested momentarily on the pile of folders. "Mind if Buck does a little snooping?"

The tall blond laughed. "Not at all. I'd welcome the help.

We're in a war here." Then leaning across the desk and looking squarely into the face of the handsome executive, he added, "But don't get your hopes up, Mike. Terrorism is not a pleasant business. They don't play fair and they make up their own rules. Most terrorists are well trained, dedicated, fanatical. They either hit, run and disappear, or they sacrifice themselves, kamikaze style. They rarely plant an inside man. If that's what happened here, we'll have a shot at him. If it's not an inside job, we may never find out who did it." The blond smiled, appearing more boyish than ever, and picked up the files. "At any rate, we'll do our best."

"Check Skinner out," Mike said to Buck after Meyers left.

"Okay. Anything else?"

"Watch out for Tisha. She's...well, just watch out for her."

Buck's leathery face folded in sympathy like a soft kid glove. And his blue eyes burned with a secret understanding. In all the years of knowing Buck, it never once occurred to Mike that his friend had ever been in love. He had always thought of Buck as a prototype of Big Foot...singular, alone, belonging to no one. It was even hard to imagine that somewhere Buck had a mother and father, although he never talked about them. Now Buck's blazing eyes said there had been someone once, someone who had been very special.

Buck thought of her now, that woman in his past, that woman he let slip away because he hadn't finished "sowing his wild oats." Tisha was a lot like her. That's why he felt so strongly for her. It went beyond friendship, more akin to family, like the daughter he never had but wished he did, a daughter so like the woman he had once loved. He didn't blame Mike for loving Tisha, he only felt sorry for him, and he felt sorry for Tisha. The two people he cared for most were in love with each other and Buck couldn't see any hope of happiness for them. "Don't worry, Mike, I'll look after both of you."

At that moment Tisha would have welcomed a guardian angel, in any form. Nolan's death had left the P2 project in jeopardy. She had relied heavily on his judgment and knowledge. Now, it would all be on her shoulders. She couldn't hand Mike another disaster, another disappointment, she thought as she finished reading Audra's notes. She rubbed her neck, already tightened by the new strain. What would Nolan have advised? All his papers concerning his meeting with Audra had been burned in the crash. Tisha looked at the notes before her. Audra's latest experiments were promising. But Audra had been right, they weren't conclusive enough to commit it to use in the reactor casing. Tisha pushed the papers away. There was little else she could do but stick to her original decision: complete testing of titanium X as the reactor casing itself in actual simulated flights. It was a short cut, a gamble, but so was everything related to this project. No, there was no other alternative.

Mike stood in the hall watching Renee as she leaned against the bar. She made a sucking noise while she drained her glass and there was something sloppy about the way she used her elbow to support herself when she shifted her weight. Her movements appeared loose, disjointed, like a slow motion picture. Except for the occasional sound of a glass tapping the bar, the house was quiet. There were no servants around. Perhaps Renee had gone on one of her rampages and fired them all. The front door was unlocked, and he had been standing there for some time. She was unaware of him, and Mike wondered at the ease in which he had entered undetected. What if he was a thief or worse? Renee was growing careless. He looked at the beige jersey dress that clung to the superb body, at the hair smartly swept to one side, and the diamond earrings glittering like miniature stars on her lobs. She had been dressed and waiting for hours, and it was obvious she was annoyed.

Mike frowned. Without a doubt, he was the cause of her agitation. After Buck left, Mike spent several hours with Tisha and Audra Shields reviewing the reports on titanium X. The three went over every possibility, over every available avenue, and finally Mike agreed with Tisha's decision. Audra was to begin immediate construction and subsequent testing of a titanium X casing on the reactor itself. Then he saw Tisha safely to his helicopter, along with a trusted pilot who would take her to Gibs Town. Mike himself would return tomorrow. He planned to work at the plant most of the night. He had come home only to pick up a few things. Even now, Buck waited outside in the company car. Since Nolan's death, Peter Meyers had insisted Mike ride only in rigorously inspected vehicles. The car was kept under twenty-four hour guard. Cars, Meyers insisted, were favorite terrorist targets.

But Mike had, at this moment, a more present problem. Irate wives could also be dangerous. Two weeks ago, when he was home last, Renee made him promise he would take her to the Everman Ball. The Mayor of Everman, along with every petty bureaucrat within a hundred miles would be there. He had promised because Renee was especially persistent. That was before Nolan's death. Now he was in a crisis situation, and balls and petty bureaucrats seemed very extraneous. He had tried to tell her that on the phone, but she remained persistent. She would wait for him, she asserted. Renee never relinquished ground gracefully. A confrontation was inevitable, Mike thought, as he studied her profile. She seemed different somehow. A gradual hardness had set in, subtle as rising dough, with deep lines of anger around the eyes and mouth. Or had they always been there and he had never seen them, had never taken the time to see them?

"Hello Renee," he said suddenly. "You still here? I thought you'd be at your party by now."

Renee quickly straightened, removed her elbow from the bar, and like a cat ready to spring, watched him come closer. She had not seen him for two weeks. Her eyes widened in concentration until they appeared like shiny patches of tar.

"Where have you been, Michael!" she asked crossly. She had begun using that tone regularly with him since her return from the Garbys. Her failure to induce Mike to go to Washington had produced unveiled disapproval in both Garby and Alexander Harner. They had treated her coolly throughout her week-long stay, as though they were punishing a naughty child. There had been no talk of a return visit. No invitations were issued. She had left in disgrace without really understanding why. The first time she saw Mike after her return she had assaulted him with her tongue, screaming that he had ruined her, and she would never forgive him. When she found out that both Senator Garby and Alex Harner would be at the Everman Ball, Renee saw a way to redeem herself. She might still be able to ingratiate herself by bringing her husband. Perhaps all was not lost. Perhaps Mecca was still within her grasp.

"Look at the time!" she screamed. She was determined to have her way with Michael this time. "You still have to shower and dress...oh, we're going to be so late. How could you do this to me! You *promised!*"

"Weren't you listening on the phone? Didn't you hear what I said about Nolan?"

"Yes...it's really a shame but... ."

"But what?"

"But life goes on. I'm sorry about poor Nolan, really I am. And I don't want to seem callous, but will brooding bring him back? Oh, Michael, this is so important to me! Come on now, hurry and get ready. If we leave soon, we shouldn't miss too... ."

"Renee!" Mike's voice was like a cracking whip that snapped his wife into silence. "I'm not going tonight. My God...a man has died! My company is in turmoil. There are armed guards crawling all over the plant. I have a schedule to meet, and if things don't go just right, I could lose everything. You know it would be nice if once, just once, you'd ask me how things were. If once, just once, you'd take as much interest in my company, in my new airplane, as you do in...in the Garbys."

"Michael, stop being so childish. The way you talk you'd think the sun rose and set over Patterson Aviation. Now be a good boy and get dressed."

"You haven't been listening. You haven't heard a word I said. I'm not going, Renee."

The cat eyes studied the grim man at the bar. "Yes, I can

see you're not. Well then, I will say, 'good-night,' Michael. I suppose I won't be seeing you for another week or two?"

"I suppose not."

"Well then...a girl will have to find comfort where she can. Won't she?"

"Don't boast, Renee."

"I'm not boasting, darling. You know I don't need to. I suppose you have taken your comfort wherever."

"You'd be surprised at what little solace I have had, in the way you mean, anyway."

"Poor dear...she must be awfully dull, your research girl. That type usually is. Pious, quaint, old-fashioned, dull."

"What are you talking about?"

"Tisha. It seems that somehow she's converted you. Oh, don't look so surprised, I know something's going on between you two. There's something about the way you say her name, the way you talk about her. So, you see, your secret is out. But I don't mind a bit. Of course I am surprised, you mixing business with pleasure. And of course she's not the least bit your type. Seems to have changed you, though. Not so long ago you wouldn't have looked twice at a woman who wouldn't put out. Well, I always did say variety was the spice of life. I guess that's what you need, a little change. Michael...call me after you've wearied of your new celibate life, after your knees begin to ache from all that praying you must do together. I mean, what else could the two of you do?"

Disgust crept over Mike's face. "You're sick, Renee."

The beautiful redhead picked up her beige clutch-bag from the bar. "I know, dear. We bring out the best in each other."

Her high heels made a dull, hollow noise that echoed through the room as she walked away. It was a strange, lonely sound that seemed to haunt him even after he went upstairs and began rummaging through his drawers. But the next sound he heard ripped through that specter as a loud explosion shook the walls of the house. Instantly, Mike knew what happened.

"Renee...oh God!" he cried, as he ran down the stairs and

toward what used to be the two-car garage, but what was now a mass of caved in sheetrock, jagged pieces of metal, shattered glass, fire, and black, billowing smoke.

Three days later, Michael Patterson knocked lightly on a door marked twelve. When the door opened, a woman in faded blue jeans and sweat shirt stood before him, her thick, black hair tied loosely back. She looked so beautiful that for an instant Mike felt his depression lift, but quickly it returned.

As Tisha stared into the troubled face, she labored to knead her lips into a smile. But the dough was stubborn, and giving it up, she squeezed Mike's hand instead.

"I'm so sorry to hear about Renee," she said softly, her eyes tearing.

The news of Renee's death had reached Gibs Town within hours after it occurred. Buck had called Tisha to let her know. A bomb planted in Renee's car had blown off the side of the house as soon as Renee tried to start the engine. The explosion had been especially fierce because a bomb had also been planted in Michael Patterson's car which was parked next to his wife's, and the explosion in one car set off the other. The force was so great that the windshield of the waiting company car was shattered, and Buck himself needed five stitches in order to close the gash in his forehead. Renee never knew what hit her.

"Would you take a walk with me?" Weariness oozed from Mike's request.

It was beginning to grow dark as they silently walked the beach. Tiny crabs scurried over the shadowed sand. Here and there driftwood and shells pockmarked the shore, and took on strange new shapes in the dusk. Tisha stopped to remove her sneakers. They were close to the water and from time to time a wave would lap their feet like a playful puppy. Mike had not removed his shoes and they began to slosh as he walked. If he minded, he did not say, and actually seemed not to notice it at all.

"My mother died when I was four," he said suddenly, as though he was in the middle of a conversation rather than beginning one. "I hardly remember her. She was beautiful though. I used to look at her picture when I was young and wonder what it would be like to have a mother like all my friends. I couldn't look at it too long, though. Her picture always made me sad and left me with a certain feeling of loneliness." He paused for a second as though he were seeing that picture now.

"I know it left a void in my education. To this day, I only understand women up to a point. I suppose that's why I never really knew what I wanted in a wife...before." Mike turned and gave Tisha a strange look, then continued.

"Once, I heard my aunts talking. They said my father had only married my mother for her money, that their marriage was a business arrangement. I knew my mother had come from a rich family. I was in my teens then and I remember feeling very shocked by it. My father had never remarried, and the way he used to talk about mom, well, I just assumed they had loved each other. Maybe they hadn't, I don't know. I never found out anymore. My aunts wouldn't talk about it when I asked them questions. And my father said, 'of course I loved her,' when I asked him. But you know Tisha, in all these years, I've never forgotten that, and for some reason I never felt quite the same about my father after that."

"Maybe you're more of a romantic than you realize," Tisha said, folding her arms across her chest, her sneakers knotted together and slung over one arm. The ocean breeze had suddenly made her feel cold.

"Maybe. But I was a terrible husband, Tisha. I...I guess I didn't know how to be a better one. Or maybe I just didn't care enough. I wish Renee could have had better. I wish she... ."

"I know," Tisha said softly, unfolding her arms and slipping her hand into his. It was the action of a friend, not a lover. Their fingers entwined like strands of hemp, strengthening, girding.

"I want you to come with me," she said softly.

"Where are we going?"

"To a wonderful little spot. I think you'll like it."

They walked silently, with hands entwined all the way up the path and along the old cracked air strip, then past the gigantic hangar. Finally, Tisha stopped by a flat grassy area at the base of the mountain. "Here it is," she said, dropping to the ground and squirming to get comfortable against the boulder. Mike settled beside her. There was barely enough room for two and they had to sit very close. Tisha reached over and once again took his hand.

"You look tired," she said.

"I'm beyond tired, but I can't sleep."

"Neither can I. So why don't we stay here and watch the sun come up?"

He looked at her sideways, at her profile. She looked so beautiful in the moonlight. "I'd...I'd like that," he said. "I'd like very much to see the sunrise." He blinked back tears of gratitude. He didn't want to be alone. He didn't want to think. He didn't want to remember that horrible sound of metal and wood and sheet-rock all exploding and crashing into a heap.

"When my father died, eight years ago, I was completely shattered," Tisha said slowly, as though experiencing the sorrow afresh. "When you're young, you never think much about death. It's something that concerns tomorrow, never now, never today." She gently stroked his hand as she talked, not even aware she was doing it. "I thought of all the times I should have told my dad I loved him, all the times I should have paid more attention to him, spent time...I thought of all my neglect. I loved him dearly, but you can neglect people, even when you love them. I was so busy, going to school, studying, being with my friends. Always time for everything but him. He loved to play golf and wanted to teach me. I think it was something he really wanted to share with me, and leave with me. But I never did learn. I never had time. I...I cried for months. Even bought a set of golf clubs. Never used them. Didn't know anyone who played. It's amazing what we do sometimes. Finally, I realized that what I was really thinking about was my *guilt*, and not my father at all."

Mike's face contorted in pain. "What did you do about it?"

"I asked God to forgive me for not being the daughter I should have been, that I could have been, that my father deserved, and then I said good-bye to my dad."

"That's fine for you, but I'm not sure I believe in God."

"I know."

"I wish I did, I wish I could believe. It would probably help now, but I don't and it just hurts. It hurts that I was such a, such a louse, and that I can never make it up to Renee."

Tisha picked up Michael's hand and kissed it. "I know, and I'm so sorry, I'm so very sorry."

The grieving executive put his arm around Tisha's shoulder and the two huddled together in the dark, trying to warm each other while they waited for the sun to rise.

Tisha and Mike walked together into the Sea Breeze looking tired and wind swept.

"Thanks for staying up with me. The sunrise was beautiful. I...I really needed a friend." Mike's eyes smiled through heavy lids. Strain and tension and a deep inner sadness marred his face.

"Any time you need to talk, I'm here," she said as they reached room number twelve.

He nodded, the smile had gone out of his eyes. "Thanks for that. Now, get some rest."

"You too," Tisha returned, then pulled his arm as though just thinking of something. "Wait here." She quickly disappeared into her room. In a moment she returned carrying a small, black, pocket Bible which she pressed into his hand. "This will help. You know, Michael, there's a 'friend that sticks closer than a brother,' and I pray you'll find Him." So saying, she gave him a hug and was gone.

It was a perfect summer day; sunny, but not too hot, with a cool, gentle breeze that wafted through the hangar. Exhilaration passed like pollen among the crew, as the laughter of men buzzed back and forth. Since the beginning of the project there had not been such merriment. The cause of it now was a huge, swan-like object in the middle of the hangar. Only moments ago the crew had mated the nose or forward fuselage with the mid fuselage. And nearby were the rising hulks that would become the aft fuselage and aft body.

Like the others, Mike experienced an incredible sense of accomplishment. He was unusually talkative and feeling better than he had felt in over a month, ever since the explosion in his home. Tisha was an attentive audience who laughed at his jokes and grew wide-eyed at his often elaborate tales of youth. Finally, he began talking about his grandfather. Tisha, who had heard Mike speak of him before and knew of Mike's special affection for the man, became interested at once.

"...It took all this time to come up with another plane good enough to be called the Patterson II. That's because the P1 was quite a machine in its time. It cost my grandfather about three thousand dollars in 1913, a large sum actually when you realize that room and board then was about fifty cents a day. And he built it all in a small garage at night and on weekends because he worked odd jobs during the day to pay for food and lodging. The P1 was small by today's standards; with a thirty foot fuselage and total weight of about two thousand two hundred pounds. But it could carry two passengers and a pilot. The most amazing thing about it was its cruising speed of fifty miles per hour and top speed of sixty. In order for you to understand how fast this was at the time, you have to know that there were only two or three designs capable of carrying two passengers, and these could only fly about ten miles per hour." Mike chuckled. "To think my grandfather made aviation history with one tractor propeller and a six cylinder water cooled engine."

"A Kirkham engine," interjected Tisha.

"What?"

"He used a Kirkham engine in the plane, and the cruising speed was fifty-one not fifty miles per hour, and top speed was sixty-three not sixty," Tisha said, smiling sweetly.

Laughter cascaded from Mike's lips like a rippling water-fall. "Who's telling this story, anyway?" His eyes twinkled with approval. He admired her vast knowledge of airplanes, her proficient use of that knowledge. During the past months she had continually amazed him by pulling one fact after another, like so many rabbits, out of her hat.

"It's what you pay me for," she once said after he had complimented her. But it wasn't true. Her knowledge surpassed what any employer could rightfully expect and strayed into the realm of a great love. Tisha loved airplanes, every aspect of them, and it was this that made her absorb these facts like a parched Bedouin. Mike had finally met someone whose ardor matched his own, and he was grateful. The only other person he knew who had had this love was his grandfather, and he had died when Mike was very young.

"Whose story is this?" Mike repeated, laughingly.

"It's yours," Tisha answered, her lips curling into a crescent. "but you don't want to mislead the audience."

Unconsciously, he reached out and touched her cheek and was surprised to see her blush. "How about going out to dinner with me tonight?" he said, not removing his hand.

"All right," she returned, flushing deeper, her skin burning under his touch. But she made no effort to pull away.

"Tell me about your dad," Tisha said, feeling like a schoolgirl on her first date. A broad, handsome man sat across from her, grinning profusely, he also feeling like a schoolboy. On the table between them was the half eaten remains of a chateaubriand.

"Not much to tell," Mike said, studying the beautiful face before him. "He was a busy man, like most fathers."

"What was he like?"

Mike laughed. "I think you've been hanging around with your doctor friend too long. You're starting to wield a scalpel." Mike knew all about Daniel, and his comment was meant to hide the immense pleasure he took in her interest. It only required Tisha's encouraging look to make him continue.

"Actually, he was a weak man. He let everyone manipulate him. Granddad began this company after building the P1 on money he earned by giving passengers a ten minute ride for ten dollars each. When he had enough to build a second plane, a twelve passenger sea plane, he legally formed Patterson Aviation. Then, right before World War I, he got a ninety thousand dollar naval contract to build a few single engine scout sea planes. That's when the company really took off, and Granddad made quite a reputation for himself. He was one of the best in his field. He was so good, in fact, that in 1946, when most airframe manufacturers were closing their doors, Granddad was still in business. He had foreseen that at the end of the war there would be a surplus of cargo and transport aircraft, so he developed the EX1, PA's first executive aircraft."

"You're taking about Grandpa again."

"He was an exceptional man, Tisha. I'm proud of him."

"Not like your father."

"My father ran the company into the ground. His weakness almost bankrupt PA. He consistently surrounded himself with ineptness. Some of his employees took bribes from competitors to spy and slow up production. My father didn't even fight them. You can't fight ineptitude and corruption with weakness! If it weren't for Uncle Jason bailing him out financially, there wouldn't be a PA today. Even with his help, my father was forced to sell about forty percent of the company's stock. I've learned from my father's mistakes, Tisha."

The dark haired engineer nodded thoughtfully. She was beginning to understand this man across from her. He was becoming amazingly transparent. "And Uncle Jason? What was he like?"

Mike's face glowed like a full moon under Tisha's telescopic scrutiny. "Uncle Jason was the funniest man I ever knew," he said, as he casually reached across the table and covered her hand with his. "He was round like a great stuffed sausage and always had a fat cigar clenched between his teeth. But he was a snappy dresser with his three-piece suits and diamond pinkie rings. I didn't know him well. He lived in the East and rarely came West. But he never forgot me at Christmas or on my birthday, and his extravagant gifts would always be accompanied by long, funny letters. I used to sit on my bed and almost cry from laughing. I love humor. My father was so serious, so glum most of the time. He rarely laughed. It was hard to believe they were brothers. They were completely different in every way.

"For my sixteenth birthday, Uncle Jason sent me three Havana cigars, and in his letter said he remembered what it was like to be sixteen. I don't know how Uncle Jason did it, but there, on the side of each cigar, was my name printed in little gold letters. And the band around each one was formed by a crisp, new one hundred dollar bill. He was something! He was a man who knew how to enjoy life. And with all his money, he never tried to make anyone feel small. I told you he was the one who saved the company. According to my father, he never had to ask Uncle Jason. As soon as his brother heard of the trouble, he just flew over and gave my father a check. He was that kind of guy. We have a lot to thank him for too, Tisha, you and I."

"We do?"

"Yes, if he hadn't saved PA, we never would have met."

"No, I suppose not." Tisha smiled as her eyes looked deeply into his. "Thank you, Uncle Jason."

"Yes, thanks uncle," Mike said, squeezing her hand.

Audra sat slumped on the bed holding a quart bottle of Corvo wine in one hand and a glass in the other. She emptied the remaining contents of the bottle, spilling it over the sides of the glass as she poured. She hated the Sea Breeze. She hated her room. She hated Gibs Town. Only her work made her life here bearable. Seeing the nearly completed mock-up of the P2 today had given her joy. The challenge of her work with the NPR910 casing gave her the same type of joy. But it was a joy constantly marred by her growing desperation and fear. Since Renee's death, even the .25 caliber in Audra's purse could not alleviate these fears. Her tension was further increased by the fact that here, there was no Groben's Tavern where a girl could go for a little comfort from time to time. The nights were long and lonely, with only the ever pounding surf as a sure companion.

Audra tossed the empty wine bottle onto the carpeted floor. This was her only consolation now; a quart of dry, red wine each night. But even this toxicant was beginning to lose its charm. It didn't seem to go as far as it used to...to last as long. And she didn't get that same warm, safe feeling she once got. It was all so unfair! Life was unfair. And it was dealing her a rather poor hand. It seemed to hold nothing but work and fear...especially fear. It was this Kamal, he was to blame; he and the fact that she had turned thirty. Oh, who cared anyway! What was there to care about? Her life was as empty as that wine bottle, spilled out upon a world that was mad. What was left for her? Was there anything that mattered...*really* mattered? Sure, if she perfected the titanium X casing she would probably be famous, that is, if she lived long enough. Life was as tenuous as the next bomb or hair trigger rifle. Well, if she lived long enough, she might get written up in the paper, even be put in the *Encyclopedia Britannica Year Book*. So what? It would just make her a more desirable target for more bombs, more hair triggers.

She thought of Bubba Hanagan and shuddered. She had never changed her lock. The day after the robbery she had been ordered to Gibs Town and there hadn't been time. She wondered if she would ever feel safe in her apartment or any place, for that matter, again. She had never reported the robbery to the police or even told Mike Patterson that valuable research notes had been stolen. Well, why should she, she reasoned? By the looks of things the P2 would never see the light of day. In fact, the entire PA complex would probably be blown to smithereens any time now. It seemed inevitable. PA was jinxed. Everyone said so. Maybe she should quit her job. Some people were doing it. But many more were staying. Yet even as these thoughts flooded her mind, Audra knew she too would stay. She was committed to her work. She would play the hand she was dealt. But she didn't have to like it. Angrily, she kicked the empty wine bottle and cursed. Maybe if she opened the other bottle of Corvo, the one she had for tomorrow, maybe then... .

Empty coffee cups and a crumpled paper bag that had held a few sandwiches from the snack bar were grim reminders that another dinner had come and gone with Tisha, Mike, and Buck consuming nothing more interesting than their daily fare of bread and cold cuts. Now all that remained were a few crumbs scattered across the table top and a brown ring of coffee, formed when it had spilled down the side of a cup. It had become a ritual, the three of them eating together, sometimes in Tisha's room, sometimes in Mike's, sometimes in Buck's. Mike and Tisha had not eaten alone together since the night they held hands over a half eaten chateaubriand. Hours whirled into days and days into weeks. Everyone at Gibs Town was keeping a grueling pace. Now Tisha and Mike sat, exhausted, listening intently to Buck.

"This Ivan Skinner's a real character. We may have stumbled onto something. All his papers are forged: driver's license, social security number, the works. And they're good forgeries too; good enough to pass his background check. But Ivan Skinner doesn't really exist. Even his home address is an empty lot. So I lifted some prints off his tools and gave them to a friend in EPD. He showed me a rap sheet that looked like a starving man's grocery list. His real name is Ivan Zorkonovich or Ivan Zor as he's usually called. Did five years in the State Pen for burglary. Safe cracking is his specialty. The thing that puzzles me is that he has no history of violence. He's not the sort of guy who would sabotage a helicopter, or blow up an autoclave, or a...car. I don't think Ivan is the type who would get involved with murder." There was no doubt anymore that they were dealing with premeditated murder.

"You told Meyers this?" Mike asked.

Buck nodded. "Seems Zor is the only one so far who doesn't check out. Meyers also agrees that Ivan is not a likely saboteur. Still, we have to follow this up." Buck winked at Tisha who sat looking at him in amazement. "I'm going to have a personal interview with our Mr. Zor and establish for myself just what part, if any, he has played in all this. I have been known to be quite persuasive in my day." The last statement was added for the sake of levity rather than anything else. It did seem to have some effect, for although Tisha did not laugh, she seemed to settle more comfortably in her chair.

"Buck, you're getting too old to play Sam Spade. Why don't you let Meyers handle it from here?" said Mike.

"You know how I feel. If you want the job done right, it's best to do it yourself. Besides, I'm not that old, yet."

"Okay," Mike returned, laughing. "Be only as persuasive as you have to. And for God's sake, Buck, be careful!"

After Buck left, Mike lingered in his chair, quietly drilling his fingers into the arm. It was unusual because he and Buck always left together.

"All this makes me nervous. I worry about you. I want you to be careful," he said suddenly, breaking the silence. "Until we get this thing figured out and under wraps, I want you to employ the buddy system. Don't go wandering around anywhere by yourself. And another thing, I don't want you driving your car until Buck has checked it out, and I mean each and every day!"

Tisha nodded. She knew there was real danger surrounding Patterson Aviation and she needed to exercise wisdom.

The handsome executive rose from his chair and walked to the door that divided their rooms. "You've become very dear to me, Tisha. Nothing must happen to you."

Tisha followed him to the door and smiled as he opened it. "I intend to be around for a long time."

He reached over and pulled her close to him, then covered her mouth with his. She responded by putting her arms around him and kissing him in return. It was brief, but Tisha had tasted his passion and her own.

"Why don't I stay the night? We could make mad passionate love," he said with a smile. Tisha looked at his lips, only inches from hers, as he spoke. She longed to taste them again, instead she pulled herself free.

"I'm desperately in love with you, Tisha. You know that."

The beautiful engineer opened the door between their rooms wider and just stood by it.

"Do you care for me? Do I mean anything to you?"

"I...I...yes."

"Then be with me, as a woman should be with a man. I've never loved anyone like I love you. I've never wanted any woman like I want you. And you want me too, or you wouldn't have kissed me that way. When Renee was alive, I knew you'd never get involved with me, but things are different now."

Tisha looked deep into Michael Patterson's eyes. She saw sincerity in them, she also saw love. What could she say to make him understand? How could she explain to him that what he asked was impossible? How could she explain to him about her wonderful, Holy God, the God of Abraham, Isaac, and Jacob? Or that this precious, wonderful God who created the universe loved her so much that He sent His only Son to pay the price with His blood, so that she and all the earth could be reconciled to Him once more. And how could she explain that to sin, to miss God's mark, His standards, was to sin against this wonderful, Holy God? She was but an earthen vessel...dust. Oh, how many times she had wanted to open that door between their rooms! But she had long ago submitted herself to the Master Potter, and He was striving to make of her a vessel of honor. There were times when Tisha thought the pressure of those molding hands was great enough to crush, to break her, like now. But how could she explain all this to Mike? There was no way she could make him understand. So instead of trying, she just pulled on the door.

"I can't ask you to stay," she said.

Confusion and anger streaked Mike's face. Then his eyes caught sight of the cross hanging from her neck. "What's the matter, Tisha, doesn't your God like sex?"

Tisha accepted his anger and managed a smile. "He's the one who created it."

Mike shook his head, "Then I *don't* understand."

"I know you don't," she said softly, her voice melting in compassion. "It's just that sex is suppose to be exclusive between a man and his wife."

"Is that what you want? Marriage? Are you one of those women who uses the promise of sex to obtain a piece of paper?" Mike regretted his words as soon as he spoke them. "I'm sorry. That was ugly, cruel. I know you believe in what you say. I just don't understand it. I've never been much for religion." His voice was softer, the anger gone.

Tisha slipped her hand into his large, callused palm. "You must have been quite a rogue as a boy."

Mike sighed and leaned against the door jamb. "Yes. And now I'm paying. Tisha, this is really important to you isn't it, this God of yours?"

"Yes."

"Where does that leave us?"

"Us?"

"Our future, do we have one?"

"I don't know. Mike, two people need something more than physical attraction between them or even common interests to make a relationship work. They need a firm foundation."

"A what?"

"'Unless a house be built upon the Rock, it cannot stand.'"

"Huh?"

"Never mind."

"Oh, some Bible talk?"

"Yes, Bible talk."

Suddenly, and almost too roughly, Mike pulled Tisha toward him. "Don't let this God of yours come between us."

The dark eyes melted with compassion. "He's your God too. If you knew how much He loved you, you wouldn't talk that way."

With a more tender movement, he folded his arms around her like a shawl. "I don't know anything about God or His love. I only know how I feel about you."

Tisha sensed the power of his body against hers. It was a power that yearned to protect, to love, to possess. But it was not enough. In the end it was an impotent power, like all of man's power. It was only the breath of the Spirit of God that could raise it from its impotency. And it was only the crucible of the furnace that could forge its strength. "If it's any consolation, I think I love you," she said softly into his hair.

Mike smiled tenderly, almost sadly, as he released her. "It's more consolation than you know." Then with a click, the door closed between them.

Everman City was noted for its civic pride. And even though it was large, and growing larger, and its growth had seen the birth of a slum, for the most part, neighborhoods were well kept. But of all that was Everman, nothing symbolized it more than the city park. It was the essence of community pride and promise. The entrance to the park lay at the northern end of Everman Boulevard, and was lined with short leaf, long leaf, and loblolly pines. Inside the park were other trees; Douglas firs, pinon pine, white pine. And sculptured clusters of yacca, ocotillo, candelilla, guayule, and maguey were positioned between these trees. Along the numerous paths and walkways were flowers, hundreds of them: red, round partridgeberries; delicate, white primroses; fluffy, pink spear thistles; and lovely blue bonnets; a sea of color to enchant the stroller. But the park was also designed for usability, for it had a jogging path, picnic area, playground, as well as scores of benches for those who wished to do nothing but watch everyone else. And to the east of the park was a sizable manmade lake, stocked with a variety of fresh water fish. But other than fisherman used the lake. Young lovers would boat on its smooth waters during a lazy afternoon, and children with their families would swim in the special section that had been roped off for that purpose. For those coming into Everman City Park for the first time, it was as though they had entered the Garden of Eden, and in a sense, to the thousands who used it every year, it was.

Buck passed a row of loblolly pines as he followed a tall, gangling man into the park, and wondered what business Ivan Zor might have here. Buck had been following by car at a safe distance ever since Zor left the plant. Even now, on foot, he held back, staying close to the bushes as he watched Zor seat himself on a vacant bench. He had been tailing Zor for days, and this sudden visit to the park was uncharacteristic of a schedule that rarely deviated from going home, to the plant, and home again.

A group of young girls came jogging up the path, and after seeing Buck crouched along the bushes, began to slow down and eye him suspiciously. Until now, Buck had paid no attention to how he might appear to others. He quickly bent down as though tying his shoe, and with a broad smile on his face, waved to the group. This seemed to relieve their suspicion, and once again the girls resumed jogging. Ivan Zor had taken no notice of this, and was looking in the opposite direction as though he was expecting someone. Buck, nevertheless, decided to take precautions against this happening again, and began working his way through the bushes until he was almost behind the bench and totally obscured from view. He touched his shirt pocket and felt the slight bulge of a camera. The new position would give him greater opportunity to use this and perhaps the miniature tape recorder he also had. He had taken to carrying them around since beginning his surveillance of Zor. Buck would be able to use them sooner than he had expected for just then another man, neatly dressed in an expensive, gray suit, sat down. Buck recognized the thin, pasty face of Robert Gunther.

"This better be good, Zor. Getting me out here... ."

"Well, what did you want me to do, go to your office!"

The pasty face marbleized into hard streaks of anger. Gunther was not a man to be trifled with. "Did you get it?"

Zor seemed to know that and instinctively changed his tone. "No, that's why I wanted to talk to you. I don't think I can do it. The place is really under tight wraps. I doubt if a cockroach could squeeze through! Ever since that guy got killed in the helicopter and the owner's wife got blown up, it's been like Fort Knox. I think something's up because... ."

"I don't pay you to think," Gunther snapped.

"I'm just trying to explain why I don't have it, that's all," Ivan reasoned sullenly.

"I don't want explanations, just results. How many times are you going to foul up? If you'd done this right the first time... ."

"That wasn't my fault! *You* didn't tell me there were so many security guards patrolling the grounds. Look, I'm trying. I even got a job there, didn't I? I'm watching things now, and when I see the right opening, I'm going to take it. It's just going to be harder than... ."

"This is your last chance." Gunther rose from the bench. "Either you deliver or you return the money I advanced you."

"I...I can't. I don't have it. I... ."

"Then you better produce. One week, Zor. That's all you have left. And don't try anything foolish. You know how I deal with double-crossers."

The thin, suited man walked away, followed by a frightened Ivan Zor. Buck could not hear the last of their conversation but waited until Gunther had disappeared before leaving his place in the bushes. His sudden appearance stunned Zor, and as Ivan began to recognize the large, square man before him, and realize that he had been nearby all along, a look of terror chalked his face.

"Hello Zor," Buck said coldly.

"The name's Skinner, Skin-ner."

"That's not what your rap sheet says."

Like a wobbly horse, Ivan hesitated, then bolted. But Buck

was in good physical condition and even though he had fifteen years on Zor, he was able to overtake the mechanic with ease. Ivan made a puny attempt at thwarting the attack but soon Buck had his arms pinned to the ground as though they were nothing more than two little twigs. Grabbing Ivan's shirt front, Buck raised him slightly off the ground. The other hand was clenched into a massive fist and positioned in the air, about two inches away from the mechanic's face.

"You have just one chance to answer my questions," Buck said. His voice was steady, hard, as his calm, blue eyes bore into Ivan's fleeing courage.

Zor nodded in quick, nervous jerks, all the while trying to put more distance between him and the large fist that looked like the end of a club in front of his nose. Even more frightening was the controlled look on Buck's face. He was not functioning on wild emotion but on calm, calculated thought.

Buck tightened his grip on Ivan's shirt. "Why did Gunther hire you?"

The thin redhead showed surprise when Buck mentioned his employer by name. "You know Gunther?"

"I know who he is, and I know you've done time for burglary. Now, what did Gunther hire you to do?"

"He...he just wanted me to keep my eyes open...to spy. Yes, that's it, to spy."

Buck jerked hard on Ivan's shirt, yanking him even further off the ground and closer to that club. "Don't be a fool, Zor, Gunther wouldn't wrinkle that gray suit of his to protect you. Eventually you're going to tell me everything I want to know. Make it easy on yourself."

"He could have me killed!"

"I could save him the trouble," Buck said, drawing back his fist.

"Okay! Okay. He hired me to steal some specs from the research lab's safe."

"And?" demanded Buck.

"And...to relay any information about that secret project," Ivan said, hopeful that the inquisition was now over.

Buck did not release him, but raised him higher off the ground until he was almost in a sitting position. "And!" Buck demanded again.

Ivan became flushed, confused. "And nothing...that's all!"

Buck's face came closer and Ivan could see little flecks like gold chips embedded in the blue iris. Then Buck drew back his fist even further and was about to strike.

"Wait! Please! For God's sake! What do you want? I've told you the truth!"

"What about the autoclave and the helicopter? What about Mrs. Patterson?"

Zor was still confused. "Huh? I don't know. What about them?" Then in sudden understanding he added, "Wait a minute. No...just wait a minute. If you think I was hired to do that, you're crazy! I had nothing to do with it. I swear! You've got to believe me. That's not my bag, man. Well, you know, you must know. I'm strictly small time. You're talking about murder...homicide. I wouldn't touch homicide for any amount of money. That's a whole different game. That's not my style. Look, you can check... ."

Suddenly, Buck released his grip and Ivan fell backward. Then the strong, square man rose to his feet. "Don't ever let me see you around the plant again," he said and walked away leaving Zor sprawled behind him.

Mike idly fingered the roll of film in front of him as he listened to Buck finish retelling the events in the park. "So, Gunther wants our specs. That must mean someone is paying him. Who and why?"

"Maybe an airline that invested in Concord and wants to protect that investment, or another airframe manufacturer checking out the competition. And then there's always the possibility that he's working on behalf of Tafco Oil. After all, nuclear fusion is not exactly in their best interest."

"Yes...maybe."

"Would you like me to ask him?"

The handsome executive chuckled. "No, Buck," he said, slipping the undeveloped role of film into his pocket along with the tape cassette that recorded most of Gunther's and Zor's conversation. "I'll interrogate him myself."

Even from the distance, Mike recognized the small frame of Bob Gunther sitting on the bench. When he called Gunther, he had insisted that they meet in the park. Over the phone, Mike had sensed Bob's reluctance and was glad. He wanted Gunther off balance, like a teetering Humpty-Dumpty about to fall off the wall. With an easy confidence, Mike erased the distance between them until at last he was standing over the pale man.

"Hello Bob," he said cheerfully. The pasty face jerked into a sickly grin as Mike sat down. "Lovely day. Haven't been here in years. I'd forgotten how beautiful it is."

Gunther's weak grin remained frozen, like a lemon wedge, on his face. He was an astute man, astute enough to know when trouble sat beside him.

"Actually, this place holds a lot of fond memories for me. I spent many pleasant hours here as a boy. It was here that I beat Nick...Nick Kelsey...the local bully, in my first fist-fight after he tried to take my baseball cards. And then I collected my first kiss, from Marylou Turner, the prettiest girl in the neighborhood. Quite a day really," Mike said with a grin, all the while watching Gunther out of the corner of his eye.

"I never knew you to go in for nostalgia," returned the thin executive.

"Shows how little we know each other. Doesn't it, Bob?"

"I suppose."

"For instance, I never knew you had such unsavory friends." Mike handed him one of the photos Buck had taken, which clearly showed Gunther talking to Zor. Then drawing a re- corder from his pocket, he added, "But you really can't appreciate the picture without listening to the story that goes with it." There was more edge in Mike's voice now. He flicked on the recorder.

Gunther listened quietly until the tape was over. "What are you going to do?" he asked, his voice surprisingly free of tension.

Mike returned the picture and recorder to his pocket. His movements were slow and deliberate. "What do you think?"

"I'd leave this alone if I were you." His voice still held no hint of concern.

Mike eyed him carefully. "I can't do that."

Gunther shrugged. "Suit yourself. But someone could get hurt if this went any further."

"Is that a threat?"

Gunther's eyes narrowed into steel blue slits as he looked squarely at Michael Patterson. "The people I work for have friends, *powerful* friends in high places."

"I have evidence, remember? And this is still a country where one is tried by his peers. I don't think your friends are pow- erful enough to buy out an entire judicial system. You know, Bob, there's more value in nostalgia than most people realize. It shows us that the past is really not so different from the present."

Raucous laughter, that sounded alien coming from such a frail looking body, and seemed almost dubbed, cascaded from Gunther's pasty lips. It resurrected the specter of Nick Kelsey. His laugh had sounded like that. But that's how it was with bullies. They thought because they were bigger or more powerful, they would get their way. Well, Kelsey had found out differently, and so would Robert Gunther.

The rich, dark paneling, the expensive, oak furniture, the soft, plush carpeting, gave the feeling this was someone's home rather than an office. Abraham Levi seemed to complete this illu- sion as he mixed drinks on a small corner bar. When he finished, he handed them to the two men sitting on his beige, velour settee. The large diamond ring he wore on his right pinkie flashed as his hand moved about. He was a good host and he smiled pleasantly. "The Levi charm," that's what people called it; that intangible quality that made clients not only trust him but like him. Yet it was for these very things that Levi was hated by lesser lawyers, men with half his expertise and energy; a combination that had, in thirty years, earned him this expensive office, a ten carat diamond ring, an overflow of clients, and a reputation that extended coast to coast. Levi never seemed bothered by the vicious attacks he sustained from time to time. He knew that the viciousness, in most cases, sprang from those craving what they lacked the ability or ambition to earn. And over the years, he had actually come to view these attacks as perverted compliments. He walked to his oak desk, over which were spread the photographs and tape of Gunther and Zor.

Meyers moved restlessly in his seat. He had not wanted to come, even though he knew of Levi's reputation. Instead, he had wanted more time to investigate Gunther. But Mike's outrage would not be pacified, so here he was.

"Well," Levi said, in a somber voice, his diamond studded hand slapping his desk top with frustration. "I don't think you have enough here to make a case. But we could try and maybe... ."

"What do you mean?" Mike shot, his impatience oozing from him like perspiration. "The pictures... ."

"The pictures show nothing except that Gunther knows a creep like Zor. So what?"

"The tape... ."

"What does Gunther say, really? He never mentions what Zor was hired to do. A good lawyer could destroy it completely."

"But I heard him say... ."

"He says nothing," Levi returned sympathetically. "Listen to it." With that, Levi turned on the recorder and the three men sat silently as Gunther and Zor's conversation pounded home the reality of Levi's words.

"And what about Zor's confession?" Mike asked, with only

a slight trace of hope left in his voice.

"First of all, Zor confessed to Buck under duress. Secondly, I'd wager this diamond ring," Levi said, waving his hand in the air, "that Zor is long gone. Even if we did go to the police and they were able to find him, you don't seriously think he'd stick to his confession? It would become Buck's word against his. Zor isn't crazy, and he's been around. If Gunther's friends are as powerful as Gunther claims, Zor won't dare cross them. If he did, chances are he would never live long enough for the trial. No, Zor is dug in somewhere like a mole and isn't going to be found easily."

"So what you're saying is that we have to let them get away with it." There was weariness in Mike's voice and a resignation that said he had accepted Levi's statement.

The lawyer's aging, white head bobbed up and down. "In a manner of speaking, yes. But actually, they haven't gotten away with anything. Both of Zor's break-in attempts failed. You've already tightened security. The only thing to do is keep an eye on Gunther."

"I know you're right, Abe, but all the same it doesn't sit well with me."

Levi sighed. "Mike, your company's been bombed, your private helicopter carrying an employee, destroyed. You've lost part of your home, and then of course...Renee. You have enough problems. Concentrate on these. We've been friends for a long time. Your father and I were friends, and I'm telling you as a friend, don't waste yourself on this. Revenge can be expensive. And in the end you could still wind up with nothing."

The executive's handsome face knotted in tight determination. "You don't understand, Abe. I'm not interested in revenge. I'm fighting for my company's life." Then turning to Meyers, he added, "You win, Pete. Tomorrow I'm going to double the shift at Gibs Town. The P2 comes first, and we are going to finish her in record time. Maybe once she's completed this madness will stop."

Nine

The gentle zephyr carried the smell of ocean and sent it swirling around the hangar, like dervish dancers. And at times, when there was a lull in activity, the cry of sea gulls filled the air. Now those calls were drowned out by the squeaky noise of the huge, overhead cranes as they moved the empennage into place, and by shouting men running along the scaffolding. Slowly, the scaffolding and crane slid over the cylindrical body of the P2 like a table over a chair, and a dull thud told the men that both empennage and wings were ready to be secured. Then a symphony of air hammers and drills filled the hanger.

Tisha watched from below as someone shouted, "She's on! She's secure!" And when the cranes and scaffolding were removed, Tisha gasped with pleasure. The empennage, like a shark's fin, rose high over the sleek bullet-like back, while the wings flared out like two great fans against the sides. The P2 was beautiful and sleek like a swan. But there was power in her body; power to endure the supersonic speeds that her reactors would put her through. And Audra would see that those reactors were completed. She was having amazing success so far. Everything was going well.

But there was still much to do before completion of the

mock-up. Even so, they were very close. Those years of dreaming about and planning a fusion reactor, and then a plane that could do it justice, had paid off. The reality now stood before her like a colossus. Tisha felt like Jack after his long, weary climb up the bean stalk, only, her giant made her tremble with joy. "Thank you, Lord," she whispered.

Hours later, when Tisha tapped on Audra's door, the glow of the day's victory was still on her face. "You in, Audra?"

The door opened slowly, almost hesitantly, and a voice sputtered through the crack. "Oh...Tisha...come in."

The crack became wider and revealed a disheveled woman patting down little matted blond clumps of hair that made a patchwork design over her head. She looked like she had just gotten out of bed. "I...wasn't expecting company," she said as she ushered Tisha into the room. The glassy eyes failed to see the look of surprise on her boss' face.

"Excuse the mess," Audra said, picking up an empty wine bottle from the floor. Hurriedly, she tossed it into a small metal garbage pail. Another empty bottle stood on the coffee table. "Sorry I can't offer you anything, but I'm all out." The voice was apologetic, nervous.

Tisha smiled naively. "I guess a lot of people are celebrating tonight. It was wonderful, wasn't it? Seeing the P2 like that with it lines, its beauty. We've come so far. And we're all very proud of you, Audra, and of your achievement."

Rods of distrust stiffened the metallurgist's back, hardening her to any overtures of friendship. "Look, Tisha, please don't be offended, but it's been a long day and I'm tired."

The dark haired engineer nodded. Over and over again, Tisha had tried to disarm Audra's hostility with conversation, suggestions they go to lunch, a friendly attitude, but nothing seemed to work. She had basically given up and accepted the fact that Audra did not want her friendship. "Yes, of course," Tisha said with no rancor in her voice. "I'll keep my visit short. Actually, I'm here at Michael Patterson's request. It was his wish that I speak with you."

Audra's face paled as she eyed the empty bottle on the table. Oh, why hadn't she thrown it away? Had someone seen her leaving the liquor store too frequently, carrying too many wine bottles? Had this someone then reported it to Michael Patterson? Audra's jaw tensed and jutted slightly like a defiant child's. Whose business was it anyway? She did her job. This little diversion, this little tension reliever of hers, did not interfere with her work. She consumed two bottles a day now and had yet to be late a single minute. She was punctual and dedicated. Nobody dare say otherwise! Everyday she poured her very life into the P2, into the reactors. What life she had left at the end of the day was hers, to do with as she pleased. Now this "goodie-two-shoes" better not give her a hard time about... .

"It seems that PA has recently been plagued by an industrial spy." Tisha's voice cut into Audra's rambling thoughts and caused her already pale complexion to ashen even more. Tisha was referring to Ivan Zor. But she neither mentioned his name nor the name of Robert Gunther. "We believe the problem is resolved, but Mike wants you to take special care of your notes. Don't leave them lying around the hangar or here." Tisha's arm encircled the room.

Audra's stomach contracted in spasms as she gave birth to her fears. For a moment she thought she was going to be sick.

"I know," Tisha continued, seeing the look on Audra's face, "that's just how I felt when I first heard. But don't worry. It's all taken care of. I'm telling you this as a precaution."

Audra nodded mutely, unable to speak, trying desperately not to appear too frantic. She had not told anyone about Bubba Hanagan. Industrial spy? So, that was it! Bubba had been paid...paid to woo her, paid to sleep with her, paid to get into her good graces so that somehow he could steal her notes. The notes were incomplete, but they were valuable nevertheless.

Little bubbles of acid rose from Audra's stomach and burned away her fear, her queasiness, until all that remained was a residue of concentrated hatred, the hatred of a lifetime that was now focused on Bubba Hanagan.

"Thank you, Tisha," she said between clenched teeth. "From now on, I'll be careful. I'll be very careful."

Several weeks had passed since Tisha's talk with Audra and it was because of the blond metallurgist that Mike and the head of Patterson Aviation's Research Department sat across from each other in a small, dimly lit Gibs Town restaurant.

"It looks like she did it," said the handsome executive. "One hundred successful simulated flights without a single sign of casing breakdown."

"Yes," Tisha said. "And now you're going to pay."

"Pay?"

"That's right. This is a celebration and I'm ordering a lobster...let's say a three-pounder."

"Do you know how much that's going to cost!" Mike wailed in mock horror.

"I figure I have it coming. With all the overtime I've put in, not to mention the work I've taken back to the room with me nearly every night, I estimate I've been making about eighty-two cents an hour."

Mike laughed at her obvious exaggeration. "What do you want? *Everything*? After all, I did give you the weekend off. And not only that, I've taken you to one of the poshest restaurants in Gibs Town."

"There are no posh restaurants in Gibs Town."

"After which," Mike continued, ignoring Tisha's last remark, "I will fly you to PA so you can avoid Everman's Friday night rush-hour traffic. And you complain!"

"Make that a four-pounder."

"Okay...okay, so I have overworked you a *little*," Mike chuckled as he reached across the table and took her hand. He looked at her tenderly, his feelings scrawled across his face like an ardent Browning poem.

"I have something to ask you," he said, his voice becoming

more serious. "But I don't want you to say a word until I'm finished, okay?" Tisha nodded. "What I want to know is if...if we can build on this Rock of yours, if it's possible, would you marry me? Right now we have to finish the P2, but when it's completed I want to spend time working on us. I love you, Tisha."

The fragrance of Old Spice drifted across the table. It was strange how each person had his own particular odor, like finger prints. She loved his. It was clean and fresh, predictable and constant. Yet if that spoke of his exterior, inside was quite a different matter. It was mysterious, changeful. She lovingly squeezed his hand. How she had longed to hear him say these words! She had dreamed of them having a life together. But not like this. It would never work. Convictions couldn't be tied on like a plastic heart.

"I want to say 'yes.' You can't imagine how much!"

"But?" returned Mike, his smile yielding to the blow of disappointment. He tried to pull his hand from hers, but Tisha wouldn't let him. She held it tightly as she looked into his face.

"You said, 'if we can build on this Rock of yours,' would I marry you?"

"Yeah?"

"Well, that's the problem. Until you can say 'my Rock, my God,' I can't say 'yes.' God isn't a convenience. He won't ever be real to you as long as you're using Him to please me. Your commitment to God can't be because of me, but because God is, and because He is worthy of that commitment. Oh Mike, please, *please* try to understand."

The handsome executive relaxed his hand. But his smile didn't return. "I'm trying, Tisha, believe me, I'm trying."

Audra Shields' hand trembled slightly as she inserted the key and turned the knob. The ever present pocketbook, with the .25 caliber inside, was pressed tightly against her body. Everman's Friday night rush-hour had been especially hectic, and her head throbbed with tension. When the door was open, she stood outside for a moment and shuddered as she thought of Bubba Hanagan. He had taken from her everything he wanted. There was no need for him to come back, the blond metallurgist reasoned as she stepped into her dark apartment. She flicked on the light switch by the door and immediately the living room brightened. Everything was in its proper place, just as she had left it. Nothing had been disturbed. She began turning on lights throughout the apartment. Finally, re-assured that all was well, Audra went to her bedroom and threw her pocketbook on the mattress. Tomorrow she would have the lock changed. This evening she would go to Grobens. There was always Ace Corbet. He would help pass the night. First a quick shower and fresh clothes, she thought as she rummaged through her drawers.

This was the first weekend she had had off in months, and all she could do was wish she was back in the security of her job, even if that meant Gibs Town. But Gibs Town was as deserted as the Hampton Bays in winter. Michael Patterson had given every-one the weekend off. Suddenly, the thought of having to go out again, to drive the streets, to walk down dark pavements beneath the shadow of a thousand dangers, made her feel queasy. Maybe she'd stay home, Audra thought, as she pulled a pair of white lace stockings from her drawer and then replaced them. She failed to see the shadow that stepped from her bathroom. She failed to see the large muscular arm as it moved to encircle her. She only no-ticed a faint sweetish odor and then a cloth was suddenly pressed violently against her face. She felt her legs buckle, felt herself sliding downward, onto the floor, onto a pair of very large, tan work boots, and...darkness.

Tisha puttered about, feather dusting the languid rattan and macramé. She hadn't realized how much she missed her apartment. It was here she relaxed best, amid the tranquillity of muted earth-tones. It was late. She missed the Friday night rush-hour as Mike promised. But they had sat for hours at the restaurant talking. By the time they left, he was smiling again. Her heart warmed as she pictured his face. She had seen such tenderness on it, but also confusion and anger. His was a difficult road ahead, with difficult choices. Years of preconceived axioms would have to yield to God's truth. She would pray diligently for him. She wanted so badly for things to work out. But ultimately, the decision was his. Yet, she couldn't help feeling an inner excitement. The possibility of becoming Mrs. Michael Patterson thrilled her beyond words. She had even practiced saying the name aloud several times. It had a nice sound, like a melodious love song. It was a most wonderful name she thought, as the doorbell rang. It startled her until she remembered Daniel Chapman. She had called him from Gibs Town after Mike had given the entire staff the weekend off. They had written to each other often. Buck flew periodically between Everman and Gibs Town with the mailbag. All mail filtered through PA. It was never sent directly. She had promised to let Daniel know when she had some free time. She was eager to see him and to find out about Joshua. Her knowledge of the younger Chapman's whereabouts was sketchy. She knew that he and his friends had finally linked up with the Zionists. They had undergone rigorous training, especially in desert warfare, and had even seen some action. Yes, she and Daniel had much to talk about, and that included Michael Patterson. She wondered about his reaction, if they would still remain friends. Suddenly, she felt a little nervous about telling him. Perhaps she would wait a while, she thought, as she glanced at the grandfather's clock in the hall. Ten minutes to eleven. Daniel had told her if he finished with his emergency before it got too outrageously late, he would stop by.

"It's not *too* outrageously late," Tisha said, as she opened the door. To her surprise it was not the face of Daniel Chapman that greeted her, but the face of a dark, menacing man. He was holding something in his hand, and before Tisha could react to her brain's message of danger, the man grabbed her roughly. Holding her in a head lock, he pressed a chloroform soaked cloth against her face. A strange, sweetish odor filled Tisha's nostrils. "Oh God!" she gasped. Then everything went black.

***

"Any news?" asked a disheveled Mike Patterson. Strands of hair fell into his eyes as he looked imploringly at the man who had just entered his office.

"No, nothing," Peter Meyers responded.

It was Wednesday morning. Neither Tisha nor Audra had shown up for work Monday. Neither had called in. Neither answered their phones. Neither was at home when someone went to check. Panic swept through Patterson Aviation and Gibs Town. The ISS, along with the Everman Police Department were feverishly searching for them, but so far, nothing. No one had seen or heard anything unusual. Neither apartment had been broken into. There were no signs of struggle, nothing amiss. It was all very strange. But in the end, there was a silent consensus, the Jihad. Who else would abduct two employees from the same company?

Mike looked haggard and worn. He had eaten and slept little since the news. His eyes darted nervously between Meyers and the telephone, as though expecting something from one of them momentarily. When Mike had found out about the missing women he had demanded answers and results. None were forthcoming. As the hours passed he became less demanding, and by Tuesday night, when he and Buck were alone, Mike had broken down and wept.

"My men haven't been able to come up with anything."

Mike slammed his fist hard against the desk top in frustration. "For God's sake, Pete! You're talking about two lives here!"

Meyers bobbed his head soberly. "That's what worries me. It's been too long without a word. I mean, if they were kidnapped for ransom, somebody would have contacted us by now. We may have to face the possibility that they have already been...killed."

A strange look crossed Michael Patterson's face. His skin became ashen, and for a moment the powerful body shuddered with a deep, inner grief. "I...I can't accept that possibility," he said.

Suddenly, one of the ISS agents came running into the room, flushed with excitement. "We just got the call," he said. "It's official. The Jihad claims responsibility for both abductions."

Mike took a deep breath. "Are they still alive?"

The agent nodded and smiled. "Yes! Both women are alive! And we will be contacted regarding terms and negotiations for their release."

"Thank God," Mike sighed, as if saying a prayer.

The handsome, muscular executive leaned backwards in his chair as though backing away from the clutter on his desk. His sleeves were rolled up and the front of his white, rumpled shirt was partially open. Absently, his fingers combed through his hair.

His chiseled face formed a frown as he studied the pile before him. Although he had been sitting here uninterrupted for hours, he had not done any work. His desk top still looked like a white paper mountain. He had hoped to scale it in an effort to keep his thoughts off the kidnapping. But his mind had been uncooperative, and no matter how hard he tried to hurl it to the peak of that white mountain, it would stubbornly slide back to the one thing that had made the past few days the most wretched in his life, Tisha's disappearance. To not know where she was, if she was well, if she was being mistreated; to be totally separated from her was unbearable. He felt like an amputee, part of him was missing.

Slowly, he pulled out a small, pocket Bible from the desk drawer. It was the one Tisha gave him after Renee died. She said it would help. He desperately needed that help now. He opened the book randomly and began reading. "'The Lord is my light and my salvation; whom shall I fear? The Lord is the strength of my... .'"

Tisha sat propped against the cold stone wall of the semi-dark room trying to get her bearings. The past several days had been like the canvas of a bizarre Picasso. The hours overlapped, twisted, ran into blur after blur. A mist-like fog had surrounded her, and was lifting only now. She struggled to concentrate, to re-create her last clear action. Then it came to her: the sinister man at the door, the brief scuffle, the darkness. And since then it was mostly darkness, with a period of dusky gray in between. She was sure she had been drugged. Possibly she had been drugged for days. She had a vague recollection of strange faces, movement, shoving, positioning. She remembered someone feeding her, giving her water. And then there was a dark, locked room and a plane ride, or...was it a hallucination? Part of that dusky gray? There had been a ride in a truck. She was sure of that. It had been hot, very hot...a very hot and bumpy ride.

Tisha's head slumped against her chest like a heavy pouch. She felt weak, strange. Her head ached. She tried to lift her hands to her face but her arms felt laden like sinkers and fell to the floor. As they did, she noticed the slight tenderness in the bend of her arms. When she checked, she saw needle marks, eight in all. Did that mean she had been with that sinister man for eight days? Or had she been given more than one injection each day? Whatever the drug, it was powerful enough to practically obliterate all memory of her captivity thus far.

She noticed she was still in the same clothes she wore that Friday when everything went blank. Oh, where was she! She began shaking her arms and legs, trying to shake the lethargy from them. She breathed deeply, hoping to clear her lungs of the fog, to replace it with healthy, mind-sharpening oxygen. It was beginning to work. She didn't feel so dopey, and was able to focus better. She looked around the room. It seemed strange, almost foreign. The walls were whitewashed mud brick. On the floor were thin rush mats and goatskin rugs. On the opposite side was a closed door. The room was dimly lit. The only source of light came from a very small, glassless window that only a tiny child could squeeze through. It had to be near sunset because even as Tisha watched, the light coming through the window grew dimmer and dimmer. Soon it would be dark. Tisha rubbed her eyes. She would have to get her bearings quickly. She looked around again. Aside from the heap of material in the corner, the room was completely empty. There was no furniture, no wall hangings, no odds or ends.

Still a bit unsteady, Tisha struggled to her feet and wobbled like a newborn doe to the window. She pushed her face through the opening as far as it could go and squinted in the twilight at the barren landscape, at the adobe-like dwellings which formed strange shapes, some rectangular, some square, some rounded like giant over-tuned beehives. Here and there were little walled courtyards attached to the adobe buildings. Some appeared empty, others held small flocks of sheep. She breathed deeply. The air was full of the smell of dung, grain, fodder, all mixed together to make one singular odor that was neither offensive nor pleasing. Tisha could see people too, walking about the dusty streets in long robes and covered heads. It looked like a primitive village straight out of Lawrence of Arabia.

Yet for all its strangeness, it seemed very familiar. It was as though Tisha had felt the heartbeat of this village before. She watched two women shuffle into their homes and thought of the flute playing its lonely melody in the hills of the Cheyenne reservation. Yes, she knew this village. There was suffering here. And there was sadness.

Suddenly, a loud, eerie wail floated over the adobe town as though it came from a high place. It was a sound Tisha would get use to, for she would hear it five times a day when the *muezzin* called the faithful to prayer from the minaret. But now it sounded sad and forlorn. Tisha shuddered and hugged herself. Then all was silent and dark, and Tisha stood frozen by the window. The drug had almost completely worn off, and her mind was sharper now. It was beginning to grasp the gravity of her situation. She knew she was somewhere in the Middle East. What danger awaited behind that closed door, she could only guess. If it came down to it, she was not afraid to die. But the unknown, that was always a bit scary.

"'In thee, O Lord, do I put my trust; let me never be ashamed: deliver me in thy righteousness,'" she prayed through the small window, dulling the blade of fear that had begun cutting through her courage. Gradually, a peace fell upon her, and when Tisha heard a low, muffled sound behind her, she stiffened, not with fear, but for action. She called out, "Who's there," and listened intently in the dark for an answer. The only response was a moan which seemed to come from inside the room. But that was inconceivable since she was quite alone. Or had that door opened and she not heard? The moan grew louder. This time there was no doubt. Someone or something was in the room with her. Tisha faced the direction of the sound, listening, straining hard against the darkness. It was then she remembered the heap of material in the corner. Could there be something under the pile? An animal perhaps? The moaning continued, becoming more pronounced, until finally the noise turned into words.

"Ooh...ooh...where am I...what...what is this...ooh...I'm sick. Please...somebody help...ooh please...somebody."

Positioned on all fours, Tisha began crawling towards the pile. It had taken a while to recognize the voice. Groping and feeling her way in the darkness, she finally reached the corner and gently touched the quivering mound. "Audra! Audra it's me! Tisha!"

The mound began to wail. "Ooh...I'm sick...help." Like Tisha, Audra apparently had been drugged, but Audra had not fully come out of it. In addition, she appeared ill. She was perspiring profusely and her body shook uncontrollably.

Tisha cradled the whimpering mound, and began gently stroking the damp head. "It's okay. You're going to be alright," she said softly, all the while hoping someone back home knew where they were. She suddenly thought of Mike and wondered if she'd ever see him again.

The night seemed like a protracted black mirage, full of shadows that looked alternately friendly and menacing. Throughout it all, Tisha tried to do what she could for Audra; patting her, speaking softly to her, praying for her. But Audra was still heavily drugged, and the nature of her illness remained a mystery. Those times when Audra seemed more comfortable, Tisha dozed restlessly against the hard, cold wall.

In the morning, Audra awoke first. She was surprised to see Tisha's sleeping face above her, and partially raised her head. But feeling ill and weak, she let it drop hard against her boss' lap. That made Tisha jerk upright. She shook off her sleep quickly, remembering their danger, remembering she didn't want to alarm anyone outside that rough, wooden door. Her voice was low, serious.

"Are you alright, Audra? Have you been injured?"

"Ooh," was the reply.

Tisha began rocking the groaning woman like a baby as she scanned for signs of an injury. Perhaps she had been shot or stabbed. There were no blood stains.

"Drink, I need a drink," Audra muttered.

Tisha continued rocking the woman in her arms, not comprehending the problem.

"Please."

"Audra, try to understand. We're prisoners. We've... ."

"A drink. I need a drink!"

"Audra." Tisha shook her companion. "Listen to me... ."

"Please! Help me. *Please* give me a drink."

Finally, Tisha understood. The symptoms were beginning to making sense. At the reservation she had seen them in other alcoholics who staggered, shook and begged for a drink or the money to buy one. Tisha's hand stroked the perspiring head. She knew this was a real crisis. Alcoholism was the one addiction in which withdrawal, without the proper medication, could kill a person.

"Audra I have nothing. We are...we are captives somewhere," she said, scanning the room. Both sun and noise now streamed through the narrow window as the village began to rouse itself. Tisha wanted to go see if she could spot something that would tell her where they were, but she dared not leave Audra.

"Help me," Audra implored through chattering teeth.

"Try to understand. We are... ."

Suddenly, the door flew open, hitting the wall with a loud bang. Two men in khaki uniforms stood like coiled vipers in the entrance. One was very dark, lean, and tall, with black threatening eyes. Two bandoleers of ammunition formed an X over his chest. In his hands he cradled a repeating automatic Russian rifle whose barrel was pointed ominously at Tisha's head. For a moment, she was not sure if he intended using it, but the moment passed, and it remained just resting in his hands like a silent menace. The man next to him was also very dark, but shorter, and somewhat stocky. His eyes too were hard, hate-filled, but he wore neither bandoleers nor carried a rifle. There was no sign of the man who had abducted her. Tisha knew, without being told, she was in the hands of the Jihad.

"Up!" growled the man with the bandoleers, in English. "On your feet!"

Tisha stared numbly into the face of madness and hate.

"Get up, slut!" barked the man with the rifle as he moved towards her.

"My friend is ill," she said, putting up one hand as if blocking his advance. "I don't think she can move."

The gunman, ignoring Tisha's statement, came forward. Standing over Audra's reclining body, he nudged her with the toe of his boot. She moaned. Tisha prayed silently that her companion would not open her eyes. If Audra did, and saw the tall man with his rifle pointing toward her chest, she might panic. Tisha feared that any show of panic could produce a violent reaction in him. Mercifully, the blond metallurgist's eyes remained closed, but she began to whimper. Even an untrained eye could see she was sick.

"Bring the *daya*!" ordered the gunman crossly, seemingly annoyed that the prisoners could not comply with his demand.

Moments later, a woman wearing a black robe-like dress and black shawl over her head, stepped quietly through the door. Her face was unveiled. She looked to be a woman in her fifties. Her large, doe eyes stared shyly at the two strangers. Her eyes mirrored fear and suspicion, but there was a gentleness in them, and compassion. They had seen their share of suffering, and for a brief, fleeting moment, the pupils shone with a secret understanding, as though in some way she identified with the two captives. She was the daya or mid-wife, and aside from delivering babies, often tended to the sick women in the village. Quickly, she examined

Audra. Never once did she look up at Tisha, upon whose lap the patient still rested. When she was finished, she said something in Arabic to the gunman whom she called Mustafa. Her words caused him to expel peals of abrasive laughter. When he tired of the joke, he bellowed out a caustic order which seemed to displease the Arab woman greatly. She made a feeble attempt to argue, but in the end, he won, and she left hurriedly. Then Mustafa focused all his attention on Tisha, completely ignoring the pathetic mound on her lap.

"The daya has seen this sickness before, in the Russian soldiers she once attended," he said, his voice harsh, cold. "It is the curse of the drink. Allah in his wisdom has forbidden Moslems to partake of this poison. Naturally the daya, being a true believer, did not want to defile herself. But I have sent her for some. What is it to us or to Allah if the infidels want to pollute themselves." He gestured with his rifle toward Audra as though he was gesturing toward a rodent.

Tisha said nothing, as her large, dark eyes unflinchingly met Mustafa's fierce gaze. A supernatural peace had settled upon her. It was as though God had woven together those countless insecure threads, forming instead one rod of iron that braced and strengthened her for whatever was to come. She felt no fear at all. It was amazing how fearless one could be once the question of death was settled. She knew her life was not in Mustafa's hands, but in God's.

Her steady gaze seemed to anger Mustafa and he began cursing in Arabic. "Lower your eyes!" he finally screamed in English. Tisha obeyed instantly. She saw no wisdom in needlessly provoking him.

All the while, Nabil stood silently watching everything with sadistic relish. "Infidel pigs!" he said in English, and made a spitting noise with his tongue. After sufficiently purifying his mouth, he again released a string of insults, calling the two women all manner of vile obscenities. As Nabil finished, the daya returned carrying a bottle of Russian vodka. Mustafa took it and barked an order. Immediately the woman disappeared, returning moments later with a small, shallow clay bowl. Mustafa handed his rifle to Nabil, then poured some vodka into the bowl. At this point, Tisha's eyes were again uplifted and she noticed the disgust on the woman's face as the gunman poured. Then Mustafa put the saucer-like bowl on the floor, opposite where Tisha sat.

A vicious smile creased Mustafa's face as he took his rifle from Nabil and walked over to the women. With his gun butt he pushed and prodded Audra until her eyes opened and she partially sat up. She gaped stupidly at the man standing over her. Then terror swept the vapidity from her face, as bits and pieces of the abduction came sliding from the slopes of her memory.

"You want a drink?" Mustafa asked, looking rather like a sadist about to pull the wings off a fly. The metallurgist was too frightened and sick to grasp what he said, even though he spoke in perfect English. Her lack of response angered the gunman and impatiently he held up the vodka bottle. This time Audra understood and nodded. Mustafa then pointed toward the bowl across the room and bellowed, "Then get it!"

Audra wasn't quite sure what she was supposed to do, but she wanted that drink, and obediently tried to rise. Immediately the rifle butt shoved her to the floor.

"No!" Mustafa snapped. "You will not walk. You must crawl like the dog you are."

Audra moaned with pain, and began slowly making her way on all fours, to the saucer of vodka. The room was not more than twelve feet across, yet Audra's progress was agonizingly slow, painful. With each foot of ground covered, a layer of dignity was being stripped away. Finally, after what seemed like hours instead of minutes, she was near enough to reach for the saucer. But as she did, Mustafa's boot pinned her hand against the floor. With his rifle butt, he roughly shoved her onto her side.

"No! You will lap it, infidel!"

Obediently, Audra again positioned herself on all fours, lowered her face into the bowl, and began lapping up the liquid.

Tisha, unable to watch Audra's degradation any longer,

turned her head and began to weep softly. Her tears seemed to please Nabil, for he believed them to be tears of fear.

"It is well that you cry, whore. For Allah has reserved a most fitting fate for all infidels."

Then suddenly the two men and the daya were gone.

It was slightly over twenty-four hours since Peter Meyers' staff had received the call from the Jihad claiming responsibility for the two kidnappings and a quiet panic had gripped the very heart of Patterson Aviation. This last assault on the company brought another rash of bogie-men. Because of this and the series of previous PA catastrophes, more and more employees were beginning to leave. The pile of ghostly bodies was becoming too high. Those that stayed would, two or three dozen times a day, put themselves in the shoes of the women captives. "It could have been me!" was the silent cry. Managers tried hard to keep these cries silent. If these fears were verbalized or dwelled on, mass hysteria could leave the plant unmanageable, perhaps even empty.

In R&D the mood was slightly different. Their co-workers had been abducted. They took that personally. It made them angry. So anger had snuffed out hysteria; anger, then depression, as a sense of almost helplessness and hopelessness smothered them like poisonous fall-out. But nowhere was this fallout heavier than in the executive office.

"It's five days, Pete. Five days since we found out Tisha was abducted," said a rumpled Michael Patterson. He had developed a habit of mentioning only Tisha's name when speaking of the kidnappings, as though she was the only one who was missing. "The waiting, the not knowing anything...it's hard."

Handsome Peter Meyers sat in his three-piece suit and nodded thoughtfully. The waiting was always the hardest part. That's when time seemed like the enemy. And Mike's feelings were typical of other's who had had a friend or loved one abducted by the Jihad. The more time passed, the more fearful they became of never seeing that person again. And in most cases they were right.

"I don't like sitting around doing nothing," Mike said, as he began to pace back and forth behind his desk.

"Believe me, everything is being done."

"I know, Pete, but somehow it doesn't seem enough. I thought the Jihad would have called back by now. What in God's name do they want? You don't think they've...killed her?" There was a gulping noise as Mike finished the sentence.

Meyers pulled a small, silver clipper from his pocket and began manicuring his nails. He used this activity to relieve tension. "No, the women are safe, for now anyway. Had the Jihad wanted them dead, they would have been executed instead of abducted. It would have been easier than going through all this. They'll be safe until the Jihad get what they want. There's a reason they're being held, and in due time, you'll find out what it is. They may wait a little longer though, before telling you. That will make you more frantic, more desperate, more receptive to their demands."

The pacing stopped as Mike looked at Meyers. "You don't pull any punches."

"Would you want me to?"

"No. That's why I trust you. And Pete... ."

"What?"

"You know I don't pull any either."

"What's that supposed to mean?"

"Just this: I want Tisha back, and I'll do whatever it takes."

Hours later, Mike stood ringing the bell of a posh Everman condo. Within seconds, the door opened, revealing a tall, lean man with delicate hands.

"Dr. Daniel Chapman?"

"Yes."

"I'm Michael Patterson from Patterson Aviation. I've come about Tisha O'Brien. I need your help."

Ten

Tisha peered out the small, glassless window and surveyed the strange, dusty village below. Her dwelling was slightly higher than most, being partially built on the side of a mountain, and this afforded her a good view. After seven days of gazing through this opening, she could recall every detail with her eyes closed: the white-washed mud brick houses with their flat roofs, where crops were dried in warm weather and water was collected during the rainy season; the houses huddled together for better defense; the walled-off pens where the sheep and goats were kept at night; the water well; the village square; the large beehive-shaped communal ovens; the small mosque with its minaret from where the muezzin's wail called the faithful to prayer, five times a day.

And from her window she had watched the people move about. Most of the older women wore long, black dresses and head coverings. The younger ones looked more modern, but no more stylish, in their mismatched, ill-fitted skirts and tops that appeared as though they had been pulled from a Salvation Army bin. Then there were the men. Almost all wore an Arab head covering or *kaffiyeh*. And those not in khakis, wore loose fitting trousers.

174

The women seemed a solemn lot, toiling long and hard; washing clothes in the nearby stream, baking in the communal ovens, tending children who never seemed to smile. The men, in contrast, appeared idle. By day, they grouped in doorways or the village square, talking, arguing, laughing. Many would spend long hours in the cafe drinking *finjans* of coffee. By night, they gathered in the village square, lighting smudge pots to drive off the mosquitoes, then lighting their own pipes filled with crumpled hashish. Before long the music of reed horns, *tambours* and the *dhamboura* would fill the air. Then eight or ten males would begin the *dabkah,* a dance only for men. At first, the men would move together, bodies rigid, arms draped over the next man's shoulder. But it would end wild, frenzied, with maniacal war cries and daggers slashing the air. It was an awesome sight.

Several times a day, when the guards would take the women to the outhouse, Tisha was able to see even more clearly how closely, almost claustrophobically close, the people lived with each other and their animals; and paradoxically, how distant they were to one another, the men and women especially. Tisha scrutinized every detail during these trips. She noticed the houses that looked like sand molds on a beach; the wash hanging on clothes lines; the women carrying heavy bundles on their heads, the glaring, angry men.

It was all so strange yet so familiar; so like her mother's reservation. It was a place where people struggled to survive, and in their survival, perished. It was a place ensnared by the tentacles of tradition, superstition, and fear. They trusted no one, not even each other. The sperm of their hostility and dread was virile, and had reproduced itself throughout the centuries. It ultimately shaped the basic canon of their life. This offspring was enmity; brother against brother, Cain verses Abel; and all against the infidel. Yet, if a villager was asked why this was so, he would not be able to explain, any more than a salmon could explain why it swims upstream.

Still...it was not hopeless. Nothing was hopeless. Tisha thought of her mother and smiled. She wondered how she was.

Tisha had not seen her for some time. The Gibs Town activities had prevented her from making those Sunday trips to the reservation. But Tisha wrote often, and her mother responded with happy, enthusiastic notes of her own. The change in the elder O'Brien could only be described as miraculous. She had painted the shanty, and even planted flowers in front. And every Wednesday night, she and some of the other women would get together and make hand crafted jewelry. Once a month, they would take their handiwork into town and sell it to a small boutique. In one letter Mrs. O'Brien had confessed, with obvious pleasure, that most of her jewelry were highly polished, ivory-colored crosses.

A feeling of homesickness swept over Tisha. She longed to see a friendly face. Audra provided poor company, and usually sat sulking in the corner. Communication between them had collapsed. Three times a day a saucer of vodka was prepared and Audra obliged her captors by crawling on all fours across the room. Tisha tried to talk to her, to encourage her to stop participating in this sadistic prank. But although Audra's shame was great, her bondage to alcohol was greater. So, the daily treks continued, followed by wakes of self-hatred and humiliation. These, ironically, were turned not inward, but outward to Tisha, as if she was the cause of it all. Audra's periodic outbursts of bad temper and bad language were always aimed at the dark haired engineer. And many times she tried to pick a quarrel over the most minor incident. With each passing day, the tension mounted, heightened by the anxiety of not knowing what tomorrow would bring. Tisha was able to release that tension daily, by praying incessantly, even while gazing out that small window. Audra found her release in the small clay saucer.

Sometimes Tisha would risk her companion's bad temper and try to get her to look out at something unusual or interesting, like the time they had market day. The entire village had bustled with confusion and noise as scores of peddlers arrived on their donkey-carts, their wares stuffed in enormous clay jars. There were medicines for every known ailment; amulets to ward off evil spirits; combs and mirrors, cloth, used clothing, and shoes. There were jars of condiments and spices, sesame seeds, currants, pomegranates, saffron, and dill, sour cherries, and cinnamon. Other peddlers sold their services; grinding knives, scissors, and gardening tools; repairing everything from pots and pans, to guns and rifles. Still others dealt in frivolities and luxuries; glass beads for necklaces, perfume in alabaster jars, gilt-handled daggers. There was even a craftsman in gold and silver who could produce almost any shaped object out of these precious metals.

Yet Audra had refused to leave her corner and missed market day completely. Tisha wondered when it would happen again. It had only occurred once in the seven days she had been here. She also wondered how many more days she would be here. She still didn't know why she had been abducted. Neither she nor Audra had been interrogated. And other than the cruelty with the vodka, they had been well treated. A large clay jar had been brought into the room and was filled with fresh drinking water daily. Outhouse privileges were frequent. And a woman, dressed in khakis, faithfully brought them vegetable and lentil soup twice a day, and a small cup of goat's milk at noon. Only once did this vary, and that was on market day. Their lentil soup had been brought in at breakfast as usual. But there was no goat's milk for lunch. And dinner was a complete surprise. Instead of the familiar soup, they were given *falafels* or deep fried balls of crushed wheat and chick peas, steamed grape leaves filled with pine nuts and currants, and two pieces of roasted chicken covered with *couscous*. It was a feast, and Tisha had had that uneasy feeling of someone eating her last meal. She chuckled as she thought of it.

"Remember that wonderful dinner we had on market day?" Tisha asked suddenly.

"I don't want to," Audra returned unexpectedly. She rarely responded to anything Tisha said. "It will make me hungry."

Tisha turned and smiled. "I know what you mean." It was noon time and soon they would be getting their goat's milk. But it never satisfied, and they were left famished for dinner.

"I hate lentil soup!" Audra complained. "If...if we ever get out of here I'll never eat it again."

Tisha was so moved by her companion's friendliness, she left the window, walked to where Audra sat, and squatted next to her. "Well, I certainly wouldn't recommend this restaurant," she said.

For the first time in a week, Tisha heard Audra laugh. "At least we never have to wonder 'what's for dinner,'" the blond giggled. Now they both began to laugh. They laughed so hard that tears rolled down their faces, not because it was very funny, but because their laughter was like a corkscrew that had popped a tension filled bottle. And as they laughed, Tisha's hand encircled Audra's, and the metallurgist did not pull away.

Suddenly, the door flung open and Mustafa stood in the entrance, tall, lean, with bandoleers of ammunition across his chest. At first, neither captive paid any attention, thinking it was the woman with the goat's milk. Audra looked up first, and when Tisha saw her companion's smile mangled by terror, she too directed her gaze to the door. Mustafa was pointing his finger at them, his eyes blazing with hatred. Instantly, both women knew that their seven day routine was about to be altered.

"You," he shouted, "come with me!"

Audra squeezed Tisha's hand so tightly that her fingernails turned white. But neither moved because neither knew who Mustafa was shouting at.

"I said *you*, come here!" The blazing eyes of the terrorist seemed to explode with fury as he saw his command go unheeded. After taking a few long strides, he stood over the two women. With his boot he nudged Tisha's leg roughly.

"Get up!" shouted the guard. And swinging his boot once more, Mustafa kicked her hard in the shins.

An excruciating pain shot through Tisha's legs. It was so severe Tisha wasn't sure she could stand. She began praying under her breath, "'I can do all things through Christ Jesus who strengthens me,'" then found herself rising to her feet. But as she rose, Audra's grip tightened and she wouldn't let go. "It's okay, I'll be back," Tisha said, not really convinced of the statement herself. It seemed to convince Audra because she released her hand. Then, Tisha quietly followed her jailer.

Mustafa's office was a room much like the one they had just left. The walls were whitewashed mud brick, the floor covered with goatskin rugs. But attached to the far wall was a long, mud brick bench, upon which the stocky Nabil half sat, half laid. A gray, metal desk dominated the center of the room. Tisha was surprised to see a rather scarred, but usable telephone perched on the desktop. The sight of it comforted her somewhat as if here, at last, was something familiar, something friendly. Mustafa pointed to it as he slid onto his metal folding chair.

"I have just received orders to begin interrogations," he said. "And you will tell me everything I want to know. I have been instructed to use any means necessary." He opened one of the side drawers and pulled out a large, curved dagger with a rough, wooden hilt. It was not ornamental in any way, but was rather crude in appearance. He placed it on his desk, with the blade facing outward.

"What is it you wish to know," Tisha asked calmly, her eyes unflinching and looking squarely into Mustafa's face.

"She is proud, this infidel," growled Mustafa.

Nabil rose from the bench and began walking around the dark haired engineer. Today he was armed with a revolver which was strapped to his waist. "Yes," he said with a hiss. "We may have to teach her some manners."

Mustafa ignored his stocky friend. "We know that the corporation which employs you is owned by Zionist pigs," he said with an air of authority. "We also know that you are building a secret superplane which your employers will use to slaughter thousands of innocent Moslem women and children."

Tisha's eyes grew wide, and before she could stop herself she blurted, "That's ridiculous."

"By Allah's beard, how this infidel lies!" shouted Mustafa, thumping the desk with his fists.

Nabil nodded. "Has not the Koran accurately warned us

about nonbelievers, especially the dirty Jews? The Surahs wisely caution us against befriending a Jew. Jews are corrupt and untrustworthy. It is unfortunate for this daughter of a camel that she does not know the wisdom of our holy book." As Nabil spoke, he continued to encircle Tisha; watching her, studying her.

"Jewish entrails will be used as fertilizer!" shrieked Mustafa, picking up the dagger. "Their eyes will be torn from their sockets! Their skulls will be used as kick-balls by our children! May the Prophet strike us blind if we do not exterminate every living Jew who breathes the air of Allah's earth!"

Tisha watched madness sweep over Mustafa as his voice grew louder. The blue, bulging veins on his neck formed a road map pattern. Herein traveled his hot, flowing hatred, pumped throughout every artery, vein, and capillary of his body. And his eyes mirrored this ardor as he looked at his dagger wistfully, as though longing to see Jewish blood drip from its blade. For a moment, Tisha wondered if he would substitute hers in appeasement. But presently, the guard replaced the knife on the desktop. "You will furnish us with the details of this superplane, with every minute detail." Tisha said nothing, but only stared at him in disbelief.

"Are you deaf, whore? I said you will give us the details of this airplane. And you will write it on this paper." The lean guard poked a pad of lined, yellow paper with his finger. Still Tisha remained silent. "Well!" shrieked Mustafa, the veins on his neck beginning to bulge again.

The beautiful engineer stared boldly and deliberately into his eyes. "No," she said, her voice calm and firm.

Mustafa convulsed in amazement. "Has there ever been such an evil, treacherous woman? We give her the chance to repent, to strike a blow against the Zionist pigs, thereby endearing herself to Mohammed the Great Prophet, the Ultimate Messenger of Allah, and she insults us! We who have shown her Allah's compassion. It is her Jewish friends; the scum have defiled her beyond redemption. It would be a good and just act indeed, to spill her blood with this dagger." Once again Mustafa picked up the weapon.

"No, not yet," returned Nabil quickly, putting up his hand like a traffic cop. "This whore is proud. Perhaps all she needs is a lesson in humility. Perhaps we can still make her see the truth and justice of our words." Nabil had stopped walking, and was standing very near the engineer. Slowly, and with deliberate ceremonial motions, he pulled the revolver from his waist. "You will take off your clothes, slut, and once nude, kneel before us, ask our forgiveness, and beg us to spare your life."

The look on Nabil's face told Tisha he was prepared to kill her on the spot. She shook her head no, and held her breath. She was not afraid to die. But the horrible ache in her shins reminded her how much she hated pain. She prayed for a swift end.

Nabil took his revolver and pressed the barrel against Tisha's temple. "You will do as I say or die!"

The dark haired engineer closed her eyes. Her legs began to shake underneath her, and in an effort to stave off fear, she began singing in a low, quivering voice, "'Jesus, Jesus, He's as close as the mention of His name.'" As her fear began to dissolve, her voice grew louder, firmer. "'Jesus, Jesus, He's as close as the mention of His name,'" she repeated. She waited for the sound of an exploding gun. There was only silence. Then she opened her eyes and saw a frightened Mustafa looking at her wide-eyed. She began singing again, and the louder she sang, the more terrified Mustafa became. Finally, his hysterical shrieks silenced her.

"Majnun! Majnun! Majnun!" he shouted, as he backed away from the desk. Majnun, so Arabs believe, is the spirit that makes people insane. "She is possessed! See how crazy she is! Remove her! Take her away!" Mustafa had backed to the far wall trying to put as much distance between him and the possessed woman as possible.

While Nabil was cautious, he was not nearly as intimidated as his companion. "It is best that I kill her," he said, the revolver still pressed against her temple.

"No! Are you so foolish? If she dies, the majnun will jump from her body and take control of one of us. Away with her! Take her away!" Mustafa then covered his face with his hands as though warding off any possibility of demon possession. This time Nabil obeyed, and after strapping his revolver to his waist, lead Tisha out of the room.

As she left, she turned to see Mustafa still shielding his face. "Thank you, Jesus," she whispered.

When Nabil returned Tisha to her room, he ordered Audra to follow him. The metallurgist paled under his order, but rose quickly in obedience. When they entered the office, Nabil angrily slammed the door behind him. It was obvious that both he and Mustafa were in very rancid moods. Their experience with Tisha left them even more ill-tempered than usual.

"I know your company is the tool of Zionist scum. Do not deny it!" Mustafa said, his words curdling in his mouth.

Audra stared blankly at her interrogator. "I...I don't understand," she stammered.

"May Allah the Merciful grant me patience!" bellowed Mustafa from behind the gray metal desk. He had returned to his seat. "We are dealing with another lying whore."

"No...please," mumbled the blond metallurgist. "I really don't know... ."

"Silence!" screamed Mustafa. Then, looking over at Nabil who was once again sprawled across the mud brick bench, added, "This one is worse than the last. She is of no more worth than a camel chip. See how uncooperative she is!"

Nabil pulled out his revolver. "Then it is best we dispose of her immediately. It is obvious that Jewish depravity has infiltrated these women completely. They are impossible. One is crazy. And one is a liar and a thief. She does not want to return to us what is rightfully ours. I say, kill her."

"Please!" pleaded Audra, her bottom lip quivering. "I do want to cooperate."

Suddenly, Mustafa smiled. "Ah! Perhaps she is not as depraved as you thought, Nabil. Perhaps there is hope. Maybe the light of Mohammed's truth can still penetrate her blackened soul."

Audra nodded, desperate to please. "Yes...yes I'll do whatever you say. Only...don't hurt me." The lip quivered even more, and little droplets of tears worked their way, like a stream, down her cheeks.

Nabil began slapping the black pistol against his palm. It made a dull, sickening noise, and for a moment Audra thought she was going to throw up all over Mustafa's metal desk. She clutched her stomach in panic.

"We do not want to hurt you," Mustafa said. "It was never our desire or intention. Do you take us for your cut-throat Jewish friends? Well, do you!" His voice was demanding, threatening, and quickly Audra shook her head, no. "Of course you don't," he resumed. "And if you cooperate, you will continue to be treated as an honored guest."

"What is it you want?" Audra managed to stammer.

"We know that your Zionist owned company is building an airplane which they intend using to slaughter our people. Because of this evil intent, they have forfeited their right to it. We claim this plane for ourselves. It is, by the will of Allah, ours. You can see that this is so, can you not?" questioned Mustafa.

"Yes," responded Audra weakly.

"Good. Excellent. Then you will furnish us with the details of this airplane; all the details."

"I...I don't think I can do that," she whined.

"May Allah make my teeth fall from my gums if I show this whore such mercy and patience again!" Mustafa bellowed.

"We are getting nowhere. She is corrupt beyond hope," Nabil returned dryly. "We should kill her and be done with it."

"No, wait!" Audra wailed. "Maybe I could. I mean...I don't know if I can remember everything without my notes. I...I could try."

Mustafa glared in satisfaction. "On your knees then. Beg for mercy and forgiveness. And maybe, if Allah wills, I shall allow you to give us that information."

Fear buckled Audra's legs in instant obedience, and she

knelt before the gray metal desk. "Forgive me," she whispered.

"What did you say? Speak up!" ordered Mustafa.

"Forgive me," Audra said, a bit louder, choking on the words that tasted like vomit in her mouth.

"You will demonstrate your sorrow by kissing our boots," Mustafa returned, his piercing, hate-filled eyes drilling through any will Audra had left.

The blond captive struggled to keep back the tears as she crawled, first to Mustafa, and then to where Nabil sat on the mud brick bench. By the time her lips touched the stocky guard's dusty, black boots, the trickling stream of tears had turned into a raging waterfall. She convulsed with uncontrollable sobs.

"We must forgive her, Nabil," Mustafa said. "It is our weakness to be merciful. Can we fight against our own weakness?"

"It would be most unwise," returned the reclining guard.

"That's it then. We forgive you, golden haired woman!" Mustafa said, magnanimously, as he watched the sobbing female.

Nabil also watched the blond as she wept into her hands. "Ah! She is overwhelmed with gratitude!" he cried. "That is good." So saying, he took his boot and shoved her onto the ground. "And now I think we can make her even more grateful."

There was a questioning look in Mustafa's face as he watched Nabil unzip his pants. "Yes, it would be an honor for her to service us," he returned, as the realization of what his friend was about to do, became obvious. Audra watched in horror as Nabil moved towards her. "She is, after all, only a whore."

For the next week, Audra was called into Mustafa's office every day. The routine never varied. Her progress was questioned. It was always poor. Audra had lost, temporarily at least, the ability to think clearly. Her notes were disjointed; her diagrams incomplete or inaccurate.

The guards lacked the knowledge to interpret the accuracy of her report so they were unaware of Audra's impediment. But her slow progress angered them greatly. They viewed this as an effort to sabotage their plans. So everyday Nabil would wave and point his gun. And everyday there would be loud cursing and name calling, accusations, and threats. And always, always it would end with one or both of the guards shoving her onto the floor saying, "She is, after all, only a whore."

Those times on the floor especially, were times Audra tried to block everything out. Survival was, after all, everything. Maybe if she didn't resist them, if she did all they asked, they would eventually release her, and she could go home.

Her thoughts were fuzzy about home. At times it was difficult to recall the color of her kitchen, or how the living room was arranged. More and more she seemed to fade into a world of cobwebs and pea-soup fog. Sometimes she would even forget where she was.

There was one good thing though, she didn't have to take her vodka from a saucer anymore. The guards had tired of that game. Instead, they gave her half a bottle a day, to drink whenever she wanted. Audra thought she would have gone out of her mind if it were not for this one comfort. She especially needed it after her daily interrogation. When it was over, she would go to her half of the room where the bottle was kept in the corner; slide down against the wall onto the goatskin rug; and then propped by the mud brick wall, she would take one large gulp. It always burned going down and made her eyes tear. After this, she would take five or six smaller sips, then cap the bottle for later. It was only then that she was able to turn and look at Tisha O'Brien.

She had grown to hate this woman with the thick, black hair and chocolate colored eyes. That brief moment of friendship, when the two had held hands, was smashed and forgotten. After the first day of interrogation, Tisha had never again been called into the office. *She* was not shouted at, or scratched by a gun barrel, or threatened, or pushed to the floor and used as a whore. And Audra hated her for that.

"Was it bad today?" Tisha asked softly, as she looked over

at her companion.

"I keep telling you to mind your business!" Audra snapped, pushing back the honey blond hair that hung about her face. Her hair was lusterless, straw-like, its protein dried up and blown away like flakes of dandruff.

The chocolate colored eyes fastened themselves onto Audra's shoulder where her blouse had been ripped. Nabil had been particularly vicious today, and in demonstrating his power over her, had torn her sleeve.

"And stop staring at me!" Audra said, self-consciously trying to repair the rip with her fingers.

"I just want to help. We all need someone," Tisha persisted. "Don't isolate yourself. If you'd only... ."

"Shut up! Just Shut up!" Audra screamed, her face looking much like a hernia ready to rupture under the strain. "I don't need you or anyone! Do you hear that! I don't need anyone!"

Eleven

Joshua Chapman sat in Michael Patterson's paneled office watching the handsome face of Peter Meyers contort in an array of emotions. It was not the same Joshua who left Everman several months ago. Outwardly he was still youthful. But his greenish eyes revealed that inwardly there was a much older man. He was flanked by his brother, Dr. Daniel Chapman, and by another member of the Zionist Underground, Iliab Nahshon.

"I've been told of your efforts in helping the ISS, and I want to begin by thanking you," Meyers said smiling, while his forehead crinkled in a slight frown. He was still perturbed with Mike Patterson. Two weeks ago, Patterson had gone to the home of Dr. Daniel Chapman, to enlist the aid of the Zionist Underground. Meyers had been furious, and told Mike he should have let the ISS handle things. The frustrated Patterson's rebuttal had been a curt accusation that the ISS didn't seem able to handle a bus transfer across town. More choleric words had followed. Meyers had been, and was even now, angry and embarrassed over his agency's failure. The women had been missing eighteen days now. It was only in the last few days that any intelligence on their whereabouts had been gathered. And this information had been gleaned, not by the ISS, but by the Zionist Underground.

"Make no mistake in thinking this is a purely unselfish act on our part," Iliab said, with a thick accent. His voice was deep, but almost gentle, in contrast to the rugged, scarred face. Hidden beneath his clothes, a network of other scars plated his body. Some he had sustained in combat. But most were received while in an Arab prison. "We are hoping these efforts on our part will encourage greater cooperation between your agency and ours."

"I understand," Meyers said, deferring to Iliab. It was obvious that he was to be the spokesman. "But you must understand that any commitment I make to you now is strictly unofficial."

"It is a pity we must play these silly 'cat and mouse' games when lives are being lost daily."

"I don't make policy. The bureaucrats in Washington... ."

"Politics do not interest me," Iliab interrupted curtly. "And quite frankly, there are many in the Underground who do not trust your government and do not wish an alliance between us. Fortunately, there are more who do. But all of us have a long memory and we still mourn our martyred Mossad brothers."

Meyers blushed. "Our agency had nothing to do with that fiasco," he returned weakly. Iliab was referring to a former Secretary of State who had given the PLO the names of three top members of the Mossad. The Mossad was Israel's intelligence service, their counterpart of the CIA. These Mossad agents had successfully infiltrated two different terrorist groups. Trying to bring Arafat to the peace table, the Secretary of State had used these men as barter. It cost the men their lives, and years later there still was no peace. The name of the former Secretary of State continued to be used as a curse word among many in Israel.

"What is it you want?" Meyers finally asked, trying to take control of himself and the discussion.

"I will come directly to the point. I will, as you Americans say, lay my cards on the table. We want to be recognized by your government as a legitimate anti-terrorist organization. Our primary concern is and will continue to be Israel. Our membership includes

Jews from all over the world and we want to eventually network with every government, to operate jointly and in collaboration with these governments when it pertains to terrorists. This will make us more effective and, in addition, aid in controlling global terrorism. The US could help get this started. America still has influence, and with your endorsement...I believe you get the picture. If we pool our intelligence, our resources and efforts, we will be able to successfully deter terrorism. If we do not, then we are all just so many splinter groups, each accomplishing only a fraction of what we actually could."

"You are an Israeli?"

Iliab nodded

"What can you expect from us? Your own government doesn't recognize you."

"Off the record, I will tell you that we work very closely with the Mossad. It is all unofficial, of course. The Israeli government would recognize us except for fear of displeasing the United States. We are unconventional and we strike hard. That is why we are so successful. The world hates terrorism, but all too often does not have the stomach to do what is necessary to stop it. I believe recognizing our organization will be a giant step in the right direction. If your government made it known that it views us in a favorable light, then the Israeli government would have no trouble in doing the same. And soon, the rest of the world would follow."

Meyers nodded, the frown on his forehead deepened. He knew Iliab spoke the truth. "I understand, and I agree, off the record, of course. But again I'm asking, what do you want from me?"

"We would like you to be...shall we say...a friendly spokesman for us in this area. Plant seeds in the right ears," Iliab returned. "Use this abduction as a test case. Work closely with us, pool intelligence, have on-going communiqués. Perhaps your government will see the benefits of such an alliance and something more permanent will result. After all, terrorism is not just a Jewish problem."

For the first time all eyes were on Mike Patterson. They

knew about his relationship with Tisha O'Brien. There was sympathy on everyone's face, except one. Mike looked into that face, into the eyes of Dr. Daniel Chapman. Both men desperately wanted Tisha safely back. But both knew that it would be into Mike's arms she would go for solace and comfort. It had been an awkward confrontation, that night in Daniel Chapman's apartment; each man sizing up the other. If Daniel Chapman had had any doubts who Tisha loved, they were dispelled that night. Still, it was hard to stop loving someone, even if that love was not returned. In the end, there was no hesitation on Chapman's part. He would do all he could to ensure Tisha's safe return. It was Daniel Chapman who had served as liaison between the ISS and the Zionist Underground.

"We will help you rescue the two American women if you can agree to these terms," Iliab resumed, turning his gaze from Patterson back to Peter Meyers.

Meyers hesitated. "As I said, I can't commit my government. But for what it's worth, I assure you I'll do my best on your behalf."

"Is this all that can be done?" quizzed the scarred-face man.

"No," Mike Patterson interrupted forcefully. He was still looking at Doctor Chapman. He owed him something. If he couldn't repay him directly, then perhaps his brother. Mike knew all about Joshua from Tisha.

"Now look, Mike," Meyers said crossly, "this is ISS business. Leave it to us."

"If I had left it to you, we still would have nothing," Mike responded without any rancor in his voice. "Sorry, Pete, but I think you can come up with something better."

"Meaning?" questioned Meyers, flushed with embarrassment over Patterson's remark.

"Meaning...Joshua is a US citizen."

"So?"

"He can be the ISS link with the Underground."

"I...I don't get it," Meyers stammered in confusion. But Iliab's scarred face lit up as he began to see the possibilities of

Mike's proposal. "You mean make Joshua an ISS agent?"

"That's right," Patterson said. "Through him, all ISS and Underground intelligence could flow."

"That would take mountains of paperwork, red tape, a lot of convincing the higher ups... ." Meyers' voice trailed off as his mind began racing. "Yes...yes I think it might be possible. What do you say, Joshua?"

The lanky blond turned to Iliab and smiled. A deep friendship between the two men had begun to develop. They had fought side by side and lived to tell about it. They had also buried friends who did not. "I say, you have yourself a new agent."

Iliab extended his hand to Meyers. "We have a deal then?"

"Yes, we have a deal," Meyers said as they shook hands. "Now tell us about this Bozrom, where they are holding the women."

A thin smile arched upward on the scarred face. "Bozrom is a Syrian village about fifty miles from the Israeli border."

"Why Bozrom?" quizzed Meyers, as he watched Mike pale.

"It's a known terrorist stronghold. And, it's pretty inaccessible; surrounded by desert and rough, mountain terrain."

"I understand you have been contacted by the Jihad; once to claim responsibility, the second time with demands," said Joshua Chapman, looking at Mike Patterson.

The handsome executive nodded. "Yes. They want two hundred thousand dollars or they will...kill the women." He had trouble getting the last few words out. "I will be contacted in three days for my answer and further instructions."

"You cannot pay the ransom," Iliab said.

"What? But...I must or they will... ."

"They will kill your Miss O'Brien and Miss Shields the minute they get the money," Iliab returned.

Instinctively, Mike knew he was right. "Then what can we do?" he asked, unwilling to give up so easily.

"We can go into Bozrom and get the ladies out."

"Is that possible?" Mike returned, leaning forward in his

chair, his face blazing with hope.

"Yes," answered the scarred man.

"You would need an army. Dozens of men would lose their lives," Meyers interjected solemnly.

"Quite so. It would take an army if we wanted to conquer Bozrom. And the guerrillas would kill the women before we reached them. That is why we will use only four men," Iliab returned. "We are not looking to vanquish a village, only to rescue two women."

Meyers shook his head skeptically. But Michael Patterson, who had been appraising the Israeli, doubted if Nahshon was the type who spoke idle words or made boastful claims. "You have a plan," he said, more as a statement than a question.

"Yes," Iliab answered. "Bozrom is surrounded by desert on three sides; on the fourth it is flanked by the treacherous Bab el Wad. Strategically placed sentries patrol twenty-four hours a day. It would be impossible to penetrate the village without being discovered immediately. And once the village is alarmed, well, we have already discussed the hazard to the women. But Bozrom has market day every two weeks. On that day a variety of peddlers come to sell their wares. There is always great confusion and excitement. It would be easy for us to slip in during this time."

"Maybe," said Meyers, not completely convinced. "But wouldn't four strange faces arouse suspicion?"

"There is a risk, certainly," Iliab responded. "But only two of the men would be new. The other two are Underground agents, and have already successfully entered Bozrom many times. One agent poses as a peddler of precious metals, the other as his assistant. Being a terrorist village, Bozrom is rich compared to the average Moslem village. Money flows like the Euphrates from the coffers of Iran, Libya and Syria to fund terrorism. Believe me when I say our silver and gold peddler does a good business in Bozrom."

"Fine," Meyers said. "But how are you going to get the other two men in undetected? "

"Peddlers are easy prey for the Bedouin or nomadic Arabs

who often lay in wait for them. A peddler of precious metals is an even more desirable target. We will stage a false robbery of our agents; let the word get around. Then, when they show up with two heavily armed bodyguards, no one will question it. In fact, they will expect it."

"Alright, so you can get in. But how are you going to get the women out?" Meyers asked.

Nahshon frowned. "This, of course, is the difficult part. We know the exact house where the women are being held, and the number of guards with them. Our peddler agent was able to get that information the last time he was in Bozrom. The fedayeen love to boast of their conquests." Iliab paused as though thinking of the perilous journey. "Yes, it will be difficult, but you must leave the rest to us. Understand this, if I did not think it possible, I would not attempt it."

"Then you will be one of the bodyguards?" Meyers asked.

"Yes." Nahshon looked over at Joshua Chapman and smiled. "My young companion here wanted to be the other, but it is too risky. He could never pass as an Arab. But he will be our back-up. He and a team of men will wait for us in the wadi."

The boyishly handsome Joshua Chapman shifted self-consciously in his chair. "My friends all volunteered to come with me," he said with pride.

Mike had been listening quietly, struggling hard to subdue his impatience. Finally, it ruptured like a boil, and spewed from his mouth. "When...*when* will this rescue take place?"

Nahshon looked sympathetically at the executive. "In seven days the peddler is due to return."

Patterson closed his eyes. "One week," he said more to himself than to anyone in particular. Then opening his eyes he continued. "The terrorists will contact me in three days. What should I say?"

The scarred face of Iliab contorted in a frown. "You must stall. And you must be convincing. If the terrorists suspect anything, your...woman will be killed. There is much riding on this.

Do you understand?"

"Yes," Mike returned. "I understand."

"Mr. Patterson?" asked a thickly accented voice over the telephone.

"Yes," answered the executive as he rolled his eyes indicating to Meyers that contact had been made.

"Are you prepared to deliver the two hundred thousand dollars?"

"No," Patterson replied, sounding calm. He had rehearsed a wide range of possible dialogue a thousand times until he could say his lines matter-of-factly. Internally, however, he was far from calm. His heart raced, and his throat felt dry and constricted.

"What?"

"These women have few family members. And they are not wealthy. But then, you knew that, otherwise you wouldn't have contacted me." Mike paused to give the voice a chance to comment, but there was only silence on the other end. Finally, the executive continued. "Therefore, I have assumed responsibility and am, even now, in the process of liquidating some of my assets."

"Do you think this is a game and you can make up the rules as you go!" snapped the accented voice. "Perhaps you need evidence of our serious intent. A finger or toe of one of the women delivered to you in a package should convince you that *we* dictate the terms!"

Mike's heart pounded wildly at the prospect of Tisha being maimed. His mind raced for what to say. If he panicked or showed any sign of weakness, the outcome could be disastrous. "Do you expect me to pay for damaged goods!" he shot back. "These women aren't family! They are valuable to me as employees. But everyone is expendable. If you're so eager for bloodletting, I can't stop you."

There was silence as the terrorist grappled with his confusion. "Then...you do not care what happens to them?"

"Of course I care, in the business sense. I assumed you were a businessman as well; that we could come to equitable terms."

"You have a proposal?"

"I do. In five days I will have liquidated enough assets to pay your ransom. In addition, I am prepared to pay you twenty thousand dollars a day interest, beginning today, until everything is settled."

There was a long pause as the terrorist digested Mike's words. The ransom price was two hundred thousand dollars. Anything over that amount could be pocketed and who would know? "I will call you in five days," came the reply which sealed the agreement. Then the phone went dead.

Peter Meyers had been listening to the conversation on a nearby telephone. "You handled it well, Mike," he said. "You kept a cool head. Now, there's nothing more we can do."

In four days Iliab Nahshon and his men would be in Bozrom. In four days Tisha would either be rescued or killed. "We can pray," Mike returned.

After driving up and down the streets of the Cheyenne reservation for over twenty minutes, Michael Patterson finally stopped and asked the directions to the home of Mrs. Paddy O'Brien. He followed the prescribed route, then stopped in front of a small, white-washed cottage. He studied the house as he squinted out the open window. It was not what he expected. Tisha had described her mother's shanty and then explained her mother had since renovated. But she had yet to see it. Still, this was nothing like Tisha's description. He could tell the cottage had been freshly painted and sported new hunter-green shutters. Large clay pots of flowers, clustered here and there on the porch, formed little rainbows of color. A wooden rocker, with a thin, summer, calico blanket thrown over one arm and an open sewing basket on the seat, looked like it belonged on Martha Stewart's porch. A red brick path led from the porch to the street, and packed along the sides of the path were shrubs and flowers that seemed to smile at the passerby. Two stone cranes, three feet high, peeked from behind the bushes, and Mike had to look twice before he realized they were not real. All this on a back-drop of lush green grass that carpeted the front like a short shag rug. This was a house that beckoned people to enter, with the promise that they would find a warm welcome inside.

The overall look was incredibly charming, and Mike wondered if Tisha had not exaggerated her description of decay. Could the person who lived here, who created all this warmth and appeal, be the same person who was able to live in the squalor that Tisha had described? He wondered if he hadn't misunderstood the directions and was about to pull away and inquire all over again, when suddenly the cottage door opened and out stepped an elderly woman in a blue house-dress. She waved at him and smiled, and began walking down the porch stairs.

Quickly, Mike Patterson got out of the car. After Tisha was abducted, he had sent the elder O'Brien a telegram informing her of what had happened. Now that the Underground had gotten involved and there was the possibility of a rescue, Mike thought he should give Tisha's mother this news in person.

Before he could take a step away from the car, the elderly woman was beside him. She was in her seventies. Tisha had been a change-of-life baby. Mike could see that the woman had been pretty once, but not a beauty like Tisha. Her features were too angular, too harsh. Still, this could be Tisha's mother.

"Mrs. O'Brien?" he asked hesitantly. Mike was surprised to see such a wide smile for a stranger. Her eyes literally sparkled.

"Yes. How can I help you?"

"I am Michael Patterson, from Patterson Aviation."

Mrs. O'Brien took his arm and began pulling him towards the house. "You have news about Tisha. It is best we go inside."

He glanced at her as they walked to the porch and noticed her forehead was wrinkled in a frown and her smile was gone.

"I have good news," he said quickly, before they got to the

front door. He wanted to relieve her fears. He didn't want her to think the worst.

Mrs. O'Brien gave him a grateful smile as she blinked back tears. Yes, her thoughts had suddenly become morbid. This was how it was when Paddy died. Someone had come personally to the house to tell her. Now this nice young man was saying he had good news, not bad. She squeezed his hand gently. "I am so relieved!"

She made him sit down at the new butcher-block table while she fixed coffee for them. Mike sensed that he should wait until Mrs. O'Brien was finished and seated before telling her anything. He understood that she did not want to miss a word or have her attention divided. As he waited, he looked around. The inside was actually a large studio apartment. It consisted of one great room, where kitchen, dining room and bedroom were all together. He could tell that the appliances and furniture were new. Also, the walls had been freshly painted. The bedspread, the stuffed chair in the corner, and the curtain were all color-coordinated and in various shades of blue and green. Mrs. O'Brien's tastes were simple and practical, but also pleasing.

"You have a nice place here," he said, trying to make idle conversation.

Mrs. O'Brien just nodded her head, put the steaming cups of coffee on the table, prepared a small platter of assorted cookies, then sat down. "Tell me about Tisha," she said.

Mike told her about the Zionist Underground, about Iliab Nahshon and his plan to rescue the two women.

Mrs. O'Brien listened carefully, without interruption. When he was finished she said, "It sounds dangerous."

"Yes," Mike returned. There was no point in trying to soften or distort the truth. If the mother was anything like Tisha, she would see through it anyway.

"Tisha is in big trouble."

"Yes," Mike said, again not blunting his answer.

"But she serves a big God. Nothing is impossible."

Mike looked into the pleasant face, at the large, hopeful

197

eyes, and watched as a bright smile appeared. But he did not respond. He only marveled at her conviction. He wished he had such faith.

"You do not believe," the elderly woman said, covering his hand with her gnarled fingers. "It is a sad thing to face trouble alone. I know, I tried." She was thinking of those lonely years after her husband's death. Now, she saw the familiar signs of grief on this man's face.

Mike turned away. Her tender, compassionate gaze had looked upon his loneliness. In truth, he had never felt so solitary, so frantic. These past weeks Mike had been desperately struggling to hold onto some firm ground, something that did not ebb and flow with the tide. Instead, he had been tossed back and forth, like a helpless, bobbing cork. The tide could be cruel, bringing you just short of land, then dragging you out again. This time, even Buck's friendship was not enough to anchor him.

"Michael," she said, breaking in on his thoughts. "You are a man in authority. A man used to controlling himself and others."

"Tisha wrote you about me?"

"No. Your name tells me this. Michael Patterson, of Patterson Aviation. You are the owner? The President?" The executive nodded. "It is often difficult for a person of position and power to surrender, to give his life to God. To say, 'I am tired and weary. Take what I have, what I am. I give it all to you, Lord.' But if you wish peace, the peace that only God can give, then you must surrender. It is the only way."

The handsome executive sighed. "Tisha has talked to me about God, but quite honestly, Mrs. O'Brien, I don't believe. I just can't seem to take that leap of faith."

"It does not take a leap of faith, but the sincere cry of a longing soul. Search the scriptures with a sincere heart. When you do, you will come face to face with Jesus."

"I...that is, Tisha gave me a Bible. I've tried reading it, but it doesn't penetrate. It doesn't mean anything to me."

"When you are ready to humble yourself before God, that is

when you will find Him. God stands, as a loving father, with out-stretched arms, waiting for us to leave our folly and turn to Him."

"You make it sound so simple."

"It is so simple."

Michael Patterson took a sip of coffee as he studied the woman in front of him. Outwardly, Tisha was nothing like her, but inwardly, Mike could see Tisha's depth and warmth mirrored in her mother. He couldn't help but like the woman. "Well," he said, at last, putting down his cup, "I just wanted to come in person and let you know what's going on. I know you have no phone. I'll keep you informed by telegram."

Mrs. O'Brien sat across the table and smiled. They remained this way for a long time; Mike twisting in his seat, Mrs. O'Brien smiling and staring. There was a strange expression on her face.

Finally, the executive leaned over the table. "What are you thinking, Mrs. O'Brien?"

The elderly woman sank comfortably into her chair. "I am thinking how fortunate you are to have Tisha's love. And how fortunate Tisha is to have yours."

The donkey cart and the two heavily armed men on horse-back who flanked it, kicked up a large mushroom of dust as they entered the village square. "May Allah and the Great Prophet curse the scorching heat," shouted a stout gold and silver peddler to no one in particular. Finding a satisfactory spot, he stopped the cart. As his assistant rolled back the goatskin covers exposing their wares, the peddler stood up and addressed the villagers.

"Warm greetings and all manner of blessings on your head," he shouted into the crowd. "All gratitude and thanks to the merciful Allah, God of the seven heavens, for guiding me safely into your blessed village. I, Izzat, merchant of precious metals am your humble servant and await your pleasure." So saying, he seated himself in the cart, and began picking over the items laid out by his assistant. Then, with incredible dexterity he began working a tiny piece of gold foil. With a gas flame and quick expert movements, he began to twist cobweb like filaments of gold into a minute Koran. The villagers had seen him do this dozens of times, yet they looked on in amazement. Meanwhile, the peddler's assistant quietly held up shiny, silver worry-beads for their inspection. Within minutes he sold one. In Bozrom there was much to fret about: crop failures, the hostile desert elements, the next raid. These things were best dealt with on the beads.

About this time the guards began mingling among the crowd. Their presence had caused no alarm. Everyone had heard how Izzat had been robbed; how both he and his assistant had been left with good size lumps on their heads and an empty donkey cart. And everyone agreed that the shrewd Izzat always got his money's worth. Were there any fiercer looking guards in all Syria? His two looked so fierce in their Arab headdress and baggy shirt and pants, with fully packed bandoleers of ammunition crossing each chest. Both had an automatic repeating rifle slung over their shoulders. And large daggers, with highly polished rhino horn hilts, were lashed into scabbards on their waist. The villagers viewed them with admiration.

Iliab Nahshon and his companion moved slowly throughout the square, allowing the villagers to satisfy their curiosity. They took pains not to appear rushed, but stopped here and there admiring the different wares. Iliab even purchased a new harness for his horse from the leather merchant. As the novelty of their presence wore off, and with it the sideward stares of the villagers, the pair was able to move further away from the hub of the square. At its perimeter, the men were now free to study the topography of the village, to commit its layout to memory. They whispered in low tones devising their strategy. Both agreed that exiting to the right of the square was the best route. That way, there were only three walls, in all, to scale. They would have to pass through a small animal courtyard, then a long alley which, from what Iliab could see, would take them to the base of the mountain, where the next cluster of houses began. There were at least twenty in that cluster, most of them attached by twos and threes, and rising steadily like giant stairs, four tiers high. The last row of houses was butted into the mountain rock itself, with one raised slightly higher than the others. This house was their target. It was a difficult objective. And the danger of being spotted by the half dozen lookouts that were forever positioned on the rocks was great.

"We must stay close to the walls and the houses as we move upward," whispered Iliab in Arabic. They could not afford to speak Hebrew. Just the sound of the language, without anyone even hearing the words, was enough to put them in danger. So it was previously agreed that only Arabic would be spoken. "We will let their shadows hide us," continued Iliab. "Our most vulnerable time will be when we scale the three walls."

His companion, Nathan Yehuda, nodded thoughtfully. "Yes. We must move quickly."

"Then, that is it. We know what to do. Remember one thing, in the house we must use only our daggers or our hands."

Again Yehuda nodded. "Of course."

"Then, that is it," Iliab repeated. But as he spoke, he clasped Nathan's wrist in a type of well-wishing handshake. Then they moved back through the crowd. More peddlers had arrived and a carnival atmosphere prevailed throughout the square as vendors shouted exaggerated claims or boasted about their wares and villagers scrambled for a bargain or an exhibition. Again the pair tried to appear unhurried. Once they even stopped to allow a curious, young Moslem to inspect one of their rifles.

Finally, they were able to make their departure to the right, then into the animal courtyard and alley, and over the three stone walls, keeping close to the sides of the houses as they moved. From time to time they would stop, huddle against the mud brick side of a house or wall, and listen for any sounds of alarm. There were none. Slowly, but steadily, they moved forward. The trek seemed tedious, long, though only minutes had passed. Once or twice Iliab had to get his bearings, to see if they were going in the proper direction.

The alleys formed a labyrinth, and they could easily get lost. But his eye always found a landmark that he had previously engraved in his mind.

The journey continued, now up the tiers of houses that seemed to be chiseled into the very mountain itself. One tier, two tiers. Iliab signaled Nathan to stop. Still no sound of alarm. Miraculously, they had not encountered any villagers. They were all at the square. It was going exactly as they had hoped. Three tiers. Finally, they were by the very door of the house. At the entrance they removed their daggers from their sheaths, then gingerly entered. Large jars and tins, used for fetching well water, cluttered one side. Nathan's foot barely missed knocking one over as he passed. They were in the kitchen now. There was no fire in the open hearth where the cooking was done, but the room was well stocked. Lined against a wall were clay jars full of coffee, salt, ground dates. To the other side were clay bins of nuts, grains, and dried fruit. On the third was a narrow doorway. Through the closed door, male voices could be heard. Izzat the peddler had found out that only two men guarded the women. Iliab raised his dagger in preparation. It would be necessary to throw it quickly. He would only have one chance to get his man. Yehuda's dagger would have its own target.

Iliab's eyes searched Nathan's. Are you ready? they asked. Nathan nodded in answer. Iliab put one hand on the knob, twisted and pushed. The door flew open, and both daggers sailed through the air, hitting their marks with a sickening thud. At once, Iliab and Nathan were upon the prone bodies. With an easy motion they withdrew the daggers from the torn flesh, and used them to slit the guards' throats. It was not an action born out of blood lust or barbarity, but out of caution. An injured man could still sound an alarm or even bury his own dagger in an unsuspecting back. Then, the Zionists wiped their knives clean, and put them in their scabbards. Nothing must be amiss when they returned to the square.

That done, the pair moved toward another closed door. It was Iliab again who opened it. In the heat-laden cell-like room were two women, very much alive. Iliab was relieved. He had not been certain in what condition he would find the ladies. From a first glance, they appeared well. One woman, with beautiful, black hair twisted into one braid down her back, stood peering out a small window. The other woman, a blond, her hair matted and pasted to her face, sat hunched in a corner sucking on a bottle.

It was the blond who saw Iliab and Nathan first. Her eyes grew large with fear. She clutched her bottle closer. "Don't hurt me," she whined.

The dark haired woman turned immediately from the window and stared with amazement into the scarred man's face. The men had penetrated and conquered the house so quietly that neither woman had heard anything.

"We will not hurt you," Iliab said in English. "We have come to rescue you."

A broad, sunny smile spread over Tisha's face. "Praise God! I've been praying for this! I saw you coming...from the window. I've been watching you and your friend darting by the houses and over the walls. Then I lost sight of you. I was hoping... ." Tisha's voice broke and tears welled up in her eyes. "I'm so glad you're here!"

"If she saw us, then maybe someone else did too," said Nathan. "Perhaps one of the guards on the cliff."

"No, I doubt it," Tisha returned calmly. "They are probably smoking hashish in the shade. On market day, everything is lax."

Iliab grunted, "Possibly. But let's not wait too long to find out. Let's move quickly." Then he and Nathan began unbuttoning their shirts. Audra gasped as she watched, then sank deeper into the corner.

"It's okay," said the scarred-face man as he pulled out a black dress and scarf, not noticing that he had pulled out his new leather harness as well, and that it fell to the floor. "Put this on," he ordered, throwing Audra the clothing. Nathan took a duplicate outfit from his shirt and handed it to Tisha.

Immediately, Tisha grasped the purpose and slipped the

dress over her clothes. With the long, black scarf, she covered her head. Then she moved to Audra and pulled her to her feet. "Come on. You must wear these."

Even through the veil of intoxication, Audra was beginning to grasp what was happening, and allowed Tisha to put the dress over her head. Tisha also helped her with the shawl, taking pains to cover all the blond hair. "Okay," she said. "We're ready."

Iliab led the group through the living room where the two Arab guards lay dead, then into the kitchen. He stopped by the old kerosene tins that were now used to haul water, and began shaking them until he came upon one that was full. In the meantime Nathan pulled goatskin pouches from his shirt, and began filling them with dried food from the clay bins. He tied them and handed them to Tisha. All the while Audra stood clutching her vodka bottle. When that was done, Iliab ushered the group out the door and onto a steep, narrow path that led into the Bab el Wad. He would find a cave to hide the women until he could return for them that night.

The terrain was extremely rough, and Audra kept slowing them down. As the sun began moving further west, Nahshon realized he could not take them as deep into the mountain as he had hoped. He would have to find a cave soon. There were many in the Bab el Wad and the men scouted several before coming upon a suitable one. It was large, having many passageways. The lack of light made it impossible to explore deep in its interior. But after Iliab's eyes had grown accustomed to the shadows, he spotted a ledge quite high off the ground. If a person lay flat and against the far wall, he would be impossible to see from the ground. It was a perfect hiding place. Iliab explained his plan to the women. After promising he would be back for them that night, he and Nathan lifted, first Tisha, then Audra onto the ledge. Then the food and water were handed up.

"Make sure you eat and drink your fill. After this, you will be on rations," Iliab said. Then the men were gone.

Once alone, Audra began to cry. Her wails bounced off the ceiling in eerie, hollow echoes. "It's like a casket," she sobbed, "a casket in a tomb. We're going to die. We're never going to get out of here. Never!"

The platform was close to the roof of the cave making it impossible to sit upright. Tisha hunched over Audra, cradling her like a baby. "Hush," she said gently. "It's going to be all right."

Iliab and Nathan trudged through the mountain. The climb downward was vastly easier than the ascent, and the two men made good progress. All along the way, Iliab's mind sketched the terrain, the pathways, the shape of the boulders, the position of the village. He would have to know these things when he returned for the women.

Finally, they arrived at the outskirts of the village, very near the house where the women had been held. All was quiet. So far, no one had discovered the dead guards. Carefully, Nathan and Iliab moved along the shadows of the buildings. Their most vulnerable position was still over the three walls. Cautiously, they scaled the first, the second, and were about to scale the last when Iliab noticed that some of the villagers were beginning to drift away from the square.

"Do exactly as I do," he whispered, and then with a quick motion, dove over the wall and landed on the ground. He then propped himself against the mud brick wall, and pulled from his shirt a pipe and bag of hashish. He crumpled some hashish into the pipe bowl, lit it, and took one long, heavy drag. Nathan had followed him over the wall, and now sat silently beside him.

"Allah Akbar! Allah Akbar!" Iliab said in a loud voice as he passed the pipe to Nathan. Yehuda took it without hesitation, and after a full, long drag, released the smoke from his mouth.

"Join us! Join us!" invited Iliab laughingly, as two men approached. His breath reeked with the drug, but his mind remained alert, cautious. His cold, sharp eyes searched for any sign of hostility. There was none. They were simply curious, and of course hoped they would be invited to share the pipe. At once, Nathan offered it, and each man took his turn before passing it to Iliab.

"Allah Akbar!" Iliab roared again.

And a chorus of three repeated in unison, "Allah Akbar! Allah is great!"

"So this is where you have gone," said the younger of the two as he gazed at Iliab. Nathan recognized him as the one who had inspected the rifle. "I want my friend to see your beautiful weapon."

"By the Prophet! It is a day that man must find shade or die!" exclaimed Iliab as he gestured for the two men to sit in the shadow of the wall. They eagerly obliged. "I am honored that you find my unworthy weapon of such interest," he said as he handed the friend his rifle.

"Unworthy!" cried the young fedayeen who had already seen it, and who even now caressed the barrel as though it was a beautiful woman. "It is a most wondrous instrument, a most magnificent instrument!" Iliab's weapon was a new, high powered, Russian made rifle. Its balance and precision were impeccable. In addition, it had added ornate features that were specialties of certain type of black market weapons. The entire rifle butt was overlaid with a latticework of sterling silver.

Iliab sighed. "Perhaps to the eye, it pleases. But it has yet to be used to end the life of a single Zionist. Does not the Koran, in Surah fifty-seven, tell us of the punishment due unbelievers? And does not Surah twenty-two tell us that because the Jews were lead astray from Islam they must be humiliated in this world?"

The other three men nodded. "Yes, it is so," they all agreed.

"Aha! So you see, this unworthy weapon has yet to humiliate one Jew! It has only been used to protect a gold and silver peddler from our poor unfortunate brothers; the very brothers who were driven off their land by Zionist pigs, and so have been forced by their regrettable circumstances to squeeze out a living from someone else's pocket. A thousand curses on the dirty Jews! It is they who steal Moslem land, rape Moslem women, butcher Moslem children. It is they who have forced our brothers to live like barbarians! By Allah's beard, I swear I will kill a hundred of them with this rifle before I am through!"

The young fedayeen holding Iliab's firearm nodded. "It is our duty to relieve the earth of all Jewish scum. You are correct. This is an unworthy weapon," so saying, he handed it back to Iliab.

The scarred-face man waved it high in the air. "Allah Akbar! Death to the Jews!" The three immediately joined in with similar shouts, pausing only long enough to drag on the pipe when it was passed. When the last ember in the bowl went out, the two fedayeen departed, feeling content. Nathan and Iliab, on the other hand, were not so disposed. They had only pretended to inhale the drug. Their senses were sharp. They would need them to dissect the hazards before them.

They were able to reach Izzat's donkey cart without further incident. The gold peddler and his assistant were already packed. Two or three of the other carts were also packed and Izzat prudently waited for them to leave before pulling out.

As the wheels of the cart once more churned the desert dust, Iliab had to resist the impulse to look back. He envisioned an angry mob of fedayeen with swords brandishing behind him. But his ears told him it was not true. There were no shouts or hoof beats, no angry, blood-curdling cries. Their deed still remained undiscovered. And only the hollow, rather lonely sound of the donkey cart caravan filled the air.

The peddler's assistant had, by previous instruction, partially disabled one wheel of the cart. The disability was of no consequence for they had with them the means to quickly repair the damage. And after about a half hour into their journey, the sabotaged wheel finally gave way. This caused great excitement among the other cart drivers as word of Izzat's distress traveled throughout the caravan. There were offers of help, but Izzat refused. He had three able-bodied men, he insisted. There were wails of protest and feigned distaste at leaving the gold peddler, but in truth, all the drivers were anxious to be off. No one wanted to be caught near the Bab el Wad at night. So, after invoking Allah's blessing and protection upon Izzat and his companions, everyone hastily departed.

Quickly, the wheel was repaired, and two more rifles with

extra ammunition were pulled from a secret compartment in the cart. Within twenty minutes they were again moving, not north as the other carts had gone, but eastward, deep into the wadi.

At a designated spot, the cart stopped. Izzat and his assistant would remain here until early morning. They would cover the other two men. If anyone followed, it would be up to the peddlers to stop them. About ten miles away, Joshua Chapman and his three friends waited. Iliab was to meet Chapman with the women in three days. Now, taking his rifle and extra shells, a goatskin flask of water and his hashish pipe, he led Nathan through the Bab el Wad, back toward the village. The horses remained with the peddler.

Iliab knew the wadi well. As a youth he had spent much time exploring its great expanse. He was a tough, disciplined man who had mastered the art of survival in a hostile country. Born in Jerusalem, he had been weaned on firearms. By ten he could take a rifle apart and put it together in a matter of minutes. And like all Israelis, he had buried his share of dead. He had seen friends maimed, and mothers weep. He himself had wept a sea of tears until finally that sea dried up. He had no tears left. Now, the only way he could discharge his anguish was at the end of a rifle. But his years of bloodletting had sickened him to killing. And at forty-one his desire was no more toward revenge, but to the survival of Israel. All his work in the Zionist Underground was toward that end. He hoped this alliance with the ISS was the beginning of other worldwide alliances. To Iliab, more was riding on this mission than the rescue of two American women.

Iliab stopped and sipped from his flask. Nathan carried his own, and he also took a drink. "You know something, Nathan, I'm tired," Iliab said, speaking Hebrew for the first time in almost two days. "I'm tired of the fight." He smiled at the look of surprise on his companion's face. "Maybe I'm just getting old."

But hours later, it was Nathan who was feeling old, as he and Iliab picked their way through the rough terrain, in the dark. Iliab, who was in superb physical condition, didn't seem tired at all.

"I must rest," Nathan whispered. Immediately, Iliab put his

hand over his companion's mouth. They were near the outskirts of Bozrom, and sentries were posted all around. In the Bab el Wad one man could be a foot away from another and remain undetected. Speaking was dangerous. Communications would have to be made by gestures or by whispering directly into the ear. Nathan nodded in understanding, and Iliab released his mouth. They rested awhile against the rocks. Even from where they stood, shouts and angry cries could be heard, twirling upward in the night breeze. And periodically, a rifle fired into the air. It was obvious that the bodies of the dead guards had been found and that the village men were whipping up their courage and their wrath. Iliab gestured to Nathan to continue. They would have to reach the women before the fedayeen took action. The cave was nearby, Iliab was certain, as he studied the terrain in the moonlight. In spite of the poor visibility, he was still able to follow the path he had memorized earlier.

Finally, the pair crept stealthily into a cave. It was impossible to see in the utter darkness. But Iliab could not use a torch for fear that light shining from the cave would attract the fedayeen sentries. Fumbling in his pocket, the scarred-face man found his book of matches. He broke off a stick and lit it. The radius of light was extremely small, being about two feet in diameter, and dwindled rapidly as the fire burned down the stem. But there was enough time and enough light for Iliab to determine that the ledge where he had left the women was only about a yard to the right. He took a few steps in that direction, then lit another match. "Miss O'Brien," he said softly. "It is Iliab." The match went out. There was no answer. Not even the sound of breathing could be heard overhead. Iliab struck another match. "Miss O'Brien! You must come quickly! There is great danger here!" Suddenly, a face peered over the ledge, and before the match went out, Iliab recognized the beautiful, dark haired engineer.

"Leave the tin of water. It is too cumbersome to carry," he said, relieved the women were safe. "Throw down the bags of food. Then Nathan and I will assist you in getting off the ledge. But quickly, ladies. You must move quickly!"

Tisha tossed over the food bags. "There's a slight problem," she murmured. "It's Audra. She's unconscious."

"What has happened?" Iliab asked, his voice tense from this new danger.

"She became hysterical," Tisha answered over the ledge, "and began gulping vodka. I tried to stop her. I told her you would be back, that we must have clear heads. But she became even more irrational. She said she was going to leave on her own. That you were never coming back. I could not let her wander around by herself. We struggled in the dark. She knocked her head against a rock. I'm sorry, I know this makes things more difficult."

"What is done, is done. There is no time for apologies. Quickly! You must roll Miss Shields off the ledge," said Iliab. "We will catch her."

With great difficulty, Tisha managed to maneuver the limp body to the edge, and after saying a quick prayer, she rolled Audra off the stone shelf into the darkness and hopefully into four waiting arms. There was a slight groan as Audra's legs struck Nathan in the face, but even in the pitch black, the men managed to keep the unconscious metallurgist from landing on the ground.

"She is alright," Iliab said as they gently laid Audra down. "We have her. Now you must lower yourself over the ledge, feet first. We will catch you. Have no fear."

Again, Tisha was quick to obey. The danger was great and every minute valuable. As she hung from the ledge, she could feel the hands of the two men grope for her. Once they had a good grasp, she let go, and in seconds found herself standing next to them.

"Gather the food bags," the scarred Israeli instructed as he lit another match.

Nathan and Tisha crouched on the ground and began searching in the dark with their hands. They were able to retrieve all but one. It had burst upon landing and its contents were scattered all over the dirt floor.

Iliab struck another match to find Audra's reclining body,

then moved closer to it. After the light went out, he stooped down and felt for the unconscious woman's arm. Pulling slightly on it, he slipped one of his own arms around her torso, and lifting her into the air, deposited her, like a sack of grain, over his shoulder.

"Hold on to me," he ordered both of his companions. "We must move together." Slowly, the three inched toward the faint glow that marked the entrance, holding onto one another until they were out of the cave.

The moonlight seemed bright in comparison to the darkness of the cave. Even so, the path was difficult and treacherous. At times it became so narrow the trio had to pass single file. Progress was measured in inches, and inspired great fatigue. They rested a moment against the rocks, but this lull was fractured by voices overhead. Instantly, they shoved themselves into a crevice between two boulders.

"May Allah choke me with my own spit if I don't kill the scum!" said a loud, angry voice. A small group of villagers had gathered and one of the more zealous was talking to the fedayeen who had been positioned on the cliff as a guard.

"Yes, word was passed earlier to be on the lookout, that the women have escaped. By the Prophet! I pray it will be my bullets that bring down those daughters of a camel!" It was the guard, and Iliab recognized the voice as belonging to the young Moslem who first inspected his rifle in the square. Apparently he had taken his place at guard duty before the bodies of Nabil and Mustafa were discovered. He was hungry for more details.

"We are sure there are others," added the zealous villager.

"Others? But who could they be?" questioned the guard. "None entered our village that was unknown."

"Surely you can not believe that two frail, American women could overpower and kill our glorious fedayeen?"

"No...no of course not. Impossible!" lied the guard. The prospect had indeed occurred to him. "Why, it would take five such women to equal even one of our females. And everyone knows that even one of our women, even if she is a fedayeen herself, is not equal to any of our males. Absurd! Impossible! But...But who then assisted these women in their crime?"

"We are not sure. It is possible...but we are not sure...that Izzat's two guards had a hand in it."

"Izzat?" returned the young Arab. "The gold peddler?"

"Yes," answered the village spokesman.

"But I myself spent much time with his guards. We smoked the pipe together. I inspected one of their rifles. We cursed the dirty Jew. No...I do not believe these are the ones."

"We found a new leather harness in Mustafa's house. Someone remembers seeing one of these men purchase such a harness from the leather merchant."

The young guard shook his head in disbelief. "Can it be? But they... ." The guard stopped as the village spokesman began eyeing him suspiciously. To defend Izzat's men any longer would be risky. Comfort and safety were found within the walls of conformity. So even though he remained unconvinced, he began shouting, "Yes...of course...the deceiving pigs! They were the ones! May Allah blind them! May Allah make their flesh rot! May buzzards eat their carcasses!" Then the young guard spat viciously on the ground.

The spokesman nodded his approval. "Be alert," he commanded. "And may Allah give you the eyes of an owl to see into the night and bring down the traitors."

"Allah Akbar!" screamed the young guard, waving his rifle in the air. Then the group of villagers moved onward, themselves screaming and waving their weapons.

When they were out of ear shot, Iliab gestured instructions to Nathan. Immediately, Nathan rested his rifle against the large boulder, removed the dagger from his sheath, and disappeared. Tisha knew the nature of Nathan's errand. The position of the guard overhead made it impossible for them to progress any further undetected. She listened for any signs of alarm. All was quiet except for the distant trailing voices of the villagers moving from one check point to another. Suddenly there was the sound of footsteps and small pebbles being accidentally kicked in the dark, then scuffling noises. After awhile, Nathan stood before them, his face locked in pain. With his knife he began cutting cloth off the bottom of his shirt and stuffing it into the area by his left underarm. His entire left side was soaked with blood.

"Is it bad?" Iliab asked, his voice void of emotion.

"Yes...I think it is serious," Nathan returned with a grimace. Nathan had not taken the guard by surprise. Just as he was about to strike, he had lost his footing on the rough terrain. Instead of a quick, clean kill, a scuffle had ensued. In the end, Nathan did get his man, but not without a price. He was certain his left lung was pierced. Breathing was extremely painful.

"She will dress it for you," Iliab said, nodding to Tisha.

"No...it is no use," Nathan returned weakly. "Go. I will cover your back. If anyone follows, I will stop them."

"No!" returned Iliab in a harsh whisper, as his feelings finally worked their way to the surface. "I will not leave you."

"So, we all die. How foolish! And what of the mission? Remember, there is much at stake."

In the moonlight Tisha could see glistening tears in Iliab's eyes as the truth of Nathan's words tore at his heart. "Then...it is good-bye my friend," he said softly. "I shall miss you."

With great effort the injured man picked up his rifle and propped himself against the boulder. He was protected on three sides. The open side faced the pathway and offered him a good view. From here, he could stop anyone who tried to follow his companions. "I have loved you like a brother," Nathan returned. "Farewell."

For three hours Iliab labored under the burden of Audra's limp body and his own heavy heart. Progress was much slower than he had hoped. Finally, in utter exhaustion, he searched out a suitable cave. They needed rest. It was while helping to settle the women that he heard a faint, far away sound coming from the direction of Bozrom.

"What is it?" Tisha whispered, sensing something wrong.

"Rifle fire," he returned dully. And the two stood by the cave entrance listening until finally the popping noise stopped and all was quiet again. And both knew that Nathan Yehuda was dead.

"Get away from me!" shrieked Audra Shields, her voice high pitched, hysterical. The blond, matted hair seemed glued around her dirt-smudged face. She was pointing to something neither Iliab nor Tisha could see. But by the look on Audra's face, it had to be something horrible; this image that slithered around in her mind.

"Keep it away from me," she whined, diving into Tisha's arms and burying her head into the engineer's shoulder.

"It's gone," Tisha answered softly.

"You said that before, but it keeps coming back."

"It won't if you sleep," Tisha responded, as she led the disheveled blond to the rear of their small cave. "Lie down and rest."

Audra nodded her head dutifully. Large drops of perspiration streamed from her face. "I'm cold," she whimpered. Although the heat of the day had begun to make the interior of the cave feel like one of Bozrom's communal ovens, the blond metallurgist began to shake. Her teeth chattered and knocked against each another. Tisha removed the black dress Nathan had given her, and covered Audra with it. She knew she would have to guard against shock.

Iliab walked over to the women. There was a curious look on his face, a mixture of both concern and disgust. "Will she be all right?" he asked. He knew Audra had delirium tremens or the DTs. She had been without alcohol for twenty-four hours. He knew all about the drinking from Tisha.

The beautiful engineer pushed her hair from her face as she watched Audra convulse. "I don't know. If she goes into shock we could lose her."

"What does she need?" Iliab growled. "Besides a drink?"

"She needs a sedative, and she needs to be kept warm."

Iliab removed the pipe and small bag of hashish from his

shirt. He always carried this when he was on a mission posing as an Arab. It was not for personal use. But rather, it was invaluable as a bribe, or to loosen a stranger's tongue. Skillfully, he filled and lit it, then handed it to Tisha. "Make her take several puffs of this," he ordered. Then he removed his shirt. Across his chest were stripes of wide scars, made by the lashes of a whip. There were other scars too, all over his back and sides, as though small patches of skin had been cut off and were now replaced by scar tissue. These were the souvenirs from an Arab prison. "Use this. It will help keep her warm."

Tisha smiled. "Thank you, Iliab."

There was an agitated look on her defender's face. "Are all American women as spoiled and self-indulgent as that one?" he finally asked crossly.

Tisha looked away. She knew what he was thinking; that Nathan had given his life to rescue two self-centered Americans. For although Iliab had not said it, Tisha was sure that in his mind he had included her with Audra.

"Make sure she is ready to travel by nightfall!" he growled, taking up his rifle and moving once again toward his post by the cave entrance.

"Iliab," Tisha said softly. The scarred man turned towards her. "I'm sorry about Nathan."

They were traveling by moonlight again. Day travel was too dangerous. They couldn't take the chance of being spotted by any of the fedayeen patrols that were scouting the wadi for them. Tisha struggled trying to help Audra maneuver over the dark, rocky path. The dust of the wadi seemed to line her mouth like a carpet. They were on water rations. No one had thought to take Nathan's flask. Now they only had Iliab's; one goatskin flagon of water for three people. Already too much of it had been used. During the worst of Audra's DTs Tisha had persuaded Iliab to give the metallurgist extra helpings. Although they were only about ten miles from where Joshua and his friends waited with fresh supplies, it would take another two days to reach them. The terrain made traveling slow. Sometimes, because of the nature of the Bab el Wad, they went backward, then forward, then backward in a zigzag pattern. It could take hours just to move forward one mile. Somehow, they had to make their water last. There would be enough food, although only handfuls of it were doled out at a time. It was rationed too. But water, that was the real problem.

"I'm so thirsty! I need a drink!" came the whiny voice of Audra Shields. The danger of shock had passed. Iliab had periodically given her small amounts of hashish. Being a narcotic, it had a soothing effect. But she remained ill-tempered and demanding. "I won't go another step unless I get some water!"

Iliab's gnarled hand covered the blond's mouth. "Quiet!" he whispered. Then he released his grip. "You must *never* speak out loud when we travel. There is great danger all around us. I have warned you of this! Why are you such a foolish woman?" Although Iliab spoke in a whisper, his words were sharp, stern.

"I'm thirsty!" Audra said, voice lower, but still whiny.

Slowly, Iliab unfastened the goatskin flask that hung by his waist. He removed the stopper, took a small sip and handed it to Tisha.

"What about me! I'm the one who's thirsty! I asked first!" Audra's voice was rising again.

Tisha looked at the flask, then at Audra. She was about to hand it to her when Iliab stopped her. "No! *You* drink. One sip, like I took." Tisha obeyed, then returned the flagon to Iliab.

"What about me!" Audra wailed.

"We must ration the water. You have already had more than your share today."

"That's not fair! I'm the one who asked for the water! Then both of you get a drink and I don't!" Her voice was starting to blare.

Iliab's hand formed a tight fist. "If you speak loudly again," he whispered, shoving his fist in front of Audra's face, "I will not hesitate to silence you."

Audra's eyes blazed with hatred, but her mouth closed tightly. And for the remainder of the night she did not utter another sound. Instinctively, she knew that Iliab Nahshon was a man of his word.

Just before sunrise the scarred guide found another cave. They stayed there during the entire day; dozing, eating their ration of dried grain, discussing the journey ahead.

There was only enough hashish left for one more pipe. Audra nursed it throughout the day; lighting, smoking, smothering the light, relighting. She even managed to have a little left at the end of the day. She was less shaky now, and aside from the partial stupor caused by the narcotic, seemed somewhat more coherent than she had been since Mustafa had begun giving her the vodka. She didn't whine as much, and even began to exhibit some spark of her former intelligence. When Iliab told her it was time to move, Audra did so without complaint. The sore spot was still water. They were only allowed two small sips each for the entire day, and one small sip during their travel at night.

"The fedayeen still search for us," Iliab said, calmly slinging his rifle over his shoulder. The women had already gathered up the small goatskin sacks which contained their food and tied them to their belts. The cave was black now, and the three stood by the mouth waiting for the last trace of sun to disappear over the horizon. Soon they would be trekking through the Bab el Wad in the dark; a dangerous experience at best. The trailing fedayeen made their journey even more perilous.

"How far away are they? " Tisha asked.

"A day perhaps, guessing from their dust." It was Iliab's practice to spend part of the daylight hours scouting. "It is only a small group of about four or five. But there are probably a dozen such groups all over the wadi. They travel by day and are able to cover more ground than we are. But unless we are very careless, we can escape detection. They cannot see us in the dark."

That night the three pushed harder than they had ever

pushed before. The thought of the trailing Bozrom citizens kept them going at a remarkable pace. It was not without incident, however. The Bab el Wad was treacherous with its jagged rocks and deep ravines. Sometimes the trail was only a narrow ledge. Sometimes there was no trail at all, and ground was covered by crawling over boulders. Night travel would have been impossible if it were not for the full moon. But even with that illumination, every step was one of chance and danger. It was while rounding one of those narrow ledges that Audra lost her footing and fell nearly ten feet into a chasm. Retrieving her was difficult, and valuable time was lost. After that, Audra limped when she walked and she began whining again. "It hurts! I can't walk! Don't go so fast!" she would say over and over in a whisper until finally Iliab threatened to leave her behind. For the next three hours Audra traveled in silence. But by the time Iliab began looking for a cave, her ankle was swollen to twice its size, and she began dragging that foot as she leaned on Tisha more and more for support.

At daybreak they were in their new cave. Iliab discovered, after he scouted ahead, that they were not as close to where Joshua Chapman and his friends stood vigil as they should be. If they did not reach this group by next dawn, Chapman had orders to pull out.

Joshua had a cart with which to transport the women, a fresh horse for Iliab, food, and...water. Once Chapman left, Iliab and the women would be completely on their own. Alone, Iliab would have a slim chance of survival. With two females to take care of, there was no chance at all. Their predicament would make day travel a necessity.

"Sleep now," ordered the scarred guide as the two women settled into the cave. "In a few hours we must travel again."

Audra rubbed her ankle. "I can't sleep," she whimpered. "The pain is killing me."

"Here. It is the last of it," Iliab said, handing her the pipe. "Maybe it will help a little."

Audra had smoked most of the hashish in the last two caves and was aware of how precious little remained. There was less than a third of the pipe left. Still, she was grateful for it. "I can't stand much more of this!" she said, after taking a long, first drag. The ordeal of the last few days, coupled with the nightmarish memories of Nabil and Mustafa had brought Audra near the breaking point. "I can't stand much more!" she repeated, her voice getting louder.

"Hush," Iliab responded. "Keep it down!"

"I'm sick of you telling me what to do!" continued Audra in a whiny tone.

"You have come this far only because you have done what I have told you."

"Well, who asked you to come! I'm sick of the lot of you. You're all alike! The only thing you know how to do is bully everyone, or kill and kill!" Audra was near hysteria.

"Perhaps. But if I had not come, sooner or later they would have killed you, Miss Shields." Iliab now stood over the hysterical blond.

"Kill! Kill! Kill! That's what I could do now, just kill someone! I could kill you, Iliab, if you're not careful!" Audra's voice was loud and booming, and seemed like the awesome noise of a cannon bludgeoning the silent wadi.

"What? Stop that! Let go! What...what are you... ." Then Audra's voice was suddenly stilled.

"Did you hurt her?" Tisha asked, worriedly, as she looked down at Audra's limp body.

"No. She is only unconscious. I had to...quiet her down."

"What did you do?"

"Pressure points."

Tisha sat down on the floor of the cave next to Audra's sprawled body. "I'm sorry," she said.

"Why are *you* sorry?"

"Because you've risked your life, and lost your friend, and have received little help or gratitude from us."

Iliab chuckled softly. "It's my trade, my job as you say. I suppose I am no longer suited for anything else. My heart has been seared by Israel's continual conflicts. It is hard now, embittered. In that respect your friend is right. Killing is all I know."

"You forget I was with you when Nathan died."

"I have only pieces of a heart left. But yes...even pieces can hurt. This is the price of a mission. Perhaps it will be worth it if we succeed."

"And will we? Will we succeed?" questioned Tisha absently, as though she was talking to herself.

"Can anyone know such a thing?" returned Iliab.

The beautiful dark haired engineer rested against the cave wall. "Yes," she said softly. "God knows."

Mike sat on a patch of grass, resting his back against the hard, smooth boulder. He listened to the distant sound of pounding waves. This was the spot where he and Tisha sat after Renee's death. He had felt very close to Tisha that night. Her absence now was sorely felt. He could no longer endure Meyers and the ISS at Everman, so he had come to Gibs Town. Surprisingly, even in the face of the present adversity, substantial progress on the P2 mockup was being made. After realizing that he wasn't need, Mike decided to slip away for the afternoon to this quiet spot.

He felt terribly alone. Even Buck was far away, somewhere over the Middle East, heading for a secret Zionist landing strip. If the rescue was successful, Buck would fly the women back. Flight plans and rendezvous points had been furnished by the Underground and cleared by the ISS. Still, it was a civilian who had to go. The ISS was not ready to publicly show a partnership with the Underground.

Mike had wanted to be the one flying that plane, but he had been overruled by Meyers. The P2 project had first priority, he was told. A fusion powered airplane had tactical applications, and the government was keenly interested. Buck had also volunteered, and being more expendable that Michael Patterson, he was chosen. It had sickened Mike, the whole rotten mess. No getting away from it, everyone was looking out for his own interests. But while Pete

Meyers and the government were covering their own backsides, Mike stood to lose, not only the woman he loved, but his best friend as well.

He had never felt so isolated and forlorn. Slowly, he pulled out a black, pocket Bible from his shirt. It had been important to Tisha. Carrying it around somehow made him feel closer to her. Stuffed between the pages was a poem of Joshua's which Tisha had used as a bookmark and forgotten when she gave Mike the Bible. He began reading it:

> What is the praise of men
> But grains of sand that shift
> With every passing breeze,
> To form small, barren mounds,
> First here, then there.

Everything he had ever worked for seemed so unimportant. Even the P2 somehow seemed insignificant. Angrily, he ripped up the paper and let the wind carry it like confetti. "Here is your parade! Here are your accolades!" he shouted to the wind. Then wearily, he dropped his head onto his chest. Everything that really mattered had been taken from him, held hostage and perhaps...killed. He thought of what Mrs. O'Brien had said. *Nothing was impossible with God.* She made having faith sound so easy. But it wasn't so easy. Not for him. *Just the sincere cry of a longing soul,* that's what she had said, that's what it took. "Oh God, why!" he suddenly wailed. "Why did You allow this to happen to the only woman I've ever loved?" Suddenly, he began to laugh a cruel, harsh laugh. "Or are You even real? Are You?" With that, he opened the pocket Bible and began shaking his fist. "I swear," he said, looking upward to heaven, "I will not leave this spot until I find out!"

"Wake up! Come on! Wake up!" said Iliab shaking the two women at the same time. Tisha and Audra had been lying near each other asleep on the cave floor. Tisha sat up immediately.

"I have scouted our position," Iliab continued, his voice tense, his speech more rapid than usual. "We are still being followed by a patrol. I saw four men. They are perhaps only an hour away. Also, there has been a great rock slide. The pathway I had hoped to take is blocked. In order to reach Chapman we must scale a very steep incline. We could never undertake it in the dark. Now we must travel by day, even though we will be easier to spot. The remainder of our journey will be dangerous on all counts. And *she* will hold us up." Iliab gestured toward the sleepy metallurgist who had just risen to a sitting position, and was rubbing her face.

"My ankle," she moaned as she became more alert. "I don't think I can walk." At once Iliab rolled up Audra's left pants' leg and inspected the injury.

"Ouch! Stop pressing on it! Can't you see it's swollen!"

The scarred man quickly cut off strips of material from his shirt. He had nothing else to use. Unfortunately, the women had discarded the hot black dresses in the last cave. He continued cutting until he had four long pieces. These he tied together. Then he began wrapping the fabric firmly around Audra's swollen ankle. Audra moaned as he worked. While she watched him a sudden, foggy memory became lucid.

"Hey...what did you do before? You did something... ."

"I rendered you unconscious. A pressure point technique. You were getting too loud."

Audra eyed him suspiciously. "And if the pressure point didn't work, you would have belted me one, wouldn't you? Well, wouldn't you?"

"Stop it, Audra," Tisha said. "Iliab is not your enemy. He's doing everything in his power to help us."

"Shut up you prig!" Audra's eyes were wide, maniacal, as though she was remembering how day after day Mustafa had called her and not Tisha into his office.

Suddenly, Iliab's gnarled hand grabbed Audra's shoulder. "Get control of yourself! If you lose it, so help me I will knock you out again and leave you! There is an armed patrol on our heels, not even an hour away. The terrain we must cover today is the most difficult yet. Eat something. And either be ready to go in five minutes or we leave without you!"

The disheveled blond compressed her dry cracked lips into a thin line as she unfastened the grain bag at her waist. She took a handful and after only a few seconds, spit it on the ground. "I'm thirsty! How can I eat when I'm so thirsty? There's not enough moisture in my mouth to even swallow the food!"

Nahshon moved menacingly towards her. As he reached for Audra, Tisha grabbed his arm. "Please, Iliab. Give her my water."

"No!" he spat as though there was fire in his mouth and he burned with anger. "She will not drag us down. Either she cooperates or by God...I will kill her myself."

Audra recoiled in terror against the cave wall. A part of her wanted to let go, to scream hysterically, to make him kill her; to put her out of her misery. But she was afraid he would only render her unconscious again, and she would be left to die a slow death of starvation and dehydration, or if the fedayeen found her...even worse. With every ounce of inner strength she could muster, Audra tried to tie together the raveled ends of her nerves. "It's okay, I don't want your ration, Tisha," she blurted. "I'm alright now. Really I am."

Iliab studied her, not even trying to conceal his doubt. "Let's move," he finally said. But somehow, Audra knew he would continue to watch her.

Four long and painful hours later, the weary blond stood by a steep jagged drop thinking that perhaps she should just throw herself off and be done with it. The pain in her ankle was unbearable. It seemed to radiate throughout her entire body, making her feel weak and nauseous. She could think of nothing else. Now she was faced with the necessity of scaling down the side of this rugged bluff. Tisha and Iliab had helped support her when she walked the path, but now even that would be impossible. It would be every man for himself. She did not see how she could make it. It was hopeless. She felt utterly defeated. She had even lost the desire to try to hold herself together. It would be so easy to just sail through the air and land with a thud on the jagged rocks below...mercifully dead. As Audra looked down, she became almost mesmerized by the view. Then suddenly she saw a pair of tan, desert boots take a step toward her and stop.

"You can do this if you want to," Iliab said, his voice reassuring. "It will be difficult, but you can manage it."

Audra said nothing, but only stared at his boots. For some reason, she couldn't take her eyes off them.

"Miss Shields, we must start now. I will go first, then you, then Miss O'Brien. You will go between us. We will help you as much as we can."

Still Audra did not move but remained staring. "Tan boots!" she finally blurted. "He wore tan boots! The man who kidnapped me!"

Iliab eyed her nervously. In a few minutes they would be hanging over the precipice. If Audra went hysterical then, it would mean disaster. She could pull both him and Tisha down with her. "We must go!" he said sharply, wondering if it would be better to leave her.

"You don't understand," Audra began babbling. "Tan work-boots! I know who kidnapped me. It was Bubba Hanagan!"

"You will have time to deal with you kidnaper later. Now concentrate on the task before you!" Iliab snapped. His hand moved for his dagger. After leaving the cave, he had decided that should it become necessary to abandon Audra, he would kill her first. To leave her to the vengeance of the fedayeen would be too cruel.

"Bubba. Bubba Hanagan," Audra mumbled over and over again, unaware of Iliab's intent. Each time she said the name, a new surge of hate filled her heart. He was the one responsible for those weeks of degradation in Bozrom. He was responsible for the nights spent sleeping in dark, scary caves, for eating out of goatskin sacks like an animal, for trudging over this hostile, rough wadi, for her terrible thirst, for her painful swollen ankle, and now, for having to dive off this cliff in the hope of putting herself out of her misery. Bubba...Bubba Hanagan! How she hated him! How she despised him!

"Iliab!" The sound of Tisha's frightened voice suddenly jolted Audra to her senses. She saw the scarred Israeli standing before her holding his dagger. She knew he was about to kill her.

"Please don't do it," Audra found herself saying. A moment ago she would have welcomed Iliab's plan. But the adrenaline of hate had pumped her up, revitalized her, and suddenly she wanted to live. "I'm all right," she insisted. "I can make it. I know I can!" The desire to live was strong now. How else could she kill the one responsible for all her problems? How else could she kill Bubba Hanagan?

Iliab's dagger moved toward Audra's throat. He hesitated. Bringing both women back alive would be more advantageous to his purpose. He wanted the ISS as grateful as possible. But the blond was a risk; perhaps too much of a risk. He studied her eyes. He was experienced enough to recognize this new driving force of hatred behind them. Yes...hate was strong enough to see her through. "Okay," he said, quickly replacing his dagger. "I will go over first. Give me two minutes, then follow."

The metallurgist nodded. "I'll be right behind you."

The descent was agonizingly slow. Once, Audra stopped and just cried with pain. She needed to use her leg with the bad ankle for balance. Often times it would have to support her entire weight as the other foot probed the rocks for the next safe foothold. Many times both Tisha and Iliab feared Audra would give up, but after a few minutes, Audra's good foot would begin probing again, and the group moved further down the incline. The jagged rocks ripped their skin and clothing as they went. But they were pressed for time and periodically Iliab would urge them to move faster.

Iliab was the first to reach level ground. Immediately, he removed the rifle from his shoulder and positioned himself behind a small boulder. He knew the patrol was not far behind, and he must be ready to defend their position.

And just as he feared, minutes later he spotted four men at

the top of the ridge. He opened fire at once, hoping to draw attention away from the women who were vulnerable and exposed as they maneuvered the last several feet of the crag. The noise, like popping fire crackers, exploded in the air and shattered the tranquillity of the wadi. Then the four men began returning Iliab's fire.

A bullet grazed a large rock next to Tisha and sent a tiny, stone chip, as sharp as a razor, cutting into her left hand. The wound was superficial, but large and bloody. As she wiped the injured hand against her blue jeans, Tisha saw a body fly past her and released an involuntary scream. It was one of the fedayeen. Iliab was an expert marksman. By the time the women reached level ground, another body had fallen. Now, there were only two fedayeen left, and in order for them to reach Iliab and the women, they would have to scale this same precipice.

To the side of the boulder where Iliab crouched was a path that cut between the mountain. It was fairly smooth and level, and would be easy traveling. At the end of the path waited Chapman and his men, food and water. Iliab was certain he could reach Chapman before the two Arabs were able to scale the bluff. But there were other patrols who undoubtedly heard the rifle fire and would also come. Iliab knew that meant someone had to stay behind when Chapman and the women left.

He looked over at the two women sitting against the boulder. Audra's cracked lips were bleeding. Her body was covered with cuts and gashes where the rocks had nicked out her flesh. Her silk blouse was shredded. Large tears streamed down white, talc cheeks. She was clutching her left ankle and moaning softly. The climb had all but finished her. Tisha sat beside her, her lips also cracked and bleeding; her body equally bruised and torn; her left hand caked with dried blood.

"Eat a handful of seeds," commanded Iliab. "You need to build your strength."

Tisha looked at the scarred man and shook her head. "We can't...our mouths...we will choke."

The guide nodded in understanding. "Come on! If you

226

don't want to eat, then we march!" he whispered gruffly. He could not afford to be soft. If he did not drive them, they would die. "Up! Get to your feet!"

Audra began to sob. But when she looked at Iliab's boots, her face hardened. She wiped her cheeks with the back of her hands, and with Tisha's help, slowly rose to her feet. She leaned heavily on the engineer's shoulder as she moved one foot in front of the other.

"Come on! Come on!" snapped Iliab sharply. And throughout their journey on the path, he drove them like cattle, whipping them with his tongue. "Faster! Move!"

"I hate you! I hate you!" Audra blurted, choking on her pain. Her ankle throbbed relentlessly.

"I'm not concerned with your feelings, Miss Shields," Iliab returned. "So, do not waste your energy on such useless words. Now...move...quickly...quickly!"

And so it went, until they were almost at the end of the path. It was Tisha who spotted the cart first, nestled between two boulders like a giant cradle; inviting, safe. Next to the cart, a group of horses were tied together. It was a welcomed sight except for the rifle barrels that dotted the periphery of each boulder and were pointed menacingly toward them. "Praise God!" Tisha shouted.

As soon as the trio was recognized, Chapman and his men were all over them, half carrying, half dragging the women to the cart; laughing and congratulating Iliab as they went. For Tisha, there were added displays of affection from Chapman as he hugged and kissed her. Both wept for joy as they clung to one another.

"Where is Nathan?" inquired Chapman, realizing for the first time someone was missing.

"He did not make it," Iliab replied, revealing only the slightest emotion. But for a time, the laughter and talking ceased.

Both women, in turn, guzzled water from the goatskin bag that Ben Cohen gave them. "Easy. Take it easy. There's more." He looked older, tougher than the last time Tisha saw him. It wasn't that long ago, yet it felt like a hundred years. A lot could happen in

227

a hundred years. "Take it easy," he repeated laughingly, then smiled broadly at Tisha. He had three teeth missing. In one of his raids, they had been knocked out by a rifle butt.

Iliab took the water bag from Cohen and swallowed only a few mouthfuls. Then he motioned with his head and the men followed him away from the cart.

He told them of the two fedayeen who were still in pursuit. He also shared his fear that other groups of fedayeen in the area were on their way. He told them that someone must stay behind to buy time for the slow moving cart. Once it had a good lead, the fedayeen wouldn't be able to catch up on foot. They discussed the possibility of them all staying and fighting it out. But Iliab feared there might be several patrols in the area, drastically outnumbering their own little group. If they all stayed, it was possible that none of them would get out alive. The decision was unanimous. Only one would stay behind and buy time for the others. Iliab said he would be the one.

"No! I will stay. It must be me," came the voice of Solomon Roth as it rose over the other intonations. "I would like to help these women...for my sister. Somehow...it would make things right." His eyes were locked passionately onto Iliab's. "We can't spare you, while I... ." He stopped and laughed sardonically. "I can best serve the cause here."

"Sol is right, we can't lose you, Iliab. You're too valuable. You must complete negotiations with the ISS. You must go and I will stay with Sol," David Rosen said.

"We do not have time to argue," returned Iliab.

"Then it's settled. Sol and I will stay."

"No!" Iliab snapped. "Am I to lose two good men!"

"Iliab is right," Solomon Roth said, clasping his friends on their shoulders. "You should go now. The sooner the better."

Tisha wept as the cart pulled away and Solomon Roth positioned himself and his rifle by the boulder.

"If we travel all day and night," Iliab said, riding on his horse along side the cart, refusing to look back, "we can reach the place where the Underground awaits you. You are almost home."

"Yes, but at such a great price!" Tisha said.

"In this world, everything must be paid for, one way or another," returned Nahshon dryly. Then he rode off ahead of the cart.

Twenty minutes later they heard a pop-pop noise coming from the direction of where they had left Solomon Roth. The popping sound continued for almost a half hour. But the cadence varied, alternating between a string of rapid pops to singular sporadic ones. It was often difficult to hear over the rattle of the cart wheels, and more than once Tisha thought the shooting had stopped. Then she would hear the noise again: pop-pop, pop-pop-pop-pop.

Finally, Iliab rode up beside her. "The shooting has stopped," he said matter-of-factly.

"You heard it too," Tisha returned, answering rather than asking a question. No one had seemed to pay any attention to the noise, and she had wondered if they were listening as she was.

"Yes. And by the sound of it, he put up a terrific fight. We will stay here for a moment." With that he signaled Joshua to stop the cart.

Audra, who had slept through the entire gun battle, suddenly awoke. "What...what's going on?" she inquired sleepily. "Why have we stopped?"

"To say 'good-bye' to a friend," Iliab returned.

The blond dropped wearily into the cart. "Oh...," she said and drifted back to sleep.

Long after the cart began moving again, Tisha continued staring into the distant Bab el Wad. She had been ripped from her friends, her home, her country, and subjected to days and nights of great uncertainty. She had seen her co-worker humiliated and abused; had escaped at great risk and peril. Two men had paid with their lives to free her. It was a bitter scenario, one that inspired bitter feelings. She knew she must fight it; hose down those smoldering embers. If she toyed with it, like a child with matches, the match could strike and ignite a fire of hatred in her heart. "Oh God," she prayed softly, "help me to forgive."

Twelve

Mike Patterson stared in disbelief at the ISS agent. "Tafco Oil was behind the kidnappings?" he blurted. Then he began to pace, back and forth, trying to control his anger. How was it possible that someone he knew, that someone his father had known, that someone who held a trusted position on the Board of Patterson Aviation could have authorized such a heinous act? He had never trusted Gunther, but could he capable of this? "Tafco Oil?" Mike repeated.

Boyish looking Peter Meyers chopped his nails feverishly with his metal clippers. "That's what Joshua Chapman said in his dispatch."

"How reliable are his sources?" asked Tisha, outwardly appearing calm, but inwardly she too was seething with anger. It had been six days since she left Solomon Roth in the Bab el Wad. The remainder of the trip to safety, and the days that followed were, for Tisha, almost as much of a blur as her initial abduction. Buck had been waiting at the Underground airstrip. There was the flight home. Then came a trip to a giant, gray-green fortress, a military installation of some sort, for a complete physical and a battery of questions and debriefings. And finally, the reunion with Mike.

She had lost ten pounds during her captivity and subsequent escape, and still looked too thin. But color had returned to her face, and her lips no longer bled when she talked. Also, the bruises and scrapes over her body were healing. It had been less than twenty-four hours since Tisha's release from the fortress and she was now staying at a small Everman motel under heavy ISS security. She had fared better than Audra, who had also been released but who was forced by the ISS to check into Everman City Hospital under an assumed name. Further observation was required.

So far, the news of the women's rescue had not been made public. Meyers had only this morning scheduled a press conference for late afternoon. An official ISS statement would be given at that time, along with a brief interview with Tisha O'Brien. Audra would not take part in the news conference. Physically, she was healing nicely, but questions had been raised about her mental stability.

Although Tisha had been given a clean bill of health, all was not well with her either. Resentment and anger continued to rob her of her peace. Since leaving Solomon Roth in the wadi, Tisha could think of nothing but her ordeal and the people responsible. She found it difficult to pray. She was moody and unhappy, and as the Master Potter ever pressed upon His mold, Tisha understood all too clearly Iliab's words. *Everything was bought with a price.* She fingered the ivory colored cross that hung around her neck. God had paid an awesome price for her. He had paid with His Son. If she was to remain true, the price she must pay was surrender to His way. She would have to forgive. She squirmed as she felt His hand press tighter around her heart. Tisha knew God was not going to allow compromise. Sometimes He asked for too much. "Well, how reliable are Joshua's sources?" she repeated.

"Reliable as any bribed information can be," Meyers returned. "Word is that orders came directly from Tafco's concession in Syria. They *paid* the Jihad to kidnap you and Audra."

"Do you know what you're saying?" asked an incredulous Michael Patterson.

"Yes," Meyers returned cautiously, but with authority. "It

means that Gunther or Alex Harner or both were behind the abduction, and probably all the rest of the sabotage aimed at PA. My guess is that they were trying to stop the P2 project. At sixty dollars a barrel of oil, Tafco stood to lose a great deal of future revenue if this plane was developed. As long as the Holy War rages, oil prices will continue to soar. And the war could last for years."

"So, it all boils down to money," Tisha said with a sick expression on her face as she thought of Solomon Roth and Nathan and...Nolan.

"Yes," Meyers answered. "And do you want to know the most incredible part? I think they're going to get away with it."

"What about Joshua? Can't he get you proof?" asked the dark haired engineer almost desperately. Forgiveness was easier if it came with a pound of flesh.

Meyers had decimated his nails and finally put the clippers away. "Nothing that would hold up in court. You must understand this information was bought in a back alley."

Tisha became increasingly more discouraged. All roads led to a dead end. Even the man who had abducted her had not been found, despite her detailed description. He had disappeared without a trace. There were many like him who were hired and transported from out of state to do a particular job. Some would be found dead, months later. Some were never found at all.

"And what about this Hanagan...Bubba Hanagan that Audra claimed kidnapped her?" Tisha pressed, trying to push back the feeling of hopelessness.

"During her debriefing she told us about the incident on the bluff. But she swore she was mistaken; that she had temporarily snapped under the pressure. She claims he's just a former boyfriend who jilted her. That could account for her hostility. But ISS will check him out. And Tisha, we'll also investigate Alex Harner and Gunther. Now, let's go over what you're going to say at the press conference."

Mike watched the beautiful engineer sink broodingly into her chair while Meyers pontificated. He was distressed by what the

ISS agent had said, but his joy at having Tisha back seemed to over-shadow any of these pangs. They had not been alone since her return. He looked forward to the time they could share what had happened. It was as if someone had ripped a page off the calendar, an entire month had been stolen from them. She would have volumes to tell him. He also had much to share with her. He especially wanted to tell her about his night on that grassy spot where he, like Jacob, had wrestled with God, and how also like Jacob, he was changed because of it. Yet he knew that like his experience, her bitter-sweet story could only be shared in part. There would always be fragments, pieces of that month, that could never be fully explained or understood by the other. And in a strange way, that made Mike feel a little sad.

"Look Pete," Mike suddenly blurted. "Can't you let up for one minute? During the last several days Tisha has been prodded, poked, examined, questioned, and grilled. Aside from that, I haven't had one minute alone with her. Come on, what do you say? Give us a half hour?"

"No!" responded Meyers sharply.

Tisha turned and smiled warmly at Mike. She had missed him terribly and had been thrilled beyond measure at seeing him again. Still, their private lives would have to be pushed aside until some of these pressing issues were resolved. But she was both grateful and pleased by his concern.

"When she's facing twenty flashing cameras," Meyers continued, pointing to Tisha with a nubby finger, "she's going to have to know what to say. And I'm going to grill her until she does."

Audra limped slightly as she walked down the corridor of a dilapidated apartment building. She scanned the numbers on the doors as she went. Finally, she saw number twenty-four, and stopped. She had been thinking about this for so long; had planned every detail so carefully. In her mind, she had stood before this door a hundred times. Now it seemed so natural, so easy. For Audra, the past six days had also been a blur. She remembered few details. Indeed, the only one consistent and clear memory of those days was the scenario she was about to enact. This had been the one overriding imagery that had preoccupied her mind. And she had managed to be very clever when the ISS questioned her about Bubba Hanagan. She was not going to allow them to mess things up.

But getting out of Everman City Hospital, undetected, had been difficult. ISS had previously retrieved her clothes and purse from her apartment upon request. But ISS agents were everywhere. Still, she managed it by climbing out a three story window. Audra chuckled to herself as she thought of it. The experience in the Bab el Wad had proven useful after all. She was able to shinny down the drain pipe with ease. After that, she had made one stop to her apartment to pick up the .25 caliber. The ISS had removed the one in her purse before giving it to her. She also picked up the key which she carried in her hand. Now, she took that key and inserted it into the lock. No, the ISS was not going to rob her of her revenge. It was for this that she had managed to survive the descent on the wadi, the long trek on the path between the mountain on an excruciatingly painful ankle. It was for this that her will to live had been restored.

Quickly, she turned the knob, but before opening the door completely, she removed the gun from her handbag. Slowly, she entered the apartment. It was dingy and ill kept, with newspapers and empty snack bags of potato chips, pretzels and the like, littering the floor. He was such a slob, Audra thought with contempt. She moved through the cluttered living room toward the kitchen where a radio blasted a country-western tune. Bubba Hanagan stood by the counter making himself a ham sandwich and singing off key. "Oh little darlin' I knowed you'd leave me some day-a."

"Your little darlin' has returned," said Audra with a sneer. The .25 caliber was pointed directly at his face. She knew what a bullet could do to human flesh. She had seen it in the Bab el Wad.

In one blast it could obliterate a nose, eyes, cheeks, and leave only a bloody indistinguishable pulp in its place. That's what she wanted to do to him.

The massive bulk of Hanagan's body recoiled backward in shock. "How in the world... ?"

"I'm going to kill you, Bubba!" Audra shrieked. Her eyes were wide, fierce. In one blast she was going to erase the memory of her crawling on the goat skin rug, the vodka bottles, the trips to Mustafa's office. They were going to be gone, all gone, wiped away like a bad dream. And she was going to wake up and be Audra Shields again: brilliant, hard working, respected.

Bubba, recovering from the shock of seeing her, straightened his huge frame. "Well hello, momma! Now don't tell me you're still sore because I walked in on you and that dude? You never did forgive me for that. But live and let live, I always say." As he spoke, he began moving slowly towards her.

"Stay where you are! Don't come any closer!"

Hanagan smiled boyishly, trying to disarm her with his charm. "Okay, momma, I'm easy." Even so, he continued moving.

"I'm warning you... ." Audra's hand began to shake. There was a crackling noise as the gun went off. The bullet grazed Bubba's shoulder. But still he kept coming. Audra had time to squeeze off one more shot. This time the bullet lodged in Hanagan's left biceps. He winced with pain. Then suddenly his muscular right arm swung away from his chest, back-handing her, and knocking her to the ground. The gun flew out of her hand and onto the floor several feet away. Picking up a metal kitchen chair, Hanagan smashed it across Audra's body, and she went blank.

"Look, Gunther, I need some money and I need it now!"

Audra opened her eyes and saw the blurred figure of a man talking on the telephone. When she tried to move she almost blacked out again from the pain. Breathing was excruciatingly difficult. She felt wet, then realized she was lying in a puddle of her own blood. She remembered the encounter with Hanagan, and knew she was still lying on his kitchen floor. She must have been unconscious for a moment. Obviously, Hanagan thought had he killed her. She dared not move. She closed her eyes and took short, shallow breaths.

"...Don't tell me to keep calm! The cops will be looking for me, not you! And remember, if I fall, I won't fall alone!"

"...You could call it a threat. You owe me."

"...Yeah, I know you paid me for the job. But you told me this bimbo had a one way ticket, that she was never coming back, and the next thing I know she's standing in my kitchen with a gun."

"...Don't you con me. I didn't bargain for this. There's a dead broad in my kitchen, and I need to get out of here quick. I'm just asking you to do right by me. That's all. Just asking for enough cash to get out of town and carry me until this thing blows over."

"...South America? Sure, I'll go there. The further away from here the better. And by the way, I need a doctor to get a slug out."

"...That's right, she shot me."

"...No, I'll live, but I don't want to travel with this bullet."

"...Okay. I'll meet you in the usual place in thirty minutes. And Gunther...thanks. I knew you'd come through."

The pain made Audra lightheaded, and for a moment she blacked out again. When she came to, she heard the noise of drawers slamming as Bubba pulled clothes out of his bedroom dresser. She had heard enough of Hanagan's conversation to know he was preparing to leave town. She held her breath when she heard his footsteps come from the small bedroom off the kitchen and finally stop where she lay. She dared not move a muscle. Her face was partially covered by her right arm. The arm itself was wet with blood and so painful she was sure it was broken. She was lying on her stomach and hoped if she took shallow breaths he would not see her breathing and think she was dead. It was her only hope. Because her eyes were closed, Audra did not see Bubba raise his foot off the ground, but she did feel the tan work boot smash into her ribs. The sudden violent jar to her body caused her to bite into her tongue. Hot, sticky liquid ooze between her lips. Apparently satisfied that he had killed her, the muscular weightlifter walked away, into the dingy living room, and out the front door. Then everything went blank.

"They've just brought Audra Shields to Everman City Hospital!" said an agitated Peter Meyers after he replaced the telephone receiver. He was still in the hotel room with Tisha and Mike. Two hours ago, his agent at the hospital had reported the blond metallurgist missing. Since then, the ISS had raked the city looking for her. But she had completely eluded them. This was the first news they had of her.

"What happened?" Tisha asked, with concern. "Why in the world did she slip out like that?"

"I don't know," Meyers returned. "And she's in no condition to tell us either. She's unconscious, and by the description my man gave, has taken quite a beating. She probably has some broken bones, possibly a concussion, and who knows what internal injuries. My man said she's a bloody mess."

Patterson shot an anxious glance at Tisha. "It's not the Jihad again, is it, Pete?"

"No...I don't think so. She was not abducted. She left the hospital on her own and, for whatever reason, didn't want us to know about it."

"Where did they find her?" Tisha asked somberly.

"Some dumpy apartment building. One of the tenants heard gun shots and called the police. When they arrived, they found the apartment door ajar and Audra on the floor, and no one else."

"Until you know more, I want Tisha to have extra protection," Mike said nervously.

"I'm going to take care of that right now," Meyers returned. "Also, I'm moving the news conference up a few hours, and it will be held at Everman Hospital. I want to talk to the press before this story about Audra gets out."

***

At two o'clock sharp, an unmarked black Cadillac pulled behind Everman City Hospital. From it, stepped Mike, Tisha, and Peter Meyers. They were immediately followed by two heavily armed men in gray suits. A side door of the hospital was opened at once by a man in a white orderly's uniform, but who was, in fact, an ISS agent. The man led the five down the hall, onto a freight elevator used only by hospital personnel, then into a large conference room on the fourth floor.

As the group entered, flash cubes popped like exploding stars, TV cameras whined, and eyes strained to see the heroine who had escaped the tentacles of the Jihad. ISS agents were positioned throughout the conference room. Their eyes continuously scanned for bulging jackets or sudden erratic movements.

"Ladies and gentlemen of the press," rang out the clear, crisp voice of Peter Meyers over the microphone. "I am sure you are all eager to question Miss O'Brien, one of the survivors of a hellish adventure. And, you will have your chance. But first, I would like to open this press conference with a statement. The other survivor of this ghastly kidnapping, Miss Audra Shields, now lies in critical condition right here in this hospital. It appears that another attempt by the Moslem Jihad was made upon her person. When she resisted, she sustained a most brutal and vicious beating. She was left for dead by her would-be abductors and only Providence knows her fate. As you are all aware, we live in perilous times; times of uncertainty and tension. And we of the ISS... ."

"Miss O'Brien! Miss O'Brien, please can we have your comments!" asked Meyers shaking her slightly, somewhat annoyed.

Tisha looked around at the faces in front of her. Her eyes stopped when she saw Mike's worried look, and she smiled reassuringly at him. She had drifted off and had been thinking...thinking of so many things. The reporters had packed the conference room in hopes of hearing a titillating, perhaps graphically gory story of violence and terror. Certainly Meyers had primed them for this. And he had briefed her on what to say. There was not to be the slightest hint of Tafco's involvement. Basically, she was to give them just what they wanted: the trying and agonizing ordeal of the kidnapping, the brutality of her captors, the hardships endured throughout her escape. The beautiful engineer stepped up to the podium and firmly grasped the microphone in her hand. Well, they would all be disappointed, all except Meyers. He would be angry.

"I am grateful to be home," she said into the microphone. "I thank God for my safe return. Truly, He went before me always. I also wish to acknowledge the brave men of the Zionist Underground whose efforts were primarily responsible for my escape."

Suddenly, the room was charged with excitement, electrified by the shock of Tisha's statement. Flashes popped, reels spun on their axis, Meyers' face reddened, and Mike's eyebrows arched in interest.

"And last of all," Tisha continued, "I want to remember Nathan Yehuda and Solomon Roth, the two brave soldiers who laid down their lives so that Miss Shields and I might survive."

As the engineer walked away from the podium, the room erupted with dozens of voices, all speaking at once. Pandemonium began to spread among the reporters, and several ISS men surrounded Tisha while others began clearing a path for her exit. A flushed and bewildered Peter Meyers jumped in front of the podium and began shouting into the microphone.

"Ladies and gentlemen of the press, I'm sorry, no more questions...no more questions please...that's quite enough. Thank you. No...I'm sorry...the press conference is over."

"Why did you do it, Tisha?" asked Peter Meyers as he paced back and forth in one of the doctor's lounges that had been sealed off for their use. His face was still flushed, and his cheeks seemed to puff out, then deflate, like two fanning billows.

"Why did you lie about Audra?" Tisha returned angrily.

Shortly before the news conference, the ISS had learned in

whose apartment Audra Shields had been found. It didn't take them long to figure out the reason she was there. A .25 caliber had been discovered on the floor after the apartment was searched. The serial number showed it was registered in Audra's name. The blond metallurgist had obviously lied to the ISS regarding Bubba Hanagan. It was clear that she had gone to his apartment in the hopes of extracting revenge. In the light of this intelligence, Peter Meyers had deliberately falsified the information he gave the press.

"I didn't intend to embarrass you," Tisha continued, her voice softer. "But this entire situation is becoming more muddled all the time. The real story is getting scrambled, like an egg, and when it's all over, it will have no resemblance to the original at all. If I had given them what you wanted, the news media would have buried the public with an avalanche of gory details. No one would have ever known about Nathan and Solomon. And they deserve more. They weren't...they aren't...for heaven's sake Peter, they didn't even get a decent burial!"

Meyers' cheeks didn't puff in and out any more, and he finally stopped pacing and sat down. "I suppose you did what you thought was right, but now I'm going to have a lot of explaining to do," he said, his anger defused.

"Okay...so the ISS relationship with the Zionists will become public," returned Tisha. "It may force our government to act, to officially support the Underground. In the long run, both agencies will benefit."

"That's true," Meyers agreed.

"Let's face it, Pete," Mike Patterson chuckled, "you'll turn out to be a hero, and in a few months they'll give you a promotion."

Meyers shrugged, "Well... ."

"How does ISS Bureau Chief sound?" Tisha teased.

"Here, here," Mike said, laughingly.

"Well, as ISS Chief I'd be in a better position to expose Tafco Oil," Meyers responded cheerfully. He too had gotten caught up in the jesting.

The smile suddenly disappeared from Mike's and Tisha's

face. The chances of bringing Tafco Oil to account were slim, and they all knew it.

"I'd like to go see Audra now," Tisha said, soberly.

Meyers nodded and was about to rise and lead the engineer down the hall when one of his men suddenly appeared.

"Sir," said the well-groomed agent. "Miss Shields has just died. We were unable to get a statement from her. She never regained consciousness."

"Come on. Let's go to the hangar," Mike Patterson said as he opened the door of the Sea Breeze lobby. "Our audience will be arriving soon." One large, powerful arm extended straight outward. Obediently, Tisha walked towards it and when she was near enough, it wrapped around her like a friendly shawl. "Listen to it, the thunderous applause, the wild, frenzied cheering," Mike said, leading her through the door. "And look at the people weeping...fainting from sheer wonderment over our 'special child.' The P2 is going to be a huge success, Tisha."

The tall, slim woman slipped her arm around Mike's waist and leaned against him as they walked towards the car. It had been three weeks since that press conference at the hospital; three long and difficult weeks of dodging curiosity seekers and hungry reporters. Much had gone on during her captivity. Mike had driven himself and his people almost to the brink of breaking. It had been his own means of filling time, of keeping his mind from thinking on the possibility of Tisha never returning. This produced a remarkable side effect. It made the P2 mock-up weeks ahead of schedule.

During the past three weeks, Tisha had purposely stayed away from Gibs Town. She did not want to bring the reporters there. The P2 was near completion and she didn't want anything to jeopardize it. She stayed in touch by phone, and kept abreast of things through briefs, and, of course, through Mike. This meant more separation for the couple, since he had to be down at Gibs Town so often. But both agreed to Meyers' wisdom regarding the need for Tisha to stay in Everman, and while shielded somewhat from the press, be visible to keep interest focused on her and away from Gibs Town. But now it was no longer necessary to do so. The P2 mock-up had been completed, and another press conference, so different from the one three weeks prior, had been scheduled for this morning.

"'The odium of success is hard enough to bear, without the added ignominy of popular applause.' I think Robert Graham put it rather well," Tisha said, kissing his shoulder.

"Tsk-tsk," Mike responded laughingly. "Mustn't sound so pompous, since you'll be eating up every last applause and sigh of appreciation, like a hungry beggar. Remember, it's for our child."

"The P2...she is as wonderful as we think, isn't she, Mike?" Tisha asked with a strain in her voice. She had suddenly thought of the terrible cost of it all.

The handsome executive chuckled, "A stage mother's jitters? Yes, Tisha, she's as wonderful as we think, and more. The world will love her. She's our first child, Tisha, a child who is about to go out into the world. We have done the best we could to raise her, now it's time to let go."

The engineer's eyes became moist. "Letting go is harder than I thought."

Mike gave her a little hug. "Yes, but we're going out there now, like two proud parents, and we're going to cut the string."

"You mean cord, don't you," she said, smiling now.

"Cord?"

"Yes. The expression is, 'cut the cord,' as in umbilical cord."

"No, I mean string, as in purse string. It's time for the little whelp to go out and make money for us!"

Rich, throaty laughter cascaded from Tisha's lips as she gazed lovingly at the man next to her. Oh, what a wonderful thing laughter was! It seemed like ages since she had laughed. She almost forgot how good it felt. "Then, by all means," she finally managed to say, "let's go cut the string."

***

The fragrance of freshly cut flowers rose above the smell of seaweed and salt, and hit Tisha at once like a falling feather pillow. "How lovely," she murmured, as she stepped from the car. Following her nose, she was led to a large canopy set up by the caterers. It shaded several tables; tables that held huge arrangements of freshly cut flowers. Around these arrangements were placed large platters of hors d'oeuvres. To one side, and slightly away from the canopy, folding chairs were arranged in neat, little rows. And here and there at the end of each row was an urn full of red and white roses, pink and yellow carnations, blue iris', purple gladiolus. In front of all these rows of chairs stood a bulletin board-like object on which were tacked large sheets of paper. This board rested on a tripod and stood very close to a podium. The guests had not yet arrived. The people milling around the airstrip were employees belonging either to PA or to the catering outfit Mike had hired for the day. And mingling throughout the area were the ever present ISS.

Tisha made a soft, whistling noise. "Impressive. Very impressive. It does prove something, that everyone is expendable. You have managed quite well without me."

Mike's dark eyes looked broodingly at her. "You'll never know how poorly I've managed," he said, kissing her on the forehead. "And today you will be most indispensable." Then he pointed to the podium. "I hope you approve of your stage, Madame."

Tisha looked in the direction of his finger and nodded. "My briefing is short."

"That's all I want. You're just an hors d'oeuvre, meant to wet the appetite."

Tisha laughed and tugged on his hand. "Okay, but first let's go say 'good-bye' to baby."

As soon as she entered the hangar, Tisha felt the charged atmosphere as, all around her, men scurried to finish their tasks. Most of them had worked on the project from the beginning, but some were newly shipped from PA to help speed completion. But no matter the length of service, each man had been touched by the spark and carried it with him, here and there, like little flashes of lightning. Now, Tisha brought fresh energy to the hangar as it exploded in greetings. Most of these people knew her well. Many had been deeply effected by her abduction. Some had even cried and prayed with Mike, and tried, in their own way, to see him through the painful ordeal of waiting. It was with genuine joy and love they greeted her now. Tisha responded with smiles and waves, with handshakes and hugs. When the commotion died down, she was free to make one last greeting and...farewell.

Her eyes strained, eager, greedy, to behold that which she had helped create. Impatiently, she dragged Mike closer. There was still some scaffolding in place. It would remain, so that the P2 could be studied closely. But even the scaffolding could not obscure the power and grace.

"She's beautiful, Mike!" Tisha said, her voice hushed in awe. "She's more beautiful than I had imagined!" she continued, staring at what her eyes settled on first, the pointed beak-like forward fuselage. Slowly, the tall engineer began walking around the P2. Her eyes took in everything; the graceful, downward slope of the forward fuselage merging into the midfuselage, the great expanse of the sculptured wings fanning outward over the wide underbelly, the sleek aft fuselage and aft body where the tall, fin-like empennage rose high into the air. Tisha was swollen with pride.

There were tears of joy she wanted to weep over her. A mother had so few occasions in which to be truly self-indulgent. A child's "coming out" was one of them. But the time for self-indulgence and joy was cut short, for suddenly Tisha heard shouts, "They're coming! They're coming!" And then the sound of many feet slapping pavement as bodies ran this way and that, seemed to stir up the electricity like particles of dust.

"Looks like you're on," Mike said, barely able to conceal his excitement.

Tisha didn't move. Her eyes kept sweeping over the body of the P2, caressing it here and there with soft, lingering stares.

"Hey you two, come on! Everyone's here. What a turnout! They all want to see the plane. I keep sending them to the tables, but it's like trying to stop a herd of stampeding bulls with a red handkerchief. Tisha, you better give them that briefing before they storm the hangar!"

Mike nodded at Buck. "We're coming." But before he moved, he looked once again at the P2 and then at Tisha. "Yes, she is beautiful," he said.

Outside, parked cars and helicopters dotted the airstrip. It was mainly by helicopter that the airline executives and PA Board members had come. The cars belonged to the host of reporters who had all arrived in keen anticipation, made keener, no doubt, by the wave of terrorism that had plagued PA these past several months.

Suddenly, a cacophony of sounds shattered the air like splintering glass, and Tisha experienced a fleeting moment of un-easiness as she realized that most of the slivers of conversation were aimed at her. But presently, she became relaxed and even ea-ger to answer the questions until she saw *him* standing almost ob-scured by the tent. For a moment she was taken back. How dare Gunther show his face here! She moved slowly to the podium as Mike quieted the crowd and invited them to sit in the chairs. All the while, Tisha's eyes were on the thin, pasty-face man. She prayed silently as that nagging feeling of bitterness once again inflamed her. This feeling had recently been heightened when Bubba Hana-gan's body was discovered in an dump-sight outside Everman. Hope of bringing the guilty parties to justice had almost totally dis-appeared. When everything was quiet, Tisha began speaking. Her voice was even and clear, and void of any hint of tension.

"Ladies," she paused to smile at the handful of women pre-sent, most of whom were reporters, the others, members of the ca-tering staff, "and gentlemen. You have been invited here today to experience a revolutionary new aircraft, an aircraft of many 'firsts,' the Patterson II or P2. It's a commercial passenger SST, the first aircraft powered by nuclear fusion."

At once a buzz arose from the audience as people began

talking to each other excitedly. Tisha waited quietly, allowing the initial impact of her words to subside. While she waited, she watched Gunther closely and noticed a redness creep, like an inch worm, to his cheeks when he discovered he was being observed. He turned away.

"My aim," she continued, "is to provide you with a brief description of the P2 and its propulsion system. In-depth details and 'questions and answers' will be dealt with during the tour that is to follow. Also, those who wish to look at these sketches of the P2 may do so after the tour.

"To begin, the P2 is a wide bodied SST; fuselage length 350 feet, wing span 199 feet, with a variable sweep wing design. It has an unlimited range, which means, in plain language, it can fly non-stop to any city in the world, at speeds of over 2,000 miles per hour, and at altitudes of 76,000 feet. The propulsion system consists of four mini-reactors or NPR910s; each eight feet in diameter, roughly the size of the Rolls Royce RB211 engine built for Lockheed."

She spoke for several minutes, further describing the plane and its propulsion system, along with their use of deuterium and Nolan's contributions and breakthroughs.

"I'd like to end this briefing by mentioning the new composite materials such as carbon fiber and titanium alloys which will be used in the building of the P2. Their use increases payloads by 20-25% over any. other type of passenger aircraft of equal size. However, most of you are already familiar with the merits of these materials. What you are not familiar with, though, is a totally new substance, titanium X, created by a former employee, Audra Shields." Here Tisha paused to allow the swell of the murmuring voices to shrivel. There was still public furor over Audra's death, and her name continued to make good copy in the press.

"This substance is so new and revolutionary," Tisha finally resumed, "that without it, the NPR910 would not be a reality. It is the only substance known to man, thus far, that is capable of withstanding the tremendous heat of a repeated thermonuclear explosion. In over 200 simulated flights the NPR's titanium X casing has not shown the slightest sign of corrosion or breakdown. We have, for your pleasure, prepared the NPR910 for such a simulated flight.

"Now the staff of Gibs Town anxiously await your inspection of both the NPR910 and the P2. They will be happy to answer all your questions. So, without further fanfare, I will close by saying it has been a pleasure to address you today. Thank you for coming."

Tisha left the podium to sounds of applause. It was obvious that those who had come were not disappointed. The P2 was years ahead of any aircraft in existence. But the applause and the victory became secondary as Tisha moved slowly toward the thin, nervous man beneath the tent canopy. She passed through the dense maze of people. Already the crowd was moving slowly toward the hangar. Those left in the seating area had also begun to head in that direction, and Tisha found herself like the salmon, traveling upstream against the current. A few people tried to stop her, but she brushed them off politely. Finally, she reached the tent.

Gunther had not moved with the others. All during her speech he had noticed Tisha's repeated stares, and then afterwards had seen her move towards him. Some basic instinct made him remain immobile, waiting for her. The pale, pasty face twitched as he forced his lips into a thin smile.

"Your disclosures were most interesting, Miss O'Brien, if not somewhat startling," he said.

"They were meant to be startling. Precautions were taken to ensure they would be," Tisha responded, feeling flames of anger lick at her heart, and feeling the Potter's hands press down as though smothering those flames. She made a low, gasping noise as the pressure continued. She had to make a choice. There was always a choice. She could choose to forgive or not.

"Yes...I had no idea you'd be so successful," said Gunther.

"I guess we've both had a shock," returned Tisha. The Hand of God continued to squeeze.

"What do you mean?"

"I mean, *I know*."

"I don't understand."

"We all know: Mike, Pete, all of us."

"What are you talking about?"

"Perhaps... ," Tisha stammered, feeling so much pressure she thought something inside would burst. "Perhaps you have fooled the law and will escape punishment here. But, there's a higher law which you cannot escape, and someday you will face it. I now release you to that higher law. And I...forgive you." Instantly, Tisha felt free. The pressure was gone. She was even able to smile into the doughy face that had begun to twitch even more.

"I assure you I haven't a clue of what you're talking about." Her smile only deepened. "Miss O'Brien, really! I...I'm not... ."

"Goodbye, Mr. Gunther," Tisha said calmly. Then she walked away, leaving the pasty-face man gaping behind her.

Once more Robert Gunther found himself gaping, as he stood before the "committee."

"We are quite grieved over you, Robert," boomed a deep, masculine voice from the head of a long, rectangular table. More than a dozen wealthy and influential men had gathered in the room. Bankers, newspaper editors, business executives, as well as Alexander Harner and Senator Garby were present. The meeting was taking place in an old, meticulously kept mansion belonging to the Chairman. The Chairman, a heavy set but impeccably dressed man, was one of the most powerful bankers in the Western world. When he spoke, he spoke with authority, and there were few who ever tried to oppose or contradict him. He leaned against the high back of his mahogany chair. As a young boy he had watched his father conduct business in this very room, the "great room" as he called it, and around this same magnificently carved twelve-foot table. Many years later, after his father died, the Chairman began having his own meetings in the "great room" and had been doing so for over twenty-five years.

The Chairman took a great puff from his cigar, and with the

other hand began thumping the newspaper that lay open before him. "This," he said with emphasis, as he struck the front page picture of the P2, "is most disappointing. You know, Robert, how I hate inefficiency. And from what I can see, you have bungled this assignment from beginning to end."

The pasty face began to turn red. "I...I have tried my best."

"That's just the point. Even doing your best, you failed miserably. I gave you carte blanche. You were to use every means to stop the P2. Your efforts were feeble, impotent. For heaven's sake, Robert, you couldn't even kill Patterson."

"How was I to know that someone else was in his helicopter? It was Patterson's private craft. I hired the best and... ."

"And still failed," continued the Chairman knotting his eyebrows.

"Well, Mr. Harner didn't do much better!" shot Gunther, losing his composure. Beads of perspiration began dotting his face like measles. "He was suppose to 'buy' Patterson; win him to our side. The autoclave would soften him, you said." Gunther had turned accusingly to Harner.

Alex Harner shrugged and smiled sheepishly. "We weren't all that confident about turning him. We figured we'd win him or kill him, whatever came first."

"Never mind that," shot the Chairman crossly. "The primary mission was given to you, Robert. And the fact remains that all your efforts failed. In addition, you were stupid and careless. You compromised Tafco Oil by contracting the Jihad through our Syrian branch. My God, man, do you know what that's going to cost! I'm going to have to call in a lot of favors and line a lot of pockets before I quell this thing. The plight of those women have aroused public sympathy. And the one that got stomped by that muscle bound idiot has become a national heroine."

"There was a million to one chance of those women ever leaving Bozrom alive. And the trail to Tafco was well covered. Only a handful could have exposed it. Am I to blame if one of them got greedy and sold out?"

"Yes! All those who knew anything should have been eliminated." The Chairman paused to puff on his cigar. Then he shook his head like a wise patriarch scolding a youngster. "Like I said, Robert, you were careless. And normally I'm a forgiving man. But this time there's too much at stake. You know how hard we've worked to get Senator Garby into position. He has won another term hands down. And when it comes time for the next Presidential election he will be a prime candidate. You know our objectives, Robert. You know there's more at stake than Tafco Oil, or you, or I, or even Senator Garby. It's a whole new world order we're talking about; an order based on economics, *our* economics. He who rules the gold, rules the world."

Suddenly, the expression on the Chairman's face changed. It became dark and ominous. "Your name has shown up in too many ISS reports. Your inefficiency has caused a cloud to hang over Tafco Oil. You've left a trail that must be erased because we can't have some wide-eyed reporter or investigator trying to build his reputation with an expose´ on you or Tafco. In short, Robert, you have become an embarrassment. And you know we can't leave around any embarrassing loose ends."

Gunther's face began turning deeper and deeper shades of red. "You're not seriously... ."

"I am most serious!" boomed the voice at the end of the table. "In our organization we do not fire. We do not demote. We *eliminate*. You understood that from the beginning."

"Yes, but...but surely... ."

"We are all expendable. Building a new world order, a new world economic system, a one world government, necessitates thinking of the larger picture. We cannot quibble over one life, more or less. I'm sorry, Robert. But you are no longer an asset to us, and have, in fact, become a liability."

Gunther's red face suddenly paled. He understood the full significance of the Chairman's words. He had only one chance left. Always in such cases, the committee had the right to overrule. If enough voted on Gunther's behalf, his life would be spared.

"Before sentencing becomes official," continued the Chairman, "is there anyone who cares to cast a contrary vote?"

Frantically, Gunther looked around the table. Not one hand was raised. His eyes rested beseechingly on Senator Garby. The senator shrugged as if to say, what can I do? Then he looked away. Immediately, Gunther turned to Harner. "Alex? Alex!"

The barrel-chested Harner squeezed out a thin, weak laugh, "I'm sorry, Bob."

Robert Gunther dropped his face into his hands, and instead of the sobs everyone expected to hear, there arose peels of laughter. Tisha O'Brien had been wrong. He had not escaped anything. The irony of it seemed overwhelmingly funny.

Three days later, Robert Gunther's dead body was discovered in the same dump-sight where Hanagan had been found. There was a bullet in his brain. Everman buzzed for days over the mysterious murder of one of Tafco Oil's leading executives. Then finally the mystery was solved. EPD received a phone call from the Moslem Jihad claiming responsibility. Everman shrugged, of course, who else? and then life continued as before.

Bodies pressed together along both sides of the runway like tissues in a box. Heads bobbed this way and that, straining to see the great silver swan descend from the sky in a perfect landing. The first test flight of the P2 had just been completed, and TV cameras and newsmen were there to record the event. The success of this flight had insured the P2 a place in history as the first nuclear powered SST in the world. It had also achieved national and international prominence in the here and now world, for it would revolutionize air travel in particular, and transportation in general. The P2 proved conclusively that man could travel by nuclear power. And the P2 would be the forerunner of all that would follow in this area. In the not so distant future it would be flying people from New York to LA in two hours, and from Washington DC to Paris in three.

Away from the crowd, Mike and Tisha stood holding hands

as they watched Buck descend the gangway. Tisha and Buck had become even closer since returning from the Mid-East. And Tisha would be forever grateful for what he had done. He was one of the many who had risked his life for her. When it came time to pick the test pilot for this P2 flight, Buck was the obvious choice. He would have both the distinction and joy of being her first pilot.

Tisha could imagine his feelings now, his pride, his exhilaration. He had flown the P2 well. Now he was the first to have carnal knowledge. He alone could answer those important questions regarding pitch control, trim, airfoil efficiency and autolanding so critical to a pilot. She watched the reporters and TV crew corral him like a prized stallion. The moment was his now...and "hers." Tisha and Mike were content to stay in the background, to watch from a distance.

Eight months had passed since Robert Gunther's murder. Everything had changed and nothing had changed. Audra Shields had become a folk hero of sorts. There was even talk of making a movie. Her story had been told and retold, embellished and changed so many times, that little truth remained until she emerged as a female counterpart of Rambo. Peter Meyers never got a promotion and, in fact, was ordered to drop the Tafco investigation. Joshua Chapman was still liaison between the ISS and the Zionists. And the United States had officially recognized the Underground as a vital bastion against terrorism. And Mike...he finally shared his "Jacob" experience with Tisha. They had wept together that day. Since then, he had continued to grow in the Lord. A wedding date had been set. They had even visited Tisha's mother together and gotten her blessing. In a few short months Tisha would become Mrs. Michael Patterson.

Now she rested her head on Mike's bulky shoulder. Both hearts swelled with joy as they looked down the runway. "I feel absolutely wonderful," Patterson said suddenly. "It's as though I feel God's smile as He looks at what we've made."

"Yes...I think I feel it too," she added softly. "We make a good team, the three of us."

Mike laughed. "That we do. But it's been a wild ride. I'll be glad to get back to normal, to have things quiet down. The most exciting thing I want on the board is this year's new interior colors for the EX4."

Tisha wrinkled up her face in thought. It was obvious that she had not been listening to her companion. "You know I've been thinking about what we should do next, and I was doodling the other day and came up with a sketch I'd like you to see."

"Oh no," groaned Mike in jest. "This sounds too familiar."

"What I had in mind," continued Tisha, ignoring his remark, on fire now, "was a new type of cargo carrier."

"Cargo carrier? Our C101 is doing well."

"Yes, yes," returned Tisha impatiently. "But I'm talking about a totally new cargo carrier, a VTOL... ."

"VTOL? Explain to me why a cargo carrier would need to take-off and land vertically?"

"Think of the many places where only a helicopter can go because of lack of airfield. But a helicopter is very limited. It can't haul or pick up really huge cargoes. Half the famine in the world could be alleviated if we could just get the food to them."

"No. The answer is no."

"And not only could it deliver goods to inconvenient places, think of its rescue value."

"This is crazy, Tisha."

"You could airlift an entire village, a community, livestock, personal possessions."

"Tisha!"

"Well, suppose you had to remove the inhabitants from the pathway of a coming tornado, or hurricane or flood or...even war?"

"Out of the question."

"I though we could begin with a stretch version of the C101 and... ."

"How many engines?"

"Well, that's the really exciting thing because I figured we would use only two NPR910s with... ."

"Why two?"

"Because I think we can achieve double the fusion capability of each engine by altering... ."